Praise for *Exit 25 Utopia*

Exit 25 Utopia is the finest memoiristic novel of a hard time for the counterculture—the 1970s and '80s. Steven Wishnia recreates the Chevy vans, the Quaaludes and smoke, reggae and punk-rock, pre-AIDS gymnastics, and the lingering, gnawing legacy of a more hopeful future nurtured in the 1960s that had all but evaporated by the time disco, and then Reagan, ruled. Wishnia's powerfully descriptive language and instinct for the comic conjures the lower echelon of the rock'n'roll band-on-the-run. This is Spinal Tap with pathos.

—Michael Simmons

Original False Prophets band member and *High Times* staffer Steven Wishnia warns his readers not to jump to any conclusions in *Exit 25 Utopia*, his semi-autobiographical work. But there's at least this much to be deduced from the intensity of Wishnia's work: This man has seen the best and the worst that America's punk-rock scene has had to offer. The trick is getting the madness and the beauty of it all on paper, and Wishnia pulls that off with sixteen sharp and insightful vignettes. If you can picture a Lower East Side cross-pollination between Henry Rollins' *Get in the Van* and Jack Kerouac's *On the Road*, you have Wishnia's *Exit 25 Utopia* in your hot little hands.

—Silja J.A. Talvi, *Heckler*

Steve Wishnia's book let me know that rock'n'roll tragicomedy, which I lived in San Francisco, was the same on the East Coast: "…as closing time impended the prospect of sex with a stranger was often far more enticing than the two-hour double-fare subway and bus ride to Queens." Well, yes. A favorite sentence about hopeful rockers: "The distance between their desire and their capabilities seemed galactic." It's a relief to read the thrilling and cryptic truth, when so many are busy glamorizing their own roles in hindsight.

—Jennifer Blowdryer, author of
White Trash Debutante

Steve Wishnia has a bad attitude, a good memory, a long FBI file, and a discerning eye for the psychodynamics of rock'n'roll on a minimal budget. *Exit 25 Utopia* presents a parade of screw-ups, idealists, and egomaniacs that will fascinate anyone interested in the anthropology of underground music.

—Charles M. Young

With pitch-perfect prose, deadpan humor, searing honesty, and keen intelligence, Steve Wishnia captures the longings and dreams of a generation of young rock'n'rollers: high on drugs, sex, philosophy, and revolution… high on music… and high on the aftereffects of too many sleepless and wild nights.

—Janice Eidus, author of *The Celibacy Club*

Exit 25
Utopia

Steven Wishnia

T**I**P
The Imaginary Press

Permissions appear on page 241, which serves as an extension of this copyright page.

EXIT 25 UTOPIA

For information address: The Imaginary Press, P.O. Box 509, East Setauket, NY 11733-0509
e-mail: swishnia@hightimes.com

ISBN: 0-9656814-2-4

Cover illustration by Mac McGill.
Calligraphy by Lynn McSweeney.

Printed on acid-free paper
Manufactured in the United States of America

First Edition December, 1999

CONTENTS

Dedicated to the memory of

Bobby Sturdivent (1956-1993)
"more fun…is that too much to ask?"

and
Kathy Alexander (1961-1987)
Gary "Scary Failure" Taylor (1956-1994)
"another gig, my ears bleed…we are the road crew"

and the future of

IAN

Author's Note: Some of this is pretty autobiographical; some of it isn't. Don't jump to any conclusions.

Acknowledgements

Thanks to my parents, Arnold & Judy, for not using birth control in the spring of 1954 and a whole lot more since then; the rest of my family; to Hooverville—English Steve, Matt the Rhythm Insurgent & Pete; Los Gatos Unidos—Charlo & Andrea the Orange Goddess; and those others who read this, encouraged it (don't blame them), partied and/or commiserated with me: Marta, Christy, Kathy M., Kathy P., Cindy, Teresa, Scott MX, Deena Rae, Faith & Rob, Edwina, the Lakeside, the kind strangers of Michigan, Marc, the Legalization Girls—Diane in Pennsylvania, Tanya in D.C., Toni in Florida, and Lynnette in Marin; the New York Police Department for arresting me on bullshit charges and the law firm of Lansner & Kubitschek for getting some money out of them for it; everybody at *High Times* and the late lamented *Guardian Newsweekly*; and a whole lot of my friends too numerous to list.

Jacqui B. from the Green Door for letting me steal some of her lines, Lisa L. for letting me steal some of hers. Eric Goldhagen at Nomad Media Lab for computer geekery. Ned Brewster and Stephan Ielpi for making history. Suzanne and Janet for putting up with our shit. Candace, whose response to some of my earlier writings was, "You should learn how to break things."

Several political causes close to my heart (and the self-interest of my ass and my class): the Metropolitan Council on Housing (preserving cheap rent in New York City); the National Writers Union; the National Organization for the Reform of Marijuana Laws; and ABC No Rio (low-budget rebel art). Everybody in "dis ya concrete jungle" who's still trying.

Special thanks to Diana, without whom this book probably would have been unwritten or a lot more depressing. Magenta for taking my 4 A.M. phone calls. Lynn McSweeney who sees more colors than most people. And Mac McGill who draws like Jimi Hendrix played guitar.

Extra special thanks to my brother Ken, who hemorrhaged a lot less red ink on my manuscript than I expected, and dripped it in the right places. Now go out and buy 23 *Shades of Black* and *Soft Money*. And Ian for being the best kid in the known universe.

"He who thinks of only vanity and no love for
humanity shall fade away."
—Junior Byles

"It's not enough"
—Johnny Thunders

INTRO: STREET MUSIC

East 11th Street and Avenue B

The neon cross
blinks 'Jesus Saves'
in red and blue
like a 1965 organ-trio blues dive

upstairs
there are immaculate white walls
digital phone tones
electronic beeps
and pens writing out four-digit checks

downstairs
the chip of spike heels
the quiet squeak of ragged sneakers
the hiss of the reptiles
three short pops
a cloud of bloody feathers
and the screams of the bereaved
and the boombox proclaims

'Nigga—It's the American Dream
Nigga—It's the American Dream.'

in a basement room
on a mattress in the back
a black-haired punk-rocker
is grunting
and a bleached-blonde stripper
is moaning
to the sound of the Clash
back in a garage with my bullshit detector
and Johnny Thunders
"This one's called, 'Get Off the Fuckin' Phone'"

Fifteen years later
the offspring of that union
will be shooting hoops
to the sound of the drums
in Tompkins Square
takes the pass fakes left
drives baseline and shoots
Yes!
I wonder wonder wonder wonder
who (bomp)
who wrote the book of love?

To the sound of the drums
Bronx rocks to the planet rock
Don't stop
Queens rocks to the planet rock
Don't stop
the beat of the future
from the technotronic tenements
amid concrete

2

cocaine
heatwave sweat
hydrocarbon soot
garbage
and gunshots
a new beat is born
this summer

To the sound of the drums
This is a beat
that survived 400 years of slavery
This is a beat
that survived 400 years of colonialism
This is a beat
that survived 400 years of genocide
and it comes out again
every spring
as reliably
as the buds on the trees

Celia Cruz in the bodega
with Ray Barretto on congas
the chunk of beer on the counter
and dominoes on the board in the back
¡ay, carajo!
This is music
about stepping out on Saturday night
in your finest plumage
and moving with abandon and grace
but here on Avenue B
it's about scratching out an honest living
and staying warm in el invierno norteamericano
a little taste of green olives
in the hawkwind

Downtown
in the highest reaches of the concrete jungle
where the well-fed arrogant
pull the levers
and tighten the screws
there is an echo of Bob Marley
reciting Haile Selassie's speech
before the League of Nations
'Until the philosophy
that holds one race superior
and another inferior
is finally
and permanently
discredited.'
There is an echo of Bob Marley
from the back of a jeep
with a Canal Street sound system
the size of two Fender Twins
Until the philosophy is discredited
Until the philosophy is discredited
I only hear one word.
Discredited.

YOU FUCKING ANIMALS
DON'T HAVE ANY RIGHTS

I hated everything Richard Nixon stood for in 1972. Both as vicious murderer and ultimate stiff. No-Dick Nixon, black militants called him, the perfect stereotype of the authoritarian pig who probably hadn't gotten laid since 1949 and was taking his frustrations out by dumping napalm on Vietnamese peasants and celebrating the shootings of student demonstrators. All with a smug puritanism, going on about how "Eisenhower restored good language to the Presidency." The tape transcripts of "the (expletive deleted) Jews control the (expletive deleted) media" were still two years away.

I was 17 that year. With six months of washing dishes at minimum wage adding an economic dimension to my teenage rebellion and antiwar outrage, I was ripe for action. So in August, four of us—me, Elliot, Rhonda and Nick, comrades from Eastern Long Island State College's radical movement, loaded into Elliot's sky-blue Chevy and drove the 1,400 miles from Brooklyn to the Republican National Convention in Miami Beach.

It was my first time down South. Steak sandwiches at a Muslim fast-food joint in the D.C. ghetto; in North Carolina, a spectacular thunderstorm split the predawn sky, the lightning illuminating a Ku Klux Klan billboard; past the Spanish moss in South Carolina and down the long Florida coast with Alice Cooper and the Raspberries blasting on the radio.

The Brooklyn-Queens-Long Island belt was turning out thousands of us, second-generation immigrants, first-generation middle class, freaky rebels loving sex, pot, rock'n'roll, and the overthrow of the American government by any means necessary. Nick had long corkscrew dark hair, a bristly beard and mustache, and angry black eyes. "We should have POUNDED those NAZIS into the SIDEWALK!" he raged after some counterdemonstrators waved swastikas at us. Straights could be forgiven for thinking he resembled Charlie Manson, but he actually was a sweet, gentle guy, one of the first serious vegetarians I knew. Elliot and Rhonda were the oldest, Elliot clean-shaven, long-nosed like a Jewish Jean-Paul Belmondo with glasses, acting like everything he did was a big revolutionary deal. He bossed Rhonda around a lot. She was thin, quiet, with long straight dark hair, a religion major who liked to wear Indian-print blouses with tiny mirrors imbedded in the embroidery. I was the baby of the bunch, with armpit-length black hair and a scraggly pubic beard, gold-rimmed Lennon glasses, and an Army jacket and cut-up black T-shirt. Some cops had stopped us and given me shit about the insignia on the jacket.

"You know that's a paratrooper jacket?"

"I don't know, I got it in a thrift shop for two bucks."

"You're lucky it's not a Marines jacket. I was in the Marines, I'd kick your ass if it was."

We camped out in Flamingo Park with a mix of antiwar Vietnam veterans—one, Ron "Born on the Fourth of July" Kovic, would get dragged out of his wheelchair and beaten when he got into the convention hall and heckled Nixon—and Quaalude freaks so wasted they probably wouldn't have noticed a cop bashing them on the head. A band called the Gooks played a free show, supposed to be some kind of rock opera about Vietnam. They did a song called "The Calley Stomp"—a caveman blues riff with the lead singer screaming, "Calley, you shithead," while choking and dismembering an effigy of the Army lieutenant who'd shot a two-year-old in the head at My Lai—and two a cappella singalongs, "Eat the Rich" an ode to revolutionary cannibalism, "Free Artie Bremer" hailing the gunman who'd made sure that Governor Wallace would never again be able to stand in any schoolhouse door. Nick was freaked about potential appeals to the crowd's latent sadism. Occasionally a Young Republican would wander by and we'd sit up in the subtropical night getting high and arguing with them.

The Republicans wanted to avoid another Chicago '68. Nixon didn't want televised images of cops battering protesters marring his coronation. The cops locked arms and clubs and kept us blocks away from the hall, except for a penned-off section in back that they pushed us out of when we got too loud. We escaped into the streets, shouting "Nixon's a murderer" and "fuck you, pig" at stray delegates and

7

occasionally smashing the windshields of Cadillacs with "President Nixon. Now more than ever" stickers. One guy I suspected as a potential agent—he'd propositioned me about blowing up an ITT facility on Long Island—jumped on the back of a delegate bus and pulled out the sparkplug wires.

The morning after the convention we picked up a guy named Dave who needed a ride to Philadelphia and had eggs and grits at a coffeeshop. On the way back to the car, he saw a toy store and wanted to get something for his little sister. Nick and I went in with him.

The owner freaked at the sight of us, like the Weather Underground and the Manson Family had just walked into his store. He screamed for us to get out. We did, but not before Nick said something like "You got a lot of war toys in here, mister." We walked the half block to the car. As we got in, about 11 cop cars pulled up. One of them blocked off our parking space.

"All right, it's the end of the road for you!" shouted the lead cop, leaping out to the driver's side of our car. Elliot didn't know what was going on and picked the moment for a display of idealistic bravado. He wouldn't roll his window down until the cop told him what we were being arrested for. When he finally did, the cop punched him in the face. The cop was wearing a "Nixon Now" button.

We got lined up against a cop car, cuffed, Maced and frisked. A crowd of old people gathered—South Miami Beach's elderly, mostly retired New York Jews who weren't particularly affluent, had been pretty sympathetic to the demonstrators, who often resembled their grandchildren. I had assumed that Nick was Jewish until one old woman said "sheyne Yid-

8

dishe kopf" to us and he asked me what it meant.

"They weren't doing anything," said one protester.

"Neither were you, buddy," said a cop. "Get over here."

Elliot and Rhonda had bail money. Nick, Dave, the bystander and I got put in a holding cell with about 20 people. Most of them seemed to be in for thoughtcrime. Their arrest warrants said things like: "On August 24, 1972 at 11 A.M., at 17th Street and Washington Avenue, said defendant did commit the crime of disorderly conduct, to wit: DID RAISE HIS MIDDLE FINGER IN AN OBSCENE GESTURE AND SHOUT 'FUCKING PIG' AT AN OFFICER OF THE MIAMI BEACH POLICE DEPARTMENT." Over 1,000 people got rounded up that day.

Periodically the cops came by to spray Mace into the cell. "I always cry at weddings," snickered one. They dragged in a longhair from Atlanta, his face bloody, his glasses smashed.

"What about my constitutional rights?" he screamed.

"You fucking animals don't have any constitutional rights," said the cop shoving him in the cell. He too was wearing a "Nixon Now" button.

Across the hall was a small, swarthy man with a cell to himself. "Hey, man, what are you in for?" I asked.

"Public display of the swastika," he said.

"Fuck you," I replied.

A few cops sauntered over. "It's a pity a good American like you has to be in jail with these bums," he said. Another one with a "Nixon Now" button.

We got moved to the overnight cell, with dirty

9

bare mattresses on battleship-gray bunks. The only reading material was old *Playboys* with the centerfolds torn out. Nick, a vegetarian, wouldn't eat the slightly rancid beef-and-carrot stew. I was hungry. I paid with diarrhea.

We went on trial the next morning. The cop who testified against us was wearing a "Nixon Now" button. The toy-store owner said all five of us had been in the store, but that there were no women. The judge tossed out the charges against Rhonda. The hundred-odd political detainees in the courtroom applauded. The owner said we had been "manhandling the customers" and shouting obscenities.

"What obscenities?" the judge asked.

"I can't repeat them," he said. "There are ladies present."

We told our stories straightforwardly. The only other customers had been leaving when we came in. "Case dismissed" said the judge. The courtroom rocked. Nick shot a raised-fist salute as we walked out. A fat blonde woman from Indiana smiled at me. We'd have a fling a couple years later.

When we got the car back there was $20 missing from my backpack, along with my Army jacket and ripped black T-shirt. They were probably adorning some undercover who needed authentic gear. We didn't stop to eat until we were out of Florida.

Nixon was re-elected overwhelmingly in November. All around radical groups were splitting up and activists cracking up. I spent the spring semester staying as high as I could and dropped out of school in May.

THE LAST SUMMER BEFORE THE GAS CRISIS

T he kid had just turned 16. It was a hot, sunny day in the development, heatwaves rising off the white sides of the houses, the green sod of the lawns, the black asphalt of the driveways, the air baking, treeless and still like a Nebraska cornfield or a Brooklyn pizza oven. This was a former Long Island potato field. It was late morning and the only cars on the street were parked. A gold Fury, a loden-green Duster. A lawnmower droned in the distance about five houses down. A car swept by the intersection smoothly and went around the curve in back.

He rounded the corner and headed out for the road. The heat made walking a trudging pain in the ass. He hoped he'd be able to get a ride before he reached the highway, but it usually didn't happen. His luck hitching usually wasn't too bad. He still looked young enough for people to regard him as a kid, and the way he looked wasn't that disreputable anymore. His black hair cleared his eyebrows in front, dropped down to his earlobes on the sides, and hung to his fifth or sixth vertebra in back. He wore a light-blue and red-tongued Rolling Stones T-shirt, moderately faded Levis, and dark blue tennis shoes.

He was on his way to buy a guitar in Paumanok, in an older development about ten miles west. The ad in the *Buy-Lines* had promised a Strat for $175 and assorted other goodies. His current guitar and amp were pieces of shit, as his friends so kindly put it. A Japanese Les Paul copy with strings almost a half inch off the frets and a five-watt Tele-Star amp. The amp wasn't really that bad. It distorted nicely when you turned it up, which was the only way you could get it to sound like an electric guitar. At low volume it sounded like a cheap acoustic played through an even cheaper transistor radio. Tinnier than a tube of toothpaste.

In any case, he had 270 dollars to change that situation. $50 in old leftover birthday money that he hadn't spent on records or weed, another $100 from his parents, $65 saved from mowing people's lawns, $10 from his allowance, and $45 scrimped from occasional pot sales. Enough to cover the guitar and maybe something extra.

Paumanok Highway was about half a mile down the road outside the development. Or rather the road that divided the C Section of the development from L Section and R Section. The names of all the streets in each section began with the same letter. C Section had Corona, Catalpa, Cox. Pity the poor girl who lived on Cox. L Section had Lilac, Linwood, Lincoln. R Section had Rosemary, Ross, and Rye. It made coming home in someone else's car late at night entertaining. Can the intoxicated, giddy rats find their way through the maze? He hitched desultorily, swinging around lazily at the sounds of cars. Really concentrating on hitching would mean walking most of the way backwards. Most people were too lame to think you'd be turning their way, so it was usually pointless.

He scored a ride as soon as he got on the highway. An old black Falcon pulled over. Young guy in a green T-shirt, about 24. He had medium-length hair and a mustache and was going to work in an electronics factory in Talmadge, just past Paumanok. They grumbled rodomontades about how boring Island life was. There's nothing to fuckin' do around here. Not completely true, but it always seemed that way when you were looking. Sometimes making the connections of friendship, deep conversations, sex, and extraterrestrial comedy theatrics, but usually just driving around taking drugs complaining about being bored and trying to get something good on the radio. If you were older you could drive around and go to bars and make the ultimate autocoital connection and three paragraphs on page 17 of *Newsday*. The 18- and 19-year-olds he knew were dying in car accidents faster than their older brothers had ever died in Vietnam.

They settled into silence. The radio was good for a change as the car cruised west. The Temptations, "Papa Was a Rolling Stone." Lou Reed, "Walk on the Wild Side." The Stones. Stevie Wonder. Alice Cooper, "School's Out." Not a stiff in the bunch, a pleasant surprise. Usually the radio stuck you with some horrible shit, syrupy and disgusting. You wondered how anyone could actually buy the record, let alone take it home and play it. Then again, if you observed the mentalities of most people…. At parties you'd watch guys trying to pick up girls, ladling out the bullshit, the girls lost in their own romantic fantasies and swallowing it from anyone who said the right lines, especially if they came pre-approved with the right status coin of the realm—car, quarterback, hunk, the usual shit—the guys later bragging about another notch on their dicks. At parties and in school he usually felt surrounded by cretins, wanting to be loved or at least accepted, hating them and their games, himself and his weakness. Other people were so easily amused.

They were stuck in traffic by the Mall. This was where the small-town middle class and hardworking or got-lucky ex-proles who populated mideastern Long Island collected their rewards from the tacky cornucopia of the American empire. A sanitized-for-your-protection chunk of downtown Brooklyn set into the mass of undifferentiated suburban tissue. Inside, husbands and wives quarreled over buying furniture, faces setting into masks of petty vindictiveness, while their resentful children dripped chocolate ice cream over their chins and chests. Teenage junkies lolled on the rim of the center fountain, ostentatiously scratching their tracks. If you lived in a two-story Colonial with wall-to-wall carpeting, a white bedroom set with gold trim in your sister's room, this was the place to cop heroin. Suburban kids returned from the city with "half-loads," "quarter-pieces," and shocked tales of shooting up in South Bronx boiler rooms with seven-months-pregnant girls and their resigned brothers. He mainly went there to buy records and act bizarre in public. It could be a fun place for theatrics. People expected you to be crazy if you looked a certain way, so you might as well act it. Let

14

them cluck and be mystified about what possessed you. The lights, floor tiles and prefab storefronts turned everything a clinical, purple-tinged white and putrid green. It made him want to puke. He actually had one Thursday night, fueled by a vilely sweet concoction of Southern Comfort and Colt 45 Malt Liquor, right into one of the fake bushes in front of Sam Goody's. That hadn't been an act.

The car eased on past a fork in the highway and onto an older, strip-developed section of road, past three gas stations, a drive-in, a McDonald's, two shopping centers, and a motel, three miles of enterprises crammed onto nearly every spot of roadside land. Occasionally a six-inch wide strip of ragged grass would straggle around the margins of a lot, blurring into dirt, gravel and asphalt, parking spaces delineated by concrete slabs.

The guy dropped him off at the light before the industrial park. They exchanged "Take it easy, mans" as the door shut, the rhythmic and ritualistic end of a good ride. He patted his left pocket just to make sure that his money was still there. Losing it would be more than a bitch. The guitar-seller lived about five blocks away. This development was older than the kid's, the houses smaller and boxier, quieter because the families had grown up and shadier because the trees had grown in. He stopped at a corner to check the directions again. The house was the third one on the left. No different from the rest, but who knew what kind of deviation lurked behind the slightly faded paintjob, the long-grown lawn, and the plenitude of old cars piled in the driveway. This time of day there were only two, a burnt-orange VW bug and an early-sixties Chevy up on blocks.

A big blackhaired guy, cut in a shag, answered the door.

"Is Billy here?"

"I'm Billy," extending his right hand.

"I'm Alex. I called about the Strat."

"Oh yeah. C'min."

Beer cans formed a skyline on the kitchen counter, partially obscuring the living-room view. Last night's spaghetti sauce was turning to crust in the sink. A trail of milkshake cups, beer glasses, Jack-in-the-Box wrappers, and empty Big Mac styrofoam boxes completed the tableau and continued into the living room. Album covers filled with marijuana seeds spilled onto the rug. Humble Pie's *Rockin' the Fillmore*, Led Zeppelin's *ZOSO*, the Allmans' *Eat A Peach*. The equipment for sale was by the wall. A big Sunn stack way out of his price range and a little Fender Princeton for $85 that was a lot more interesting, an Electro-Harmonix fuzzbox, a wah-wah, and assorted odds and ends.

"Cord's in the case," Billy said, slumping into an armchair and retrieving a half-finished 16-ounce Budweiser. A game show was on TV. Watching daytime TV for a suburban male was a sure sign of terminal burnout, nothing to do and nobody to do it with. The guitar was gleaming white against the royal blue lining of the case, a jewel on display with a maple neck and "Fender STRATOCASTER" painted in black on the headstock, the F backwards, the "STRATOCASTER" curving to the right. Billy turned the TV up as Alex plugged into the small amp, seemingly oblivious as he put the guitar through its paces. The riff from "Paranoid," a bit of "Johnny B. Goode," a minute and a half of "Jumpin' Jack Flash." Not only acceptable but even thrilling, like realizing you could ride a motorcycle for the first time. They quickly agreed on $250 for the guitar and amp, a cord and a strap.

Billy got up long enough to walk Alex to the door. "Ya sound good, Alex," he said in a gravelly Guyland accent.

"You in a band?" Alex wanted to know.

"Not anymore." Billy answered.

"What happened?"

Billy held up his left hand. There was no forefinger or ring finger. The middle one was rounded and nailless at the first knuckle. It looked like a plastic fork that had gone through the dishwasher. "Car accident," he said dispassionately.

Alex couldn't respond except for a weak "Shit."

The way back to the highway was pure drudgery. He had to stop about every fifty feet to rest his distended arms. Acutely embarrassed by it all, his mind churned with regret.

If it had been his right hand, he could at least still hold a pick.

On the highway he had to wait almost twenty minutes before a maroon Saab sputtered over. A guy with very long black hair opened the door. "Got a guitar, huh? Far fuckin' out," said the girl driving. She had very long black hair too and an armload of silver bracelets. Both of them wore all black and the guy had remnants of makeup and glitter around his eyes. "Yeah, we saw the best fuckin' band, in the city last night," he was saying.

"Who?"

"The New York Dolls," the girl said. "Fuckin' great. I saw them once before in Portchester and all these hitters and jocks were yellin' shit at them, like 'Go back to New York ya fuckin' fags.' The singer's like wearing a bra and going like 'Come up here and say that. Me and the boys, we know Kung Fu.'"

"Yeah, I felt like it was 1963 and I just saw the Stones," the guy said. He popped an 8-track tape into the dashboard and the opening chords of "Personality Crisis" cranked out.

It was like no rock'n'roll Alex had ever heard before. Well, maybe like the Stones, a lot like the Stones, but different. Guitars corkscrewing through the subway-train rhythms, wild city sidewalk boys wearing lipstick and howling at the moon, copping bratty attitudes from old tough-girl 45s, loud, crude and cool, like they knew they couldn't play that complicated but didn't give a shit because it was all so fuckin' LIVE.

Alex almost asked them to drop him off at the Mall so he could buy the album. He hitched there the next day to get it. "They look like a bunch of transvestite hookers," his mother said when she saw the album cover. He'd figured out the chords to seven songs by the end of the week.

RED DIRT REEFER

Mick Greenberg made the hard right off Route 32, onto Bronson Road. The VW engine strained up the hill, grinding and whining over the top. Another left and into the driveway. Adam's van was already home.

Mick was burnt, charred around the edges, uneasy. He'd been up until 6:30 that morning finishing a paper and grabbed two hours of ersatz sleep. The amphetamine bleaching away in his body made it more like accelerated rest. His eyeballs felt like toothpicks were stuffed under the lids. But he'd stayed awake through two classes and a four-hour shift at the record store, Resinous Vinyl.

Adam and Brian, his housemates, the guitarist and lead singer in Red Dirt Reefer, his band, were sitting on the ratty rust couch in the front room. They'd had the band for a year. Adam was leaning over the steamer-trunk table, packing a two-foot bong that towered above the detritus and clutter like the

19

Williamsburgh Bank over downtown Brooklyn. The second highest buildings were a sextet of Budweiser grain elevators. Brian and Adam had already broken the symmetry.

"Ready for the Red?" Adam asked.

"Yeah, that's what I need. I'm fuckin' fried."

Mick leaned over as Adam lit the bowl. A whirlpool of smoke twisted up the cloud chamber. No dirt reefer this, it was potent. Mick coughed convulsively. "Fuckin' lightweight," said Brian.

"Fuck you, like you never inhaled too much and spat out phlegm." Mick unsnipped a beer, easing his scorched throat. Two more hits and half the beer and he was fading, drifting in and out of consciousness as Brian flipped over *Overnite Sensation* and Adam changed the strings on his Les Paul. They had a show that night.

A loudmouthed, loud-clothed guy named Richie was stopping by to buy a half-ounce as Mick dragged himself upstairs to his room, clearing books and papers and the typewriter off his bed. The paper had been for his philosophy class, on nihilism. He'd been up all night sorting out his ideas, typing and rewriting. It was easy to write it off as inhuman, the nexus of mirror-image opposites, the space warp where the unbridled freedom of anarchism transformed into the unbridled brutality of fascism, but there was something appealing about it, its single-minded devotion, its passionless and austere willingness to acknowledge no answers and no way out in a bleak fuckin' world. Depressed thoughts an indication the speed crash was coming on soon and hard. Time to crash or I'll be totally fuckin' useless at the gig. Contemplated taking a lude, then thought better—I'll be fuckin' comatose the rest of the night. Adam and Brian will have to carry me into the club, prop me up by the side of the stage like a fuckin' cadaver, and then I'll play everything on 16 RPM. Actually he liked playing on downs, turning everything into slow metallic bulldozer sludge riffs, but it wasn't exactly gig material. And it didn't go along well with the care and feeding of his Gibson EB4 bass, whose fragile mahogany flesh already had enough nicks and scratches.

Sleep. Pile the books and papers, close up the typewriter, pick out gig clothes—a scoop-necked top with thin purple and black stripes, tight faded ripped jeans, and boots. Crawl into bed.

Brian and Adam woke him up two hours later. Mick was still bleary, his face puffy and sluggish in the bathroom mirror. Quick washup. Get dressed. Pack up the bass, flip the head inside the B-15—the Ampeg B-15, a magnificently self-contained bass amp—clip it shut, stick a spare cable in the guitar case. Drugs. Mick wrapped three ludes in tinfoil and stuck about a nickel of the coppery red Colombian he'd gone in on with Adam into a pill vial. The Red reminded him of Melissa Morganstern. She was a DJ on the college station, short and skinny with a corona of red hair the same color as the pot. They'd met at a party during the winter. She looked like a younger Alison Steele, or maybe it was just that late-night DJ aura. She was 22 and a senior and light-years more sophisticated than him, or so he felt. He'd started out stoned and inarticulate but she persisted and they got into a good rap about each other's musical obsessions and wound up back at her house. She was the first woman he'd ever made come. Sex came naturally to him—it felt good, and he loved touching and exploring women's bodies on the rare occasions when he got close enough to them to do it—but raw talent needs direction. She was willing to provide it.

The romance hadn't gone anywhere. He'd been scared awkward about calling her back. They'd gone to the movies and she'd been irritated that he wanted to get high first. Why do you have to be high all the time, she'd asked. Because reality bores the shit out of me and I don't feel complete without a little color. The next time he'd seen her was at the Aerosmith concert in the gym and she was with some big guy who looked like an English rockstar.

"C'mon, man, you gotta move." It was Brian.

"Yeah, wait, I gotta get my drugs." Still moving slow. Mick stuffed the pot and Bambu in the pocket of his denim jacket, dug out a couple whites from his stash box, crushing one up between two quarters and snorting it. He'd definitely need a lude by the end of the night.

Load the gear in Adam's van. Not much, just three guitars, Adam's Twin Reverb, and the B-15. Mike Delmonte their drummer would arrive separately. Speed creeping down the back of his throat. Bitter postnasal drip. A good sign the drug was being absorbed. This is a power surge. Or at least he wasn't going to fucking pass out on the bandstand, curled up inside Mike's 24-inch champagne-sparkle Ludwig kick drum, with the old flannel shirt Mike used to muffle the ring for a pillow.

Five miles down a country road. Into town. Klein's, an old German rathskeller in a two-story wood building, now watering hole for college students, local alkies, and dirtbag hippies. Posters for Red Dirt Reefer on Friday and the Backwoods Band on Saturday tacked on the door. Load in. Mike was already there, setting up the drums on a piece of indeterminate brown carpet on the small stage. The place had a welcoming smell of stale booze. Vincent, a wispy middle-aged black dude, was sweeping up cigarette debris and collating last night's empties. "Hey, it's the Reefer boys. How you doin'?" "Gettin' there," answered Mick.

Red-flocked walls with gold-painted eagles perched on plaques around the room. Creepy. Like fuckin' Berchtesgarten or whatever the fuck it was, hideaway in the Bavarian Alps. Roll the B-15 up to the stage, flip the top up. A few early drinkers, cocktail-hour starters now getting a full load on. Adam tuning up, the Les Paul in regular tuning and the off-white Danelectro hollowbody he used for slide in open E. Mike adjusting cymbals. Brian getting levels on the house PA. Uncase the bass, tune to Adam—da-da, da-dong, da-ding. Done. Two minutes of "Hoochie Coochie Man" for soundcheck. Ready.

Thirst. Cottonmouth and kidneys need something to chew on. Brian was already down at the bar getting a Bud. Klein's gave bands free domestic beer but charged for imports and liquor. For somebody who drank as much beer as he did Brian was still pretty skinny. Pale squarish face, long stringy brown hair, slightly buggy eyes, brown ribbed top. Not great-looking, but girls liked him. Mick drained half a Rolling Rock in one gulp. Adam—bushy Isro hair, red plaid flannel shirt—was hunched over, scribbling out set lists in Magic Marker on the back of a flyer.

Set-list time. Plenty of potential for dissension. They had to do three sets, one at 9:30, one at 11, one at 12:30. The band clustered around. If Adam got free rein to do it all himself, they'd do nothing but blues and Dead covers. For a Jew from East Meadow, Long Island he had distinctly Southern-fried tastes. The Allmans, Marshall Tucker, Robert Johnson, Elmore James and a host of country blues, some bluegrass licks he'd copped off Jerry Garcia.

Open with the Allmans' version of "Statesboro Blues." They all could agree on that.

"'Done Somebody Wrong'" second?" Adam asked.

"Nah, fuck that, we're not an Allmans copy band," Mick.

"It's not an Allmans song, it's an *Elmore James* song."

Brian intervened. "Hey. Look at what's on the album. Use some common sense. Are we gonna put a shill in the audience to yell out 'Whipping Post' next?" They compromised on "Sugar Magnolia," an upbeat midtempo rocker that would satisfy Adam's Dead obsession. Save "Crossroads" for later. A few bar-band staples, rockers, Chuck Berry and Stones covers. "Train Kept A-Rollin'" won consensus for the second set, Adam because it was the Yardbirds, Mike because it was Aerosmith, Mick and Brian because it was both. (Not one of them had ever heard the original.) Adam groaned and cringed when Mike and Brian wanted to do Bad Company's "Can't Get Enough of Your Love."

"Commercial shit, man, how can you like that?" "Commercial" was the strongest term of opprobrium in Adam's rock-critical vocabulary. No point pointing out to him that the Dead selling out Nassau Coliseum was not exactly a free concert in the Haight-Ashbury panhandle.

"Cause it fuckin' rocks." Mike. Mike was from

24

Canarsie and liked the crude, powerful beat, the drummer's penchant for uncomplicated pounding. He was short with a black shag haircut and a mustache. Another small argument over funk covers, Stevie Wonder's "Higher Ground," Curtis Mayfield's "Superfly," B.T. Express' "Do It Till You're Satisfied."

"Man, that shit is so stupid and repetitive, it's just one chord." Adam again. But clubowners liked bands to play dance music, and Mike liked the grooves. Mick wasn't a very good funk player, but liked it too. Compromise here was that they agreed to do "Laura" late in the first set, a ballad Adam had written for an ex-girlfriend that everyone else in the band hated as hopelessly sappy. Mick was willing to put up with playing almost anything anyone else wanted as long as they did the two instrumentals he'd written and the two Lou Reed covers he sang on.

Mick's drug cocktail held up through the first set, the speed warding off collapse, the beer taking the mindracing teethgrinding edge off the speed, and neither one addling him too much. He wasn't playing great or inspired but he wasn't fucking up either. They had a decent crowd, mostly students, not really happening yet, milling about with beers and drinks, a few girls starting to dance, a few older dudes and one woman a well-worn 30 sitting at the bar. They closed the first set with Lynyrd Skynyrd's "Gimme Three Steps" and took a break, Brian and Mick rushing the bar.

Brian settled in, holding court. Mick stood off a few feet away, nursing a beer. He felt a tap on his shoulder. "Hi, Mick," said a soft voice, slight trace of Spanglish, bigger trace of Long Island. It was Maria Diaz. She'd been in his philosophy class. She had large octagonal glasses, frizzy black hair, and mottled olive skin. She thought she was ugly. He thought she was fucking beautiful and that tied his tongue, as compulsively fecund as his mind was acting. After he said hi back he was stuck for a gambit to keep the conversation going. Anything routine or mundane would sound stupid and banal, anything more lofty would sound pretentious and arty. She settled the question by asking him how he was.

"Really burnt. I was up all night doing that paper. I had to do some more speed to make this gig."

"Oh, do you have any more?"

"I got one white. Wanna split it?"

They slipped back into the storage room that served as a dressing room for bands at Klein's. Mick unwrapped the tinfoil, crushed the pill on it on top of a brown Formica table. They snorted the powder through a rolled-up dollar bill. Outside the thirtyish barfly woman was wrapped around one of the old dudes, slow-dancing to a country song on the jukebox. "Oh, baby don't get hooked on me."

"Man, I don't see how people can listen to that shit." Mick, pointing outside at an abstraction. "I'm from Brooklyn, I just don't see it."

"Why do you play all that country blues and Southern rock then?" Maria. "Lynyrd Skynyrd's not exactly Brooklyn music."

"Yeah, but it's rock'n'roll. Like the Stones and Hendrix and everything comes from Robert Johnson and blues, it's not that redneck cry-in-your-beer crap."

"Did you ever hear Hank Williams?" she asked. "It's the most perfect heartbreak you could ever imagine." Mick couldn't understand why somebody would think heartbreak was perfect, but a lot of people

26

thought his ideas were insane too, so he wasn't going to argue with her and blow things.

Pause. Mick's mind racing away, jammed compulsive thoughts. The second dose was coming on. "Are you from the city?" he asked.

"Originally. I grew up in Bushwick. We moved to the Island when I was ten. We live in Brentwood. My father started out working in a bodega, and now he's got a whole chain. He thinks he's king of the world. He's always telling me and my sister we don't know anything, we've never been in the real world, he's like, 'I came here from Puerto Rico in 1953 with nothing but the shirt on my back and now you see what I have? You kids don't want to work." The speed and liquor were starting to make her blither. "And when I started going out with guys—forget it! My parents named me Maria Magdalena, ain't that some heavy shit for a Catholic girl? It's like telling you you're going to grow up to be a slut, a moral lesson for everybody. So I was. I was the school slut. I only did a few guys but they all had big mouths. This one asshole on the football team I went out with once, Bob Coleman, he comes up to me the next week, puts a big rock in my face and goes 'Let him who is without sin cast the first stone.'"

"Brooklyn's not that bad. At least the city's only 35 cents away, and there's some cool people around. It got a lot cooler when drugs and rock'n'roll came. Like before pot and acid came around you were either a hood or a nerd, nothin' in between. I knew this guy Louie C, Louie Crescenti, and he was like the first one in the neighborhood to have long hair, he played in this band the Crescent Cactus, and he was always 'The fuck-n faggot. Louie the fuck-n faggot.' Then like two

27

years later the same dudes who'd been picking fights with him would be like, 'Hey Louie, man, you got any pot?'" The speed and beer were making him blither too. Speed and alcohol was one of the worst drug combinations you could do for your body, but one of the best for getting to know somebody fast, the speed stimulating your tongue and the liquor loosening it. "But you know, I get along with my parents a lot better when I'm not living with them."

"If I ever have a daughter the first thing I'm going to tell her when she's a teenager is use birth control and never fuck any boy who goes to the same high school, or you'll never hear the end of it."

Adam came in, interrupted. Time to get back on stage. Mick was buzzing on second wind and possibilities. They opened with "Rewired," a fast, jagged sort of surf instrumental he and Adam had written, into Chuck Berry's "Promised Land." People were starting to dance and Mick was feeling like he'd been singled out and blessed by the Great Gods of Underdrive, pumping the bass faster, harder and fatter than he ever had, into a couple more rockers and a couple funk tunes. Revelation. The secret to funk was simplicity and time, using the bass like a drum, one or two or three notes in the right place and then shut up, not running off at the fingers in a constant barrage, just a few well-placed bursts. Now "Train Kept A-Rollin'," Mick and Mike locking in and revving together like a D-train express, Adam's guitar a cawing crow over it, Brian wrapping his leg around the mike stand for the stop: "She looked so good, I just couldn't let her go." Into "Sweet Jane," Mick's turn to sing. "This one's for Maria." The *Rock'n'Roll Animal* album version, plenty of room for Adam to play around, then crunch in with

28

the eight-note riff like the New York City skyline appearing over the horizon after 40 days and 40 nights in Middle America. Mick couldn't really sing but if Lou Reed could half-talk his way through it why couldn't he?

The band dropped down for the third verse. Mick looked out at Maria and she had a drawing pad out, scribbling away furiously with a Rapidograph, the band surrounded by wrought-iron curlicues, whirl-winds, flying doves, liana vines with myriad prolifer-ating tendrils. No one was dancing and the crowd at the bar was thick. They finished the set with a couple Stones covers and Bowie's "Jean Genie."

Mick went over to Maria. "That was great," she said. He was bummed. "People weren't into it." He invited her to get high. They went out back, him rolling one up in the shadow of a dumpster, fired it up. She gazed at him. "I got to go—I got a lot of studying to do tomorrow—but here's my number." She kissed him quickly. His cock sprang up like a maple-necked mushroom. Then she was gone.

Third set, traditionally time to stretch out and jam, when the customers were too drunk or tired to demand faithful cover versions, the bar slowly emp-tying. They did "Mutant Sphinx," a long Zappaesque tune by Brian, quirky with lots of changes, Mick got lost in thought and spaced out on going to the chorus, earning angry stares from the rest of the band. The warped lens of paranoia begins to impose its field of vision. Slow blues, Adam getting to wail on slide on Elmore James' "It Hurts Me Too," Mick slowing down for it, still burning away, the crash beginning to sink its claws in his temples. Try to fight it, just stay on track, you've just got to keep the bottom steady, don't fuck it up.

End the night with another Lou Reed cover, "Rock'n'Roll," Mick joining Brian on the choruses, Adam taking a long solo and rhythm jam while Brian finished his ninth beer. Life-saving powers of rock'n'roll, but not very transcendent at this hour. Mick's mood was more Black Sabbath. What is this that stands before me? A bunch of friends he didn't really know and a bunch of drunks ranging from obliviously frivolous to what-are-you-looking-at motherfucker. Time to do those ludes. Take three, they're bootlegs, they're not as strong as Rorers. He needed about 20 hours of coma. Timed right they'd kick in just as he got home.

They loaded the van. Adam and Mike went to get the money as Mick and Brian waited in the van, smoking a joint. Brian hanging out with a round-faced girl named Claudia in a lacy tanktop and brown bangs. "Claudia! You comin'?" Her friends, leaning out the windows, packed into a small blue car. "Oops. That's my ride. Take care."

Mick rolled another number for the road. Spark it up rolling home on 32, the new-leafed trees waving in the headlights, then dissolving back into the night. The radio playing a staticky guitar solo. Orange dayglo paint on the trunk of a tree, the coal of the joint glowing as they passed it, a red light blinking in the distance behind them, then coming closer. Pull over.

Cop by the driver's side window. License, registration, you got a busted taillight. Sniffing. Everybody out of the van. Electronic crackle. *Brown '68 Ford Econoline van, Roger Navy 6-7-8-6.* More cops come. ID. All his identity, the sum total of his bodily and mental and personal beings and histories, reduced in the eyes

30

of the state to computer-dot printing on a cardboard card. GREENBERG, MITCHELL T. 2120 AVENUE X BROOKLYN, NY 11235. 11/27/55. 6' 0" BR BL. CORRECTIVE LENSES. Empty your pockets. Mick had stuffed his pot vial down his balls when they first got pulled over. Walk a straight line. Adam did OK, stepping gingerly in measured paces. Brian strutted, rolling his hips like Mick Jagger, not deviating *too* far off course. Mick. The pot vial had fallen through a hole in his underwear and was lodged along his thigh in a fold of his jeans.

"Aaahh, fuuuhhcck, daw aaahI haaaff taaa daaaw thissss," he grumbled, voice whining like a chainsaw running on glacial speed.

"Yeah, you stupid druggie, you obey an order of a police officer."

"AaaI'm competely fuck-innn sober. AaaaI wuuhzn't fauhckin' driivinnn'."

Mick tried to keep his legs together. The pot vial had oozed down to just above his knee. He wished it would go back up like an undescended testicle. He tripped over his ankles and collapsed on the gravel. Meanwhile another cop going through the van had looked in the Army-surplus bag with Adam's cables and wah-wah pedal and found two half-ounces of Colombian. Mick got jerked up and the vial protruded blatantly over the top of his boot, a screaming neon cylindrical wart.

They got taken down to the new police precinct in town, tossed in a holding cell with two wood-slab benches and a steel toilet with no seat and a flush button in the wall. Six other prisoners already in there, two flash black guys in denim and suede patchwork, one with purple-tinted aviator glasses and a beard, possession of cocaine; two greaser-dirtbag types, one Italian-looking in a flame-patterned polyester shirt, the other bigger, bearded, gut bulging out of a green T-shirt, receiving stolen property, unauthorized use of a vehicle, and possession of narcotics paraphernalia; and two drunk drivers, one a blond fratboy type, the other a shamed-looking middle-aged man in a rumpled suit, what was left of his hair slicked back and boulevards of broken veins ruddying his pale face.

"Fuck, man. All that good weed gone to waste," Adam bemoaned.

"Fuckin' cops probably smokin' it up right now." The biker dude. "Or takin' your shit and sellin' it. Damn I wanna get fucked up. Couple ice-cold beers, coupla bones, and some good New York dope."

"When I get out of here, I'm gonna get sooooo high." Adam. "I'm gonna roll one up the size of a cigar."

"Fuck that," said the older of the black dudes, the one with the glasses. "You know what you gonna do? You gonna sit on the motherfuckin' toilet, smoke a motherfuckin' cigarette, and go 'I'm gonna take me a motherfuckin' shit.' You ever see a motherfucker take a shit in jail? You wanna be sittin' there gruntin' and groanin' with eight other motherfuckers lookin' at yo' ass like you a monkey in the motherfuckin' zoo? Am I right?"

Mick had other uses in mind for the toilet. He knelt at the edge of the steel receptacle, abandoning all hope of quelling the revolt in his stomach, praying to the porcelain god for deliverance, convulsively presenting an offering of all the night's mortifications dissolved in a backdrop of bitter yellow bile. Adam and Brian cleaned him off a bit and laid him to rest under one of the benches. It was easy to sleep.

All three of them were charged with possession with intent to sell for Adam's ounce. The cops said it was in plain view on the dashboard of the van. Adam got driving while intoxicated, and Mick got a misdemeanor for the 2.5 grams in the vial.

He called Maria two days later, after his parents had come up from Brooklyn to bail him out. There would be a separate price to pay for that. She was upset for him and asked him if he wanted company. He drove onto campus to pick her up, carefully hovering just under the speed limit, one eye constantly in the rear-view mirror. She was wearing a turquoise leotard and blue jeans. The lawyer said we'd probably be able to get off with probation, he told her. They sat close together on the bed in her room, staring into each other's eyes, not sure who should make the first move, then kissing with quick, tentative pecks, then imbedding themselves in each other. Later she told him he was the gentlest man she'd ever been with and the first one ever to make her come.

IN THE SHADOW OF THE BRIDGE

N o respect for the wretches, the geeks, in the outside world. Scratching out a living or dragging out a waiting, waiting for their turn in the spotlight. 15 minutes of fame? No. More like 35 minutes of obscure glory, where it didn't matter what kind of pathetic sentiment you held in the name of emotion, what kind of picayune fetishes you held in the name of flash, as long as you could crank. Better to be outrageously ridiculous than mediocre, for there were plenty of them diluting the atmosphere, sometimes completely deadening it.

And the outcasts and misfits formed a community. Public stupidities were dished ruthlessly, private sins gossiped mercilessly, but when all the passion, flash and raw power rolled together ecstasy earned respect.

Sid Berkowitz met Queenie Qualls at the Bob Marley concert at Eastern Long Island State College in the spring of 1974. Queenie was in the row in back of

Sid, holding court in the side bleachers, resplendent beneath her giant Afro. Sid passed her his joint. She asked if she could pass it on to her friend and he agreed. He believed in the 614th commandment of Jewish hippies: It is a mitzvah to share your pot with strangers at rock concerts. He was still a little irked when it didn't come back. He only had three emaciated joints for the whole show.

Halfway through the set—Marley dancing up front, undulating sinuously in back of the mike stand; Peter Tosh off to the side, tall and spectral as he chinked the rhythm, Family Man Barrett's fat, rich bass sound booming warmly through the gym—she tapped him on the shoulder. "Yo, white Rastaman," she called. "'Ere." She passed him a spliff. Rastafarianism was almost completely unknown on Long Island back then, but Sid's long raggedy hair was as close to dreadlocks as any white person there got. He'd read a magazine interview with Marley talking about the vow of a Nazarite in words and sounds worlds away from his cousin Seth's bar mitzvah speech. The vow of a Nazarite is to never cut your hair, eat meat, or drink wine. Sid was 15 then and cited the vow of a Nazarite whenever any of his relatives gave him shit about his hair. He wasn't so devout about the last part of it. He'd drank six glasses of Manischewitz, forcing his father to pull the car over at a Long Island Expressway rest area on the way home. His gastric ululations had interrupted two gay men in mid-cruise. He'd been grounded for two weeks, despite his mother's contention that the hangover was punishment enough.

They ran into each other again four years later. Sid had moved to Brooklyn, worked a succession of

36

bad easy-to-get blue-collar jobs—messenger, sorting used clothes in a warehouse; bad easy-to-get office-temp jobs—file clerk, mailroom; then landed a job as a proofreader at an ad agency. He'd lasted five months before getting called into the boss' office. They'd been working on an ad campaign for the *New York Post* and he'd loudly commented that the paper was "a lot of celebrity-scandal bullshit to fool the masses while they're ripping them off. Fuckin' prolefeed, like in 1984."

"Your work is fine," they told him, "we don't have any problems with it, but we've had several complaints about your attitude. Maybe you'd be happier somewhere else."

"Fine. Can you get me on unemployment?"

That meant 39 weeks of relief from the basic bargain of work: Selling most of your time and energy to some asshole who made more money than you and expected you to be enthusiastic about it. He hated every grey pigeonshit morning of it. He'd made enough money to get a black Rickenbacker bass, which he'd dusted with drippy nebulas of red spray paint, and a Sunn Concert bass stack. Bored to death by the state of rock'n'roll—music with all the grit and passion of a stainless-steel dildo, we're-oh-so-hip cocaine attitude—he'd discovered punk, obsessively spinning Patti Smith's raw word-jams, the Ramones' melodic chainsaw, and—one icy winter afternoon— the Sex Pistols' "Anarchy in the UK," a British 45 with the small hole in the middle. He cut his hair short, evolved his wardrobe to black, practiced daily on his bass.

That weekend he was out on Long Island, party-ing with some old friends in Whitman. Drive around, get a couple sixes, go to the graveyard and smoke shitty pot, speculate about how the woman whose tombstone was a bedpost must have been the town whore in the 19th century. There were still woods left this far out of the city. Then one of the women would see ghosts and freak out, and they'd leave. Drive around some more, developments and pine barrens and strip malls. Fuckin' pathetic, he thought, these people are almost 25 and they're still doing the same nothing they bitched about all the time in high school.

Except that he recognized the tall skinny black woman, light-skinned, oval-faced. "Yo. Didn't we party at the Bob Marley concert at E.L.I.?"

"Yeah! I remember you. What've you been up to?

"Living in the city. I'm trying to start a band."

"Yeah? What are you into?"

"Kind of punk, like that kind of energy, but not formula, you know?"

"Wow, so am I. What bands do you like?"

They swapped band names like passwords, Ramones Blondie Heartbreakers Clash Television X-Ray Spex Talking Heads Suicide.

Queenie came from East Floyd, two towns away from Whitman. Her father, a psychology professor at E.L.I., had been killed in a car accident when she was 13, three years after they'd moved there. Burnouts in the town had inevitably called it Pink Floyd. She'd been prominent among them, selling pot more to get known as the one with the good weed than to make any money. Though she'd also wangled a job as assistant manager of a McDonald's there, one of the new ones with the mansard roof instead of the garish golden arches. She'd come in to work at the front counter totally wasted one day, a grinning, goofy,

38

bantering high, and the regional supervisor had hailed her "dynamic personality." She'd done two years at E.L.I. and then dropped out, doing some volunteer work against the nuclear-power plant in Gull Point, a dark satanic behemoth on what was once beach.

They exchanged numbers. Queenie noticed his last name. "You aren't related to Marshall Berkowitz, are you?"

"Yeah. That's my father."

"Holy shit! He was my cousin's lawyer."

Queenie's cousin Jimmy had been framed in 1970 on charges of conspiracy to blow up the Department of Motor Vehicles building in Riverhead. Any number of license-renewers had harbored far more violent thoughts about the DMV than Jimmy Qualls ever had, but he was Minister of Defense for the Riverhead Brothers Collective, small-town would-be Black Panthers, and Suffolk County did not take kindly to that sort of thing. Sid's father had gotten him acquitted— he'd devastated the informer the RBC called a "Judas-goat motherfucker" on cross-examination—but Jimmy was now in Attica for coke.

"You aren't related to David Berkowitz too, are you?

"No. And he was adopted anyway."

A week later Queenie took up residence on Sid's couch in Brooklyn.

Unemployed, they hung out at home most nights, smoking pot and philosophizing. Punk, nihilistic on the surface of the image, had resurrected their dreams of cultural revolution. To insiders, the scene was dying—the Sex Pistols imploding, most of the New York bands less than a year to live—but to them it was a revelation. Grandiose dreams, basslines and screams sparking upheaval to shake the world. Upheaval and groove, soundtracks for celebration and apocalypse. And they'd be at the center of it. "Punk-rock is the sound of cities crumbling." Sid. "Yeah, two-minute songs make a lot of sense when we've got the Bomb over our heads." Queenie.

They were hated as weirdos and radicals in suburbia, scorned as bridge-and-tunnel hicks and nobodies in Manhattan, driven by an odd mix of revulsion and fun. "We should do a song called 'Geek Romance'," Queenie suggested. Sid played a '50s doo-wop progression on his acoustic, she improvised non sequiturs and innuendoes.

They talked frustration, boredom, neither hope nor desire of fitting in, jumbled with dreams of communal ecstasy. "Everyone's so fuckin' complacent," Sid complained. "I wanna play music that's gonna fuckin' shake them out of it, music that's gonna wake them up, get them off like real rock'n'roll should."

"Yeah," Queenie answered. "We're gonna be stars, we're not gonna be nihilists. We want everybody in on the party if they're cool, you know what I mean?

Who are we going to get for guitar players, they wondered. Sheila O'Neill, a witchy hippie artist Sid knew, recommended a songwriter she knew named Jimmy Keniston. Jimmy lived with his parents in a two-family home in southeastern Queens, a dead-end street abutting the Long Island Railroad embankment, next to a small factory with ailanthus trees overgrowing a chain-link fence. He used it as a base of operations, spending most of the week crashing around with friends and lovers. The rumor that he'd been a hustler when he was younger wasn't true, but

40

as closing time impended the prospect of sex with a stranger was often far more enticing than the two-hour double-fare subway and bus ride to Queens.

Jimmy showed up a week later, slight and smiling, kinky hair hot-combed into spikes. He came bearing four plastic cases full of old 45s, '60s garage-band obscurities and classics, '70s soul hits and rarities. Unlike Sid or Queenie, he had more than garage-band experience. He'd played CBGB twice and was a gofer at a small disco-record company for three months.

Sid called a guitarist named Rori Ross he'd met at a Pere Ubu show at CBGB. Her real name was Irene Rabinowitz, a short, chunky 20-year-old with dyed black hair. She lived with her parents off Kings Highway near the F train, in a 1920s Spanish castle building that smelled of old people's piss and chicken soup.

She had just bought a guitar for $125 at a pawnshop on Atlantic Avenue, a '50s Gretsch hollowbody in a hideous shade of institutional green. Jimmy had topped that in the cheap-guitar derby; he had an old copper-colored Danelectro his mother had found for $25 at a garage sale when he was 16.

It was a grey late-spring day in Brooklyn, the trees in bloom, the air dank and sweet, occasionally tarnished by car exhaust.

"We're going to be stars, but on our *own terms*, you know?" Queenie proclaimed.

All these grandiose dreams were meaningless unless translated into songs, and that wasn't the easy part. Transmuting them into actual sets of lyrics and chords was not automatic alchemy. The distance between their desire and their capabilities seemed galactic.

41

They spent the afternoon and evening sitting around the living room, batting around ideas.

Sid dug out his pot vial, began rolling a joint. "Why don't you wait on that," Jimmy interceded. "We want to remember what we play."

"Can you lend me five bucks?" Queenie asked. "I'll pay you back Monday." She came back ten minutes later with a six-pack. Her unemployment check was $20 a week more than Sid's, but she never seemed to have any money.

"Why don't we do one called 'Kill Your Boss'?" Sid.

"No, too obvious." Queenie.

"I'm never going to be a part of corporate America," Jimmy expounded. "I hate it. But I don't want to do sloganeering, it just looks silly. These people act like there's no joy in their lives. How can they deny themselves the pleasures of the world? They come off like some screaming gargoyle caricature thing almost. I'll be happy if I can just make people dance."

Queenie, playing acoustic, started a funk jam. Jimmy dismissed it. "We're not rhythmically sophisticated enough to pull that off. I played in funk bands, we're not even close enough to do it wrong right."

"We need to do one that really rips." Rori.

"Yeah," Sid enthused.

Rori's guitar playing wasn't up to it; she was trying for rage, but couldn't get it out right. Nobody had ever taught her the secret of punk guitar—nothing but downstrokes—so she sounded like on open-mike folksinger on speed, hyperactive acoustic strumming. She could do a nice British Invasion chime, though.

"We're not the Ramones or the Sex Pistols,"

Jimmy said. "It's been done. What's the point?" He wasn't that good a guitar player, but he had a good feel for the right phrase to shape a melody or groove. Sid had a lot of intensity and some chops, but was sloppy.

Queenie hit a one-chord lick, too syncopated to be punk, too messy to be funk. Sid clanked in with the bass, hammering on low notes. Queenie improvised some lyrics, and it became "You're So Tired." They had a song. Like an entry in a baby book. First Practice. First Song. Jimmy brought in an idea he'd been working on, "Television Scholar," half-written, a riff and a chorus. "That needs something more." Queenie. "A bridge?" Jimmy. Sid came up with a four-chord lick that fit. "Yeah, that works." Queenie. "Wow, we've got two songs." "It's fabulous." "Fuckin' great."

Five hours, two songs down. Queenie cooked dinner. One pound of spaghetti, dusted with most of a jar of Spice Isle Jamaican Curry. The neighbors banged on the walls when they started to play again. They stayed up late playing Jimmy's 45s and Sid's albums, smoking up the last of the herb, mooting possible names. The Fashion Victims? No, we're not dressy enough. The 714s? Too druggy.

They settled on the Mutant Queens, inspired by a James Dean bio Jimmy was reading. His full name was James Dean Keniston. "Hey, dig, new blue jeans, Jimmy Dean," Queenie twanged.

Jimmy, hunched over the turntable, played ? and the Mysterians' "8 Teen." Garage-band legends, five Michigan Chicanos whose home-recorded 45 had hit Number One in the fall of '66. The Cramps' "Human Fly," punk neo-'50s insect guitar buzz. Machine's "There But for the Grace of God," the uncensored version, about a couple who'd fled the Bronx for "somewhere far away, with no blacks, no Jews, and no gays." Wayward daughter dancing desperately, the riff reiterating in the disco night. The Soul Brothers Six's "Some Kind of Wonderful," a mid-'70s hit for the much-maligned Grand Funk Railroad.

"I never heard the original of that." Sid.

"You can hear the mike clunk on it." Rori.

"Actually I *liked* Grand Funk," Jimmy said. "Everybody was calling them the worst band in the world, the Talentless Trio, and it made me want to check them out, just to be contrary. They had that whole Detroit-chrome factory-boy thing, 'Heartbreaker,' 'Inside Looking Out.' It's pop music, you know, it creates a world for people to connect to, it's like it's imaginary and it's real, and they were like coming from this machine world, this car world, tough boys becoming hippies and trying to make sense, it was stupid but it was really touching."

"I'm getting clo-o-ser to my ho-ome," he sang, laughing. "I like when people can be stupid. It means they're more sincere. And they had good songs too."

Queenie pulled out Sid's copy of the *All the Girls in the World Beware!* album. "But some of their stuff was embarrassing," Jimmy went on. "Look at this *cover!*" It was truly tacky, the bands' heads superimposed on bloated bodybuilders. "I mean, there's *good* stupid and *stupid* stupid. This is so *egotesticle.*"

All four crashed out in various configurations, Sid and Queenie in the bed, Rori on the couch, Jimmy on the floor. They started again the next morning.

This day was more productive. Things came easier, flowing and falling into place. Jimmy's two-chord lick, underpinned by Sid's discoey bassline, fit a lyric sheet called "Obsession." They agreed on four covers, culled mainly from Jimmy's 45s. The Undisputed Truth's "Smiling Faces Sometimes," an exception to Jimmy's edict against funk covers, Sid playing the ominous-commentary bassline tough, rigid, Jimmy asking him to make it "less stiff, more melodic." The Velvet Underground's "Guess I'm Falling in Love," two dirt-simple C-chord progressions, learned off a bootleg album of Sid's. Rori wanted to do Lesley Gore's "You Don't Own Me." Queenie and Jimmy shot that idea down—Joan Jett already did it—but it led into Cher's "Bang Bang." They did a flamenco-disco version, Queenie camping it up in a tuneless punk squawk, part of her wanting to get into its schlocky heartfeltness, part of her incapable of taking it seriously, of playing anything straight. Drafi's "Marble Breaks and Iron Bends," a total obscurity from 1966, a dumb and overwrought love song with good dynamics and surge.

Everything seemed to hang together, devolving into a sort of updated '60s-garage style, basic chords and progressions, hard and hypnotic. Jimmy's quasi-operatic baritone—he'd sang in church for years when he was a kid, losing his virginity to the organist at 15—was well mismatched with Queenie's Poly Styrene yowl. Somehow it worked.

Rori pushed for at least one pure-punk song. Sid pounded out a psychedelic-punk progression, an E minor-F-G verse and an A minor-F-G chorus—awfully close to the Ramones' "I Just Wanna Have Something to Do"—and the result—lyrics out of his notebook—was "I'm Not Disposable." It was the first song he'd ever written that got played by anyone else. He was ready to pass out cigars.

At the end of the day they had half-coherent versions of eight songs, including the four covers. But Jimmy wasn't happy with the name the Mutant Queens. "It sounds like a birth defect," he complained. There was already a San Francisco band called the Mutants, Sid pointed out.

Queenie suggested All My Children, after the soap.

"All Your Children," countered Jimmy.

"Yeah, that's like who spawned these creatures—you did," Sid chimed in, and they had a new name. Queenie and Sid went to the pot store on Fifth Avenue to cop a celebratory trey bag while Rori rode the F train home.

They put ads for a drummer up in the punk clothing stores on St. Marks Place, the guitar stores on 48th Street, and a couple places around the neighborhood. The first one who called was a mainstream rocker with absolutely nothing in common with them. The next one was a total cretin, telling Queenie "I don't wanna play with chicks in the band." The third auditioned, and was way too good for them. Then one night they were hanging out with Aetern, an old friend of Sid's who lived a few blocks away, and he mentioned he'd played drums in high school. He hadn't been in a band since then—eleven years—but Queenie quickly talked him into trying it again. Aetern was a wispy, mystical glam-rock hippie leprechaun, at 27 the oldest one in the band. He'd lose it completely if he tried to do a roll, but he could keep a steady, minimal thud going.

All Your Children was too unwieldy, so they needed another new name. Queenie suggested Universal Noise, and Jimmy shortened it to the Universals. "It fits, 'cause we're not just punk, we're into lots of different kinds of music," Sid concurred, while Jimmy said it sounded like a cool 1963 R&B act. He was the only one in the band who could have pulled off wearing a gold spangled suit.

Two days after their first practice they had a show to look forward to. Queenie had met three women who were having a house party the weekend after next, and talked them into letting the Universals play.

Next practice Rori brought in a song called "Not You," a fast punk tune, a put-down with a doo-wop chorus. She'd written out every note of the song, delineating the bassline in small curved capitals, EEEE EEEE GGGG GAC, going into an A/F# minor chorus. Jimmy and Queenie resisted, but they did it. They taped four songs, and Sid lettered the cassette box in the neatest printing he could do. Another milestone.

THE UNIVERSALS
TELEVISION SCHOLAR
YOU'RE SO TIRED
OBSESSION
BANG BANG

QUEENIE QUALLS—VOCALS
JIMMY KENISTON—GUITAR, VOCALS
RORI ROSS—GUITAR, VOCALS
SID BERKOWITZ—BASS
AETERN—DRUMS

Aetern and his girlfriend Nova had a party the weekend before the show. Their parties were legendary in the set, all-night spectaculars of sex, drugs, rock'n'roll, and costuming. They had once gone to the immigration office during Alien Registration Month dressed as extraterrestrials. "We are alien from Betelgeuse. We must register," Nova chirped in an android voice.

"We come to take biochemical sample from Earthling rectum," Aetern croaked. Security guards had escorted them out, trying hard not to laugh.

Aetern answered the door for the four other Universals wearing a black caftan covered with runes like Jimmy Page. He had already done one hit of acid and three Quaaludes and was starting to slur. The Stones' "When the Whip Comes Down" blasted from his giant speakers. Pot smoke swirled everywhere, circulating on the dance floor, nitrous oxide hissed from an orange canister. Sid was talking to a woman in a blue tank top named Rea. She was thin, bony and curvy like the baby-blue Strat she coveted. He had a crush immediately.

Music war threatened at the end of the tape. Queenie, holding court on a corner of the couch with a beer in one hand and the nitrous tank and a joint in the other, ranked on Aetern for wanting to put on Pink Floyd. "Pink Floyd *is dead*."

Jimmy snapped on his abhorrence of disco. "Really, Aetern, you can't be so *conservative*. You're acting like 'I will not abide music that's not of the highest cosmic consciousness.' It's all pop music." Bowie's *Young Americans* was the compromise, trad enough to appease the hippies, modern and decadent enough for the punks, and danceable enough for the disco people.

"It's a great album to fuck to," Aetern averred. Queenie passed Sid the nitrous and the metallic taste in his mouth was his only connection to reality for 120 seconds, coming up for the lyric "Do you remember your President Nixon? Do you remember the bills you have to pay?" Nixon was long gone, but there was a whole harsh world out there. A million miles away from this capsule of pleasure, a cocoon of red light and music and sex and drugs. Sheila O'Neill in a long black dress, fluffy with chiffon underneath, her long brown hair swinging as she danced with some WASPy-looking guy. Sid with Rea, Queenie and Jimmy with a cluster of about five people, Jimmy with designs on a slender boy who looked like Rimbaud in an olive T-shirt, Nova, clad in silver body paint and a G-string, a lavender translucent scarf and blue glitter on her face, Aetern with her for one song, with Sheila for one song, one couple in an alcove with most of their clothes off, Sid still with Rea for "Fascination," electric snap beat, mysterious infatuation mood, moving in to caress her.

She edged away uncomfortably. "I'm bisexual," she whispered. "I'm not really into it." She went to get a drink.

Aetern was there, passed Sid a joint, asked him what happened.

"She said she was bi."

"Bisexual? I didn't know she was into men."

Sid accepted Aetern's offer of a lude. Consolation prize.

Rori stood alone in the kitchen. Joints and pipes circulated until no one was very conversational, the couch dwellers swirling to themselves, the couple in the alcove fucking out in the open, Nova sitting cross-legged sucking nitrous, Jimmy making out with Daniel the Rimbaud boy, Sid dancing by himself to Lou

Reed's "Heroin," the long, epic *Rock'n'Roll Animal* version, lashing and slashing slowly and deliberately like he was kung-fu fighting.

"Very Weimar. Your dance has fascist overtones," said Norman Levy, the Leninist. "Look at all this decadence. We should organize this party and go down to City Hall." Norman had once lectured Sheila O'Neill about how painting her room deep blue—she said it reminded her of the sea—was a "bourgeois indulgence."

"It's three o'clock in the fucking morning. Who'd be there?"

Actually the digital clock had just flipped over to 3:11.

Sid hadn't had sex in six months, not since his sort-of girlfriend, Tara Rizzotti, was committed. She had tried to see if she could go to work on acid and get away undetected. It hadn't worked. The mask had dropped, along with most of her clothes. "You want a sexy secretary—you got one," she screamed, throwing pens, typewriter balls, memo pads, shredding her stockings, biting off her lipstick and spitting out red goo like Linda Blair. 911 was called, she was wrapped in a sheet and strapped to a board, and the sanctity of office decorum was duly restored. He visited her occasionally in the hospital, way out in East Flatbush. She'd gained about 50 pounds in the six months.

Why do I always wind up with fucked-up women, he thought. Maybe because they're the ones who question, who chafe, who kick against the pricks. They're the ones with no choice, they can't just sail through life never wanting more than the lush spectacle, the bland cornucopia. I can't find any common ground with people who aren't outsiders.

50

"Genius is seeing small details and understanding how they're symbolic of something bigger," Sheila had once told him. "Insanity is imagining them to be omens of the dark forces controlling the universe, or your life, when they're not."

"But maybe they are," he had said.

Too wasted to walk the ten blocks home, he and Queenie scraped their money together for a cab. Rori didn't want to take the subway by herself, so she came too. Queenie was trashed. Sid bummed two ludes off Aetern for a nightcap, one for her and one for him. Aetern offered another to Rori. "Take it, it'll loosen you up," Queenie said.

"You don't know how much it means to me to be playing with you guys," Rori told Queenie and Sid when they got home. "It's so special to have you as friends, to be in a band with you. I've never been accepted so much anywhere." She was slurring a bit, the lude kicking in. She hugged them. The hug turned into an embrace, sluggish, sloppy affection slipping over into a three-way tongue kiss. Soon they were all on the bed making out, Rori lying back, one arm around Sid, one around Queenie, pulling Queenie close for a long, slow kiss, Queenie aggressively rubbing and caressing her, Sid stroking Rori's pale silky skin and Queenie's tan velvet. When Queenie unbuttoned her blouse Rori stopped, sat up.

"I can't do this," she said.

"You never did this before?" Queenie asked.

"No, I got raped when I was 17. I only had sex once since then, and I couldn't go through with it."

She stumbled off to the bathroom to throw up. "We shouldn't have given her that lude," Sid mumbled.

"Or maybe we should have given her two, she wouldn't feel so bad," Queenie answered. She rolled over and grabbed his cock. They fucked soporifically, his half-limp dick thrusting precariously into her barely-moist pussy, neither of them coming. All the 22-year-old hormones in the world couldn't counter the downs and bad karma.

They had practice from 7 to 10 the next night. Aetern showed up half an hour late, still jellified from the five ludes he did at the party. They sounded like a cassette player with dying batteries.

"We're not ready at all," Rori said. "We should cancel this."

"No way," Queenie. "We'll pull it together. You always pull it together on stage."

Sid knew they weren't really ready, but he was jonesing to play out so hard he wouldn't even think of canceling. "If we suck, we suck. We gotta start somewhere."

Wednesday night's practice—the last before the show—was better, although they were still shaky on several parts. "Can you play a more steady rhythm?" Jimmy asked Rori after they'd run through "Obsession." It set off a torrent.

"I suck," she moaned. "I can't play. I have no sense of time." Still, they got tentative versions of two new songs, both rockers, Jimmy's medium-fast "Loose Boys" and Rori's pounding "Not You," enough for a full set of ten.

Afterwards Queenie decided she wanted a Mohawk. Sid and Jimmy shaved the sides of her head, first with scissors and then with Sid's razor blades. Sid opted out of the second part on the grounds of chronic uncoordination. "You don't want me severing any vital arteries now, do you?" The next morning Queenie dyed the remaining strip a radioactive shade of canary yellow.

They used up all of Sid's razor blades. He wouldn't be able to shave until his next unemployment check came.

When Sid woke up it burned to piss. There was a nasty green discharge coming out of his cock, a shade darker than Rori's guitar. That meant a trip to the city free VD clinic on Flatbush Avenue Extension, where a doctor with an Indian accent put on rubber gloves, stuck a Q-tip into his glans, and scraped his agonized urethra for a culture. Half an hour later he received the verdict—non-specific urethritis, not gonorrhea—and a prescription for ten days' tetracycline.

When he got back home Tara was in the hallway waiting for him. "I escaped," she said.

Tara was obviously not the world's sanest woman, but Sid had been intrigued by the twists and turns of her mind, enough to indulge her phobias, like not letting anyone write with her special pen, or not walking on the same side of the street as funeral homes. And there weren't many other women interested in him either. Wired, obsessive, prolix, she got totally possessed during sex, like fighting through a hurricane of craziness to get to an eye of sweetness and peace, holding her from behind.

The hospital time had soured her. Whatever drugs they had given her, neurochemical weariness, emotional defeat, she had turned into a slug, resentful and uncomprehending.

Sid was obsessing on the gig, worrying about the state of the band, Rori's depressions, Aetern's spaciness, just whether or not they'd be able to do it at all, or crash and burn in terror as they entered the unknown territory of the stage. He put on the Clash album to practice with.

"Why do you play this punk-rock shit?" she demanded. "It's so negative, it's so depressing. Put on some *real* music." She picked a safety pin out of a ripped black T-shirt Sid had and was idly stabbing her thumb just below the cuticle.

He was glad they'd worn out all his razor blades on Queenie's Mohawk.

She stayed for the next two days. "Sid slept with *that*?" Jimmy whispered when he came over.

"I think that was about 50 million brain cells ago," Queenie answered.

It didn't happen again. She'd decided in the hospital that she was asexual, and Sid was too infected anyway.

He practiced for hours on the day of the show, running through the basslines of every song over and over. Queenie fielded phone calls.

What they were going to wear was a major decision. Jimmy had a scarlet ruffled shirt and a black vest, a 1969 psychedelic-soul look. "Nothing with other bands' names on it," he said, vetoing a homemade Sex Pistols T-shirt Queenie and Sid coveted, a handgun with a limp, dripping barrel. Queenie riffled through Sid's clothes for him, settling on basic scrawny punk-boy black jeans and sleeveless T-shirt. After all this deliberation she wound up in an old orange T-shirt and nondescript baggy pants. Aetern showed up in a scoop-necked silver velvet top; Rori in a black sequined vest over a sheer blouse, an outfit that could flip her from punk to middle-aged housewife in an instant like an optical-illusion toy. Sid used her mascara to color his stubble green.

The party was on the first floor of a yellow stone building on Seventh Street, just up the hill from Fifth Avenue. They moved the equipment over at six o'clock in Aetern's Rabbit.

Queenie knocked on the door, coming back out about five minutes later. "There's this woman Moon-daughter in there, she's a lesbian-feminist-vegetarian-separatist, and she said she didn't want any male musicians playing, this is a womyn's space." she explained. "I told her one of them's gay and two are bi."

"OK, you're my date," Aetern told Sid.

"Well, give me enough drugs and there's no telling what I might do."

It took three more trips to get all the gear over. Queenie deputized Sheila O'Neill to do set lists in black Magic Marker, which she did with an art-nouveau flourish. They opened with "Guess I'm Falling in Love," then "Loose Boys," then "Marble Breaks," Jimmy cupping his hands on the guitar bridge to mute the strings.

There were about 75 people packed into the big empty room, milling, mingling, and drinking beers from a keg. Sid was so nervous his knees were shaking for the first three songs, but then he settled down, strutting out front, hips shaking and swiveling. It was better than losing his virginity, another nerve-raddled consummation of years of fantasy. This time he didn't fall off the stage after ten seconds. Queenie was gobbling beers, singing way off-mike on "You're So Tired," Aetern never really finding the groove, but people were starting to dance. Tara was devouring a bottle of vodka and shouting "Fuck you, play some good music.

Rolling Stones."

"Can you get her to shut up?" Queenie whispered to Sid.

Rori took the mike for "Not You," rattled by Tara's heckling. It was shaky, almost falling apart coming out of the second chorus.

"Paint it black, you devil," Tara called out.

"Something always happens when we play that song," Queenie quipped in a Mick Jagger voice, and they jumped into the disco interlude, "Bang Bang," "Obsession," and "Smiling Faces." People were dancing seriously now, the whole front half of the room shaking, bouncing, and writhing, Queenie and Sid coming out to join them. They did "Smiling Faces Sometimes" much harder than usual, Sid turning the bassline into full-frontal riffage, Queenie and Jimmy trading vocals and laughing, voices blending perfectly, then ripped into "I'm Not Disposable" and the anthemic "Television Scholar."

They got an encore. "We don't know any more songs," Jimmy called out, half apologetic, half impatient like a kindergarten teacher. Queenie, several beers gone, borrowed an acoustic guitar, started "Knockin' on Heaven's Door," speeding it up as Sid and Jimmy followed. Aetern couldn't get it at first, but after a minute or so clicked into a Neanderthal dance beat. Sid and Jimmy bounced around, beaming at each other, pounding and throbbing on the newfound groove. Queenie ran out in the audience, mocking and rocking, yelping "Lick-lick-lickin' on heaven's clit," and "Suck-suck-suckin' on heaven's cock." It lasted ten minutes.

Rori hardly played at all. At the end she looked disgusted. "You can't just spring things on me like

that," she complained. "I don't know that song."
Fucking assholes, she thought, *they're so self-absorbed, they never care about me.*

"It's the same three chords all the way through," Queenie snapped. "You gotta learn to go with it, be spontaneous."

Someone cranked up *The Harder They Come* soundtrack on the stereo wired to the PA, and the whole room was up, "You can get it if you really want." The whole band was dancing in a loose circle, friends and newcomers flowing in and out, passing joints and beers and congratulations. *We did it, we actually pulled it off.* It was a feeling of warm fire, a glow inside, like there were five or ten of them in a cave and winter couldn't touch them, summer caressed them, this sweaty smoky room was tropical heaven and they were all together with their secret of bliss, and soon it was going to light up the entire world.

Tara was passed out in a corner. Sid didn't bother waking her up when it was equipment-moving time. They had another practice booked for Monday night. Aetern wanted to cancel it because he was tired from work and there was a movie on TV he wanted to watch. He showed up an hour late. Then Rori threw another self-pity fit.

"Both of them gotta go," Queenie growled afterwards.

"Yeah, but they're our friends," Sid said weakly.

"We're supposed to be professionals. We can't have anyone around who's holding us back."

Queenie promised to take him out drinking when he got off the antibiotics. She never did.

CHINESE ROCK CITY

After practice they ambled down the Bowery. Sid and Rick the guitarist and Ivan the lead singer. At Fourth Street three drunk suburban rednecks crossed their path and rammed into them.

"Watch where you're fuckin' going," one of them challenged.

"*You* bumped into *me*." Sid turned back and responded. He thought it sounded weak, but it earned a "That's telling 'em" from Rick and Ivan. The two groups were now several feet apart. Three on three and none of us into playing the game. The cretins didn't get the fight they were looking for and moved on.

Past CBGB's. Catching a whiff of stale beer, cigarette smoke and rock'n'roll out the door briefly. They had an audition there in three weeks.

They turned left on Houston Street.

"Where we going?" Sid asked.

"Just for a walk."

Something was weird. They crossed over and walked past Forsyth. As they turned right on Eldridge the jukebox in Sid's head started playing the opening chords of "Chinese Rocks."

If somebody had told Sid that in six months he'd be seriously thinking about living on that block he would have thought they were absolutely fucking demented. Five rooms for $165 wasn't such a good deal when you had neighbors who'd break into apartments in their own building. If somebody had told him that Sinead, a video artist and painter he knew vaguely from Brooklyn, was going to move in on the next block over and he was going to fall in love with her, he probably would have been quite pleasantly surprised.

A few dim figures hung spaced at intervals along the curb of the spectrally lit street. They advanced up to one of them, a tall thin Puerto Rican in an army fatigue jacket.

"Is number 7 open?" inquired Rick, sounding as businesslike and knowing-the-ropes as was necessary. The guide led them into the hallway. It was painted institutional green. Some old Lower East Side tenements never get clean, no matter how hard ambitious home decorators rip up the linoleum and scrub. They're like an old canvas sneaker that's seen more than its share of dogshit, mud puddles and tar.

Number 7 was on the second floor. The guide knocked on the door. "Yo. Flaco. Yo. Flaco."

Flaco must have been either asleep, nodded out, or taking a shit, because it took him several minutes to respond. He sounded tired. Rick and Ivan slipped a ten-dollar bill under the door. About half a minute later the bag came turtling out on top of an envelope. They went downstairs. Ivan held the bag up to the hall light. They found it lacking in quantity, so the guide suggested they exchange it.

Up the stairs again. Another knock on the door.

"What's the matter."

"It's light."

"Let me see," and the envelope oozed out again. Rick dropped the bag on top and it slid in.

"Yeah, that's a light one. Sorry," came Flaco's voice from inside, and a fresh bag turtlebacked out on the envelope.

They repeated the examination routine downstairs.

"Satisfied?" the guide asked.

"Yeah." Rick answered. They smiled and shook hands.

Sid was surprised to find dope businesspeople so honest. Every junkie he'd ever known had relied on all manner of beat schemes, from the crude "you didn't give me a five, man, you gave me a one" to elaborately concocted scenarios. Competition and steady customers had made them semi-respectable, he guessed. They probably saved the rips for desperate situations and really dumb schmucks from uptown and the burbs.

They'd reached Second Avenue and Fourth Street before he said anything.

"That wasn't coke you were copping back there, was it?" It sounded lame as hell, but he wanted confirmation.

"No, but it goes up the nose just as nice," Ivan replied smugly.

"I don't approve," was Sid's rebuttal. The same

phrase his father had used when he found out about his little brother Julius trying coke for the first time. "I've seen a lot of people get fucked up from it and a lot of people die from it, and it's one of the reasons I quit my last band, 'cause those guys were into it."

"We're not junkies. We only snort it once in a while. We use it like coke."

The standard routine. No use going into the whole story. About Nick, who died in his sleep in a rooming house at 18 after shooting up two nickel bags on top of a bottle of Boone's Farm Apple Wine, or Brian, who got stopped by the cops and ate the four hits of methadone he had just copped and never woke up again except to cough, or Byron, who stole the coins-for-crippled-children canister out of a pizzeria, or Al, a once-good musician who'd sold his Les Paul for $150 and pissed it into his veins within a week. Another standard routine. Said so many times it was a total cliche, and true so many times you wondered when people would fucking wise up. Dope glamorous, the deadly nectar of tragic heroes and martyred visionaries? Fuck that, it was Long Island dirtbags stealing car stereos in the parking lot of the East Suffolk Mall, when they weren't ripping off their friends.

He knew that Rick and Ivan were only occasional users, only snorters, and that he was coming off like a Jewish mother, dampening everybody's fun with horror stories contrived from the most innocuous situations. But he also knew this band wasn't going to last.

C-SECTION

C-Section was an after-hours club on East 8th Street between B and C. The building was a small former warehouse with a large basement. Bands played in the basement and there was a sparsely furnished bar on the first floor with a cement floor painted crimson.

The club opened at midnight to a spare crowd—often just band members, their girlfriends and roadies, and a stray tourist or couple—and kept going until it stopped, sometimes at eight in the morning. "Let's go to Leshko's for breakfast and come back to catch the last set" was a joke among its habitues.

This Saturday night the bill was the Criminal Minds and Nonoxynol-9. The bands loaded in at about ten, carrying their amps and drums down a steep concrete staircase under the metal cellar doors. They split equipment to save the trouble of moving it, sharing the Criminal Minds' bass amp and Nonoxynol-9's drums. The guitarists were too picky about their gear to share. The Criminal Minds' Jerome Vinson, an L.A. refugee with stringy blond hair, was intensely protective of his $1,200 Mesa Boogie, believing it vulnerable to the slightest bump. Nonoxynol-9's Sheryl Spermicide, a university brat from Nassau County with fluorescent green hair, adored her 50-watt Fender and flew into a rage if anyone touched it, believing a simple twist of a knob would ruin tonalities that could not be restored. "Write your settings down after soundcheck," someone had once told her. "It's not the same," she had answered.

After soundcheck they went upstairs, leaving the gear onstage. The March night was pleasantly cold, about 40 degrees. A dozen punks were hanging out in front of the club in various degrees of leather, drinking quarts of Old English 800 malt liquor and Ballantine XXX Ale wrapped in paper bags. Beer in the club was two dollars a bottle and quarts were 75 cents at the bodega on Avenue C.

"Think we'll get a decent draw tonight?" Jerome asked his bass player, Mick Greenberg, a lanky ex-hippie who'd come to the Lower East Side via Sheepshead Bay.

"Not until later," Mick said in a soft Brooklyn accent. "Stiff Little Fingers are at the Ritz and Johnny Thunders' at Irving Plaza, so we'll probably get a pretty good crowd when they let out."

Sheryl Spermicide sidled over with a fresh quart of Ballantine. "Green death," she quipped, twisting the cap off and taking a long swig. "Yeah, last time we played here the place was deserted until about 3:30 and then it was like a flood. She passed the bottle over to Mick.

"Yeah, you got to time your sets to catch the

closing-time rush," he answered. "All these kids"—he pointed to the drinking punks—none of them got any money to go out with except maybe the four bucks to get in here. Or they scam the guest list."

"They should call it the pest list," said Sheryl. "You get these assholes coming in the door with a six-pack of Heineken under their jackets going 'I got no money. Can you get me on the list?' XKI's got a song "Put Me On The Guest List, I Don't Wanna Pay."

A beer bottle smashed in the middle of the street. "Fuckin' shit," cursed the thrower, a short, skinny kid named Jimi Gimmix. Jimi had short, spiky black hair in emulation of his idol, Sid Vicious, and wore a lock around his neck and an open leather jacket with no shirt. His chest was covered with cigarette burns and X-shaped scars. He also had on spiked leather bracelets and spandex tubes over his elbows. Beneath the spandex was a veritable railyard of small red marks.

Jimi picked up an empty quart bottle and smashed it in the street. Mick walked over to him.

"Yo, Jimi," he called.

Jimi stopped and turned to him.

Mick put his hands on Jimi's shoulders. "I don't wanna come on like your father, but—"

"YOU'RE NOT MY FUCKIN' FATHER!" Jimi exploded, shaking Mick's hands off and jumping back into a fighter's crouch.

"Yo, listen," Mick said, tensing up but not wanting to fight. "I got a band and if something gets fucked up at the club they're gonna blame it on the band. Not even on us but on 'the kind of crowd they bring in,' you know? And if we lose a gig I want it to be because we fucked up and not because somebody else did. And if the fuckin' cops shut the club down because somebody was breakin' fuckin' bottles in the street then that's one more place we can't play. You understand?"

Jimi breathed out, relaxing visibly. "Sorry," he said.

"Okay. You got any money? You wanna be on the list? I got room."

"Yeah. I'm sorry."

Nonoxynol-9 did the first set at 1:15 to fifteen people. The Criminal Minds played the second an hour later to twenty-five, most of them sprawled on the couches and cushions that lined the walls. A handful drifted back and forth to the front of the stage, standing with their hands in their pockets or shaking their hips tentatively. A large red-haired woman sat on her boyfriend's lap in the back, licking his ears and biting his neck. Upstairs, L.T. Guarini from the Consolations sat at the bar in a gold lamé suit jacket, putting away beers and talking abut Motown and the wretched state of the current music scene. The Consolations, part from the Lower East Side and part from the Belmont section of the Bronx, mixed punk-rock's chaotic trashiness with a love for R&B rhythms and showmanship.

"It sucks now, it's like totally wack," he told the bartender, Eddie Cartagena. "Me and my friends used to sing on the subways back in the '70s. Friday and Saturday nights the last car of the D or the number 4 train in the Bronx was always the party car. People coming back from the city smoking joints, playing boxes. Me and Angel and Patrick would be coming home from Max's or the 9th Circle at like 4:30 in the morning and we'd get up and sing along with Donna Summer. 'Ohhhh—love to love you baby,' you know.

66

I felt like we were the Supremes reincarnated. And we'd be like totally ripped and have just seen the Dolls or whatever. There's nothing like that now. All the punks go 'disco sucks' the minute you put a funky beat in something—don't get me wrong, I hate that fuckin' Studio 54 shit too, the fuckin' cougines in my neighborhood always go 'punk-rock faggots die' at us or like 'Yo, Devo' when they think they're being cool."

"I know what you're saying," Eddie answered, turning sideways to open a beer and make change for a ten. "I turn on the radio and it's the same old shit. All the same covers my old band used to do, same songs we used to do in the park bandshell, summer of 1970. "Black Magic Woman." "Crossroads." Jimi Hendrix, "Who Knows." I'm not kiddin'. Hey, like I'm Puerto Rican and Carlos Santana's my main man, you dig, but give me something new. But you gotta have roots too. I'm trying to get a new band together, but it's really hard finding people who can do what I want."

"What happened to the old one?"

"We broke up in '73. We had some good songs—"El Viajero," "Brothers and Sisters," but we weren't going anywhere. T.C. the bass player got married, had a couple kids, he's workin' for the post office in Brooklyn. Luis the conga player's doing pretty good, some session work, I heard he was gonna audition for Ruben Blades a couple years ago. Ricky the drummer's a stone junkie. Last time I saw him he was trying to sell somebody's cymbals on 4th and B for 10 bucks, looked all faded and wasted, you know. This neighborhood went to shit in the '70s. Dope, fires, you know the cops are corrupt, the landlords want us out, the city don't give a fuck. My sister moved to the Island, she said 'I'm not raising my kids somewhere they gotta go trick-or-treating in the stores because the buildings are too dangerous. Later for that.' I don't blame her."

In between sets, band members hung around desultorily and smoked cigarettes. Jerome played pinball with Denise Morgan, Nonoxynol-9's drummer, a skinny high-school dropout with jet-black hair and a thick Queens accent. Mick and Sheryl compared life stories and talked about the Clash and the Pretenders.

"I saw Sid Vicious at Max's in '78," Mick was saying. "He was fuckin' pathetic—I don't know how he managed to hold the knife to stab his girlfriend, he was so fucked up the mike was falling out of his hand, but his band was great. Jerry Nolan and Arthur Kane from the Dolls and Mick Jones from the Clash—Mick Jones was fuckin' incredible, I think he spent more time in the air than on stage, he was jumping around so much. And the band was like this screaming wall of sound coming at you. I saw the Clash a few months later and they were as good as the Stones in '72."

"So where'd you meet Billy?" Sheryl asked.

"In the Sam Ash on Kings Highway in '77. He was in there with Chris Cazullo—his old guitar player—looking at amps and telling the guy I want like a Sex Pistols-Ramones kind of sound. And the guy's a typical guitar-store asshole, you know, kind of guy who knows six million leads note for note but couldn't play something original if you pointed a fuckin' gun at his head. So he starts telling Billy and Chris, 'No, you don't want that, those punk-rock guys, they can't play, they use whatever amp they fall over and piss on backstage.' This is Brooklyn, you know, Kiss and Rush and Zeppelin land. So I follow them out of the store and start talking to them and then we just kept running into each other around the scene. We started the band about a year ago."

"Yeah, Long Island sucks even worse," Sheryl said. "At least you could take the subway in here. The only thing out there is copy bands and Deadheads. And it's even worse for a woman. I used to answer ads and get 'Chicks can't play,' 'We don't want any girls in the band.' Those assholes think the only thing a woman's good for is to suck their dick in adoration after they finish the set. They play copies—*copies*—to twenty-five people and think they're the rock gods of the century. I get that some in the scene here but it's not half as bad. At least they know Chrissie Hynde and Patti Smith and they'll respect you if your band is any good."

Mick got up to take a piss. Billy Casualty, their singer, collected the rest of the band into the men's room. He waved to Denise to invite her inside. She demurred nonverbally.

"C'mon, you're not gonna get molested in here," called Louie Carcano, the Criminal Minds' drummer, who was also occasionally known as Mannlicher Carcano, after Lee Harvey Oswald's rifle. "The only thing that's gonna happen is Sheryl and Amy might complain you're playing too fast."

She came in and closed the door behind her as Billy unwrapped a small piece of aluminum foil in one of the two stalls. "That coke?" she asked.

"No, it's genuine London motorhead. Scorch your sinuses and keep your brain revving. Not like those bullshit Black Beauties you guys do."

Billy dipped into the tinfoil with a matchbook cover folded over and torn to fit nostril size and passed around snorts. After they went out they all had beers to get rid of the bitter postnasal drip.

Nonoxynol-9 went on again at 3:30, finishing their set just after the 4:10 rush of people crossing Tompkins Square Park from the First Avenue and Avenue A bars. They encored with the Avengers "Uh Oh," a song about a man trying to pick up an escaped mental patient.

Three women got out of a cab and pushed their way into the knot in the vestibule. They were dressed in the height of punk-rock slut fashion, a whirlwind of ripped spandex, black lingerie, fishnets, spiked belts and black and blonde hair dye. They had had a flush night at Broadway Rose, the midtown topless bar they danced at. Three electronics salesmen from Chicago had dropped $175 each plus tips on fake champagne and a half-hour of conversation in the back room, and Rosie Acerdo, Rita Andruleska, and Roxanne Sexbomb had left the club with over $200 each, minus the cost of a gram of blow purchased from the bouncer. That didn't stop them from trying to get on the guest list.

"I'm Billy Casualty's girlfriend," claimed Rosie.

"But you air not on zee list," explained Jean-Michel, the sleepy-eyed Haitian-Parisian doorman.

"We're regulars here. Give us a break," tried Rita.

The inside door swung open, letting out a gust of sound. "I got my business, I got no time for you/Said I'm goin' to a wedding/Getting married to myself," Sheryl sang. Roxanne dipped into her purse and discreetly poked Jean-Michel in the nostril with a small silver spoon, one on each side. The three of them got in for $4. They got downstairs just as the song ended.

"The answer is—The answer is NO," Sheryl sang.

The band stopped cold on one snare hit. Denise rolled around the kit twice and leaped off her stool. Bassist Amy Apathy looked at her quizzically. The DJ put on Mötörhead's "Ace of Spades," segueing into Black Flag's "Wasted."

The Criminal Minds were onstage within two songs. Rosie embraced Billy while Jerome and Mick tuned up. She pointedly ignored Jimi Gimmix, who leaned on a nearby wall, his face about to fall into his beer.

Mick knew the set would be hot from the minute they surged into the Stooges' "Raw Power," Louie smashing the cowbell three times and the snare once to set it off. Billy, barechested in tight tigerskin pants, was thrashing about on the floor by the end of the second verse. He crawled over to Rosie and licked her fishnetted knees. The guitars churned. She pulled his head up toward her crotch. He pulled it back about a foot and ad-libbed into the microphone.

They finished the set about half an hour later, roaring through "Subway Sex," "No More," "Demented," and "No Freedom." The crowd pressed against the low lip of the stage, dancing, flinging sweatdrops, and banging into each other. Mick recognized Johnny Voltage, Maria Mezzanini from Astoria and Ricky from Baby Blade in the front lines. The Damaged Kids were out, a contingent of five 18 and 19-year-olds from Brooklyn led by Kat Genovesi, a chubby girl in a ripped sweater, a kilt and combat boots, also known as Kat Kaos and Kat Litter. She'd grown up in and out of foster homes and sometimes roadied for the Criminal Minds. A couple of teenage boys banged harder, temporarily clearing an oval-shaped space.

They encored with "I Wanna Be Your Dog," another Stooges cover. "For all the girls from Detroit," Billy announced. Rosie and Rita were from Detroit.

"You guys don't mind if I skip out on moving equipment tonight?" he told the band just before Rosie spirited him off to her place.

Louie sat on the drum stool, leaning back on the wall behind and talking to Rita. His green-and-black snakeskin-print shirt, rolled to just below his elbows, dripped with sweat. Jerome didn't bother to unstrap his guitar. Mick just leaned his bass on the amp while he took a quick trip to the bar for more beers to put on his amp head. The after-hours jam was a great C-Section tradition. Anyone who was halfway sober and could play—or sometimes neither—could get on stage.

Sheryl uncased her red Gibson SG and plugged in. They kicked into "Pipeline." Mick and Sheryl pounded the rhythm like an IRT express while Jerome surfed leads over it. Denise stood by the side of the drums and whacked the cymbals.

They did the Ramones' "Blitzkrieg Bop" next. As the song ended L.T. Guarini lurched stageward.

"You guys know 'Around and Around'?" he asked. "Sort of," said Jerome.

"It's easy. Chuck Berry in A. Just watch my arm for the stops."

L.T. could sing pretty well, messing with the lyrics. "Yeah, six o'clock"—the band stopped—"and the place was packed"—they riffed with each phrase, rocking back and forth—"Front doors was locked/ yeah, the place was packed/And when the Ninth Precinct knocked—them doors flew back."

Next Sheryl hit the intro to "Chinese Rocks," an

ode to the joys of heroin addiction written by some of the East Village's leading lights. L.T. stuck the mike out to a knot of five people who shouted the chorus. The song was an anthem even among people who didn't do dope. It foundered when Mick was the only one who knew the bridge, collapsing into a wall of noise. Louie turned the drum seat over to Denise, pleading exhaustion.

"Whaddaya wanna hear?" L.T. slurred. "Whipping Post," the inevitable wiseass called out. Roxanne took advantage of the interruption to visit the band members' nostrils.

"Ya know any Dolls?" a blackhaired boy in a leather jacket asked.

"Human Being," said L.T. "Any of you know it?" He turned to the band.

"B and E, goes down to G-sharp. Just watch me," said Mick.

"That's fuckin' K-Tel Greenberg," announced Louie, grabbing the mike as he left the stage. "Knows every cover song in the fuckin' book."

Mick played the intro chords on bass because nobody else knew them, but they picked it up fast enough. The guitars flamed down to the G-sharp, sizzling fifties sentiment with distortion, hesitated, and slammed in again. "What you need is a plastic doll with a fresh coat of paint," L.T. sang. "Who's gonna sit through the madness and always act so quaint."

The band flared into the break with Jerome corkscrewing leads, twisting his left fingers low on the neck. Denise whammed the drums, rolling all over the tom-toms and crashing the cymbals. L.T. gestured for them to bring it down. "All right, kids... Down, boys, down." Sheryl poked him in the ass with her guitar. "And *Miss Thing* over here." Sheryl cupped her hand over the bridge to play savage, muted chords. L.T. sang hushed and almost whispering, messing with the lyrics some more. The crowd quieted visibly.

Now if I'm acting like a queen
Well I'm a human being
And if I want to masturbate
You know that I'm a human being

The band picked up a bit.

And if I've got to dream yeah-yeah
I'm a human being
And if I get a bit obscene WHOOOO!
I'm a human being

L.T.'s hairdo, a cross between a '50s pompadour and a '70s shag, fell sweatily onto his forehead. The band roared back, L.T. voice-jamming "yeah-yeah-yeahs" and "human beings" over the two-chord riff. He headed back to the bar after it climaxed. Now vocal-less, the band settled into a long two-chord jam which Sheryl eventually twisted into the Pretenders' "Mystery Achievement." By the time they finished the sky was the color of blue velvet and only a handful of passouts and all-night drinkers were left in the club.

Louie had borrowed his cousin's van to move the equipment back to the rehearsal space, the basement of a storefront on 6th and B. Jerome and Sheryl got the money—$113 for the Criminal Minds, $76 for Non-oxynol-9. Amy Apathy, 5' 3" and 95 pounds, and Jerome's girlfriend Diane watched the van while the others lugged equipment. The only really heavy pieces were Mick's bass cabinet and Denise's trap case, but the steps were narrow, damp, and treacherous. Denise cursed when she slipped with a floor tom in her hands.

The band members hung out in the damp, low-ceilinged basement for a few minutes, talking about the gig, splitting the money, and deciding when to practice next. Mick walked around the corner to piss on the side of an abandoned building. The speed and beer had his kidneys on overdrive. "Viva Puerto Rico Libre—Libertad Para Pablo Marcano Y Nydia Cuevas" and "Iggy Pop Is God" was spray-painted on the brick wall above him.

When he came back everybody was up on the corner by the van, guitar cases between them. Louie locked the cellar doors and drove back to Brooklyn, dropping Denise and Amy at the subway. Jerome and Diane walked back to their place on Norfolk Street.

"You mind if I stay over? I don't feel like dealing with the Long Island Railroad at this hour," Sheryl asked Mick.

"Sure. I can leave you alone if you want. You're not allergic to cats, are you?"

They walked up past Tompkins Square Park, pigeons and sparrows chirping and screaming. The sun was about to rise over the Avenue D projects. The incipient light made Mick feel like someone was beginning to stick sewing needles in his eyeballs.

"Blue tips. Blue tips," a drug hustler hawked at them as they turned west on 11th Street. "What you need? What you need?"

"C and D. C and D. Got that Ayatollah," another one chanted. For some reason the 11th and B dope dealers were busiest in the hours just before dawn. Mick shook his head, grunted negatively.

He turned the key in the front-door lock of his building, breathing relief as it clicked behind them.

The faded tan walls were encrusted with paint chips and scrambled calligraphy in black and silver. He had a two-room apartment on the top floor.

Mick leaned his bass case against the wall, pulled down the shades and went to the bathroom. Sheryl read the walls—flyers from old gigs, a poster of Richard Hell with "You Make Me" scrawled on his bare chest, Van Gogh's "Starry Night," and another poster, in scarlet Western-style letters on yellowish cardstock, for Bo Diddley and Red Dirt Reefer at a club upstate in New Paltz—and perused his record collection, which occupied five milkcrates on the floor next to a small practice amp. A six-month-old tiger-striped kitten rubbed its head against her calves and meowed. Punk purist, she noted the presence of several Aerosmith and Black Sabbath albums with some irony.

"Anything you want to hear?" Mick asked when he came out.

"Whatever you want. You've got a lot of good records."

Mick put on a quiet Velvet Underground album and sat down on the edge of the mattress to roll a joint from a manila-envelope nickel. The cat poked her nose into the buds. "Get the fuck out of here, Nebula," he grumbled, shoving her away gently with one hand while rolling with the other.

"You do a lot of drugs," Sheryl said after he lit the joint.

"Not really. I don't do dope and I don't do acid anymore. I hardly ever do coke except when people turn me on—fuck, man, it's just too much money. This is just to calm down at the end of the night."

He passed it over to Sheryl a couple times. She took a few hits and then shook her head to turn down any more. He finished it slowly, talking in between tokes.

"Yeah, I stopped doing acid about five or six years ago. It fucked up my playing too much—like it totally destroyed my timing. The last time I did it was when I was living upstate and—uh, what was I gonna say?—oh yeah, we were all jamming at this house up in the mountains and I was playing through this old Ampeg, beautiful old tube amp, and all of a sudden the thing starts to fuckin' *breathe*, pulsing in and out to the music, and the tubes started turning all these colors—you know, like gasoline in a mud puddle— and I got scared it was going to blow up and had to unplug."

He dropped the roach in an ashtray. The cat curled up on the mattress between them.

"I'm not really self-destructive," he went on. "I don't know, maybe I am. I can play straight, I like getting fucked up, I don't like to play too fucked up. I think there's something kind of self-destructive about playing out anyway, you know, sometimes I feel like it's kind of like going out and being a human sacrifice in front of the audience, like you're going out to sac- rifice yourself for their entertainment. Like you know the Dead Boys song 'Down In Flames'?"

Sheryl nodded. "Good band, but sexist lyrics."

"Yeah, I know, like 'I Need Lunch.' But it's like if you're gonna burn sometimes you need fuel. I'm not trying to die but I don't care if I get a little scorched. Like Jerome—he looks all laid-back on stage, Califor- nia dude, but sometimes he plays so hard his hands bleed. Like I'm not into maintaining an image"—this was true, the black Escher-lizards Mott the Hoople T- shirt he was wearing was his idea of dressing up for a show—"but you have to be different on stage, like fuck the Con Ed bill, burn it, forget tomorrow if we can rip tonight—I mean I can't in real life say 'fuck the Con Ed bill,' I'd be sitting around playin' acoustic and setting the place on fire when I tripped over the candles, but you know what I'm saying?"

"It's not like that for me at all," Sheryl said. "I feel like I have power, I'm totally in control of things, I let them carry me away but I like to be aware so I can feed off them and put it back. You know the Patti Smith album where she says 'And I trust my guitar?' It's like that, like there's this voice coming out of me and I can direct it, focus it. Like this is the first time in my life that people take what I'm doing seriously. You ever say something and people just go on like nothing happened, like you said it into a vacuum? I get up onstage and crank my amp and they *have* to pay attention, look at me, like I'm the center of a forcefield in the room and I control it, I can make it fast and chaotic or slow and intense and they feed off it. Like I can knock down any wall, anything that oppresses me, like they can't tell me I can't do it because I'm a woman if I can get up there and do it, you know? And it feels good. I felt it when I first really learned how to play, just jamming in my bedroom." She did a Patti Smith voice. "And I step up to the microphone and I have *no fear*."

There was a pause. Mick petted Nebula, his brain churning for something to break the silence.

"What's with Jimi Gimmix? You know him, right?"

"Not that well. Denise knows him better than I do. There was this place on 17th Street she used to go to for birth control when she was around 16, some kind of teenage counseling center. The Damaged Kids all went there too. Everybody knew him as 'the kid who looks like Sid Vicious.' She said he used to cut himself up all the time."

"Yeah, the first time I saw him he had a huge cross carved into his chest."

"What I heard was he got kicked out of his house when he was 13—he's from Jersey City, and his step-father was molesting him—came here and started hustling on 53rd and 3rd. I heard he was in Covenant House for a while but left because it was too strict—they wouldn't let him be a punk."

"That's fucked up. You know, when I had the argument with him before, I had this weird feeling like he almost wanted me to tell him what to do, like he wanted me to play father."

The record was over, the needle knocking back and forth against the final groove. Mick got up to change it, put on side one of Iggy Pop's *New Values*. "It's weird he should think that, because I don't think I could ever deal with having a kid."

"Why not? You don't get along with your parents?"

"Now I do. Not when I was living home. The worst thing that happened was when I was 16, it was a Sunday afternoon and I was down in the base-ment—my father's got a TV repair shop, he had his workshop down there, and I had my amp set up down there so I could make noise—so anyway, I'm down there, I'm playing along with the Stooges, '1970,' you know, doo-do-doo, do-do-do-do"—she nodded— "and he comes down yelling 'TURN THAT SHIT OFF!' and I say, 'It's not shit. It's the Stooges,' and he picks up a fuckin' TV picture tube and throws it at me, he misses, and it smashes all over the place, and he's screaming 'YOU FUCKING LITTLE BASTARD! SEE WHAT YOU MADE ME DO!' Turns out I had my stash in a hollowed-out Hardy Boys book, and my little sister opens it up and out pops an ounce of pot and a bunch of pills, I had a couple tabs of acid and some Seconals."

"That's fucked up. Better find a better place to hide it next time."

"Yeah, it was like the fuckin' family Altamont. My mom cooled him out. They were a lot more pissed about the acid and the downs than they were about the pot. Weird thing is, I got busted for pot when I was 19 and they were more pissed at the law than they were at me, the only thing they were mad at me for was having to drive upstate to bail me out."

"I don't really fight with mine like that, it's just like I feel I don't matter to them. Like my brother got to go away to school, but I'm going to fucking Nassau Community because they wouldn't pay extra for a girl. Who cares, I don't even want a career anyway, I don't need all that 'the more you learn the more you earn' shit, I just want to do my music, and if I want to learn something I can read the book myself."

"Yeah, you can. I get along with mine OK now. My dad taught me a lot of stuff about electronics. It's weird, all the stuff he used to do, tube circuits and shit, it's all out of date now except for music. The only thing they use tubes for now is guitar amps."

"I hate solid-state amps. The way they distort just sounds fake, it's like it's harsh and wimpy at the same time. My amp—it's like it's dirty sweet, that's what I like about it."

She got up to go to the bathroom. She came out carrying a black bra. Mick noticed her tits underneath the black sleeveless T-shirt and his brain started waxing both lewd and loving. "Listen, I'm really tired," she said.

They slipped off their pants and crawled into bed. He was almost a foot taller than her. He rolled over, stroked her hair, kissed her on the cheek. *I like him, it's nice being next to him, I don't know if I want him for a boyfriend, I definitely don't want him for a one-night stand.* "Uh—listen, I'm not really into sex with you tonight. I'm really tired." She kissed him goodnight quickly, was out within seconds.

Mick couldn't sleep, shuddering restlessly, staring longingly at her green hair streaming across the pillow. He got up and took another piss. The speed had shrunk his cock almost down to a button. *Even if she did want to fuck I couldn't do much good,* he was thinking. He took two Valiums, smoked another joint, finally fell into the endless sea.

They went out to breakfast at Odessa on Avenue A the next afternoon, walking past two men working on a sky-blue van, merengue's frenetic 2/4 blasting as they passed by. Jerome and Diane were already there.

"I know what you two did last night," Diane chirped.

"Nah, we're just good friends," Mick said. The Ukrainian coffeeshop, the only restaurant open east of First Avenue on Sunday afternoons, was a neighborhood gossip-columnist's paradise. Which twosomes were eating breakfast together was a good index of who had gone home with whom last night. Billy claimed he'd once seen Suzy P from *Oh No!* zine there taking notes for her "Gossip, Slander and Intrigue" column.

Mick rode the subway with her up to Penn Station, then walked to work, the 4-12 shift at Trisonic Rehearsal Studio on West 27th Street. Three bands coming in at 4, the Piss Missiles in A, the small room, Clear Sight in B, the big room, Penetrator in C. The innards of a Marshall head covered the reception desk, next to his tools, a voltmeter, circuit tester, wire-cutters and strippers, soldering iron. Charlie from the Piss Missiles was in first, said hi, they were from 11th Street too, noisy, basic Lower East Side rock. Clear Sight was a polished seven-piece R&B band, from Crown Heights, Harlem and New Jersey, the kind of act being wiped out by disco and worsening ghetto economics. "On bass: Tyrone. He's an Aquarius, and he likes a lady who's not afraid to speak her mind." Penetrator was a metal/hard-rock band from Bensonhurst, shaghaircut dudes starting to cop some punk influences.

Everybody in, time to get to work on the Marshall. One capacitor was obviously scorched, where was the short that caused it? He could hear bits and pieces of each band, Penetrator arguing, the singer yelling at Vince the guitar player not to solo over the verses. *If the output tranformer's blown the thing's fucked bigtime.*

Vince came out a few minutes later. "I want a Marshall, not this Fender Twin shit," he whined.

"The Marshall's broken. Can't you see I'm workin' on it?"

"I don't give a fuck. I can't play on that Twin bullshit. I need a Marshall for my sound."

Fucking prima donna. "The—Marshall—is—broken. Do—you—see—I'm—working—on—it?" Maybe if I talk slow enough it'll sink in. Asshole uses so many effects it doesn't matter what kind of amp he's playing on anyway.

Jerry their drummer came out. "C'mon Vince, it's

fuckin' busted, we ain't payin' ten an hour for you ta fuckin' argue with the dude." Mick mouthed thanks.

He leaned back, breathed in deeply, burnt from last night, headache developing, thinking about Sheryl.

Tonight I stay home and eat health food, he was thinking.

rocket, blurred with the crayon marks no matter you ha
her apple within the book. She had noticed that she
She turned back and sorted it carefully, looking for
her picking the out, and dropping it back. With. Then
She

I ought I saw some and walked on and forward.

84

COLD CRUSH

T he Bad Words' rehearsal studio was a storefront in the heart of the heroin district, on East
11th just off Avenue B, five steps down from
the sidewalk. They had an ironclad rule against opening the door to strangers. Every time they practiced,
junkies selling hot trumpets and Casios and drunks
demanding "just to hear the music, man" would bang
on the door.

It was one of the bitter New York winters they
had before global warming. Cold as the hearts of the
Reagan greedonomics people infesting the city, green
numbers on a satanic computer. Cold enough to freeze
the dogshit on the streets. The hawk wind came out in
late November, scourging the flesh of 14th Street. The
other new species of the '80s, the homeless people
who'd suddenly proliferated in the last year, curled
up in doorways, over steam vents, in abandoned
buildings, in the park around oil-drum fires. Other
people were beginning to move into the abandoned

buildings too. The one next door was home to an old hippie pot dealer and amateur guitar-maker who called himself the Green Genius of Ganja; the lead singer and bass player from the Babylon Burners and a couple other fledgling Rastafarians; and the guitar player and drummer from the Piss Missiles. Both bands had shared bills with the Bad Words, the Piss Missiles opening, the Babylon Burners headlining. The Piss Missiles' guitarist's girlfriend's roommate was going out with Sid Berkowitz, the Bad Words' bassist, so they were vaguely kin.

The studio had heat on Tuesday night, and practice was productive. They got two new songs down, ready for debut at C-Section on Friday and the Green Palace on Sunday, with a relative minimum of argument between François the lead singer and Kent the guitarist. François Monahan was from the Bronx, perpetually wired with long stringy black hair, shaved close at the temples and streaked with orange and cranberry. He was extremely skinny, his silver leather jacket and tight black jeans flopping about on his bones. People joked that he made Sid look fat, and Sid probably could have fit inside his Fender bass case. François' father was a bookie called Frankie Miracle because he'd bet $200 on the Mets to win the World Series before the '69 season. The way François told the story, he'd had to sleep on the couch until the Mets took four out of six from the first-place Cubs that July. He'd bought the family a house with the proceeds. François' mother was Italian and prone to break out in amateur arias in the kitchen.

Kent Thatcher was from the Virginia horse country. Combed-over blond hair and a broken nose and teeth suffered while "cutting himself shaving" gave him the aura of a degenerated preppie. He'd been playing R&B covers at University of Virginia frat parties when he was 16. François had never been in a real band before, only a couple of songwriting ventures that never made it out of the bedroom, let alone the garage. There were a few cultural differences between them.

Sid hoped they'd de-kink the new songs at C-Section. The Green Palace was a big gig. While people joked that he was so fuckin' spacy he had to do speed to stay conscious, he wrote most of the music. He looked like a softer Lou Reed, with black eyes that managed to be both intense and sleepy. He practiced obsessively when wired, refining hooks and riffs, rearranging bridges and choruses, playing along with records. He knew hundreds of covers.

It was time to start fucking around. Tommy Valentine the drummer broke out the weed, a nickel of White Plains Road Jamaican in a brown manila envelope. They jammed on "Blitzkrieg Bop," Kent and François singing "Beast of Burden," sinking into reggae as the herb took hold—"Police and Thieves" and "Sun Is Shining" off *Kaya*, dubbing it out, Tommy whacking the toms like timbale flams—*bok-di-biddle-a-bok*—Kent turning his reverb up to 10, Sid and Tommy trancing out on the groove and the echoes, alternating fills in the empty spaces.

Emerge. Resurface. Kent hit the the riff from Ted Nugent's "Cat Scratch Fever."

"You guys…you fuckin' guys…do you have to play this stupid shit?" François. No tolerance for dumbass rock'n'roll, especially the kind that brought back memories of the assholes in high school. He'd been an equal-opportunity target, a loudmouthed

87

oddball who was fair game for both whites and blacks. "Why don't you do fuckin' Kiss covers next." He finally yielded, dealing with it by mocking the lyrics, "Well, it's been two years and seven months/Since I changed the litter box/It gives me Cat Shit Fever/Cat Shit Fever."

Knock at the door. Tommy opened it without asking. Eight teenage homeboys in sneakers and sweatshirts poured in.

Sid and Tommy were too stoned to react. François discreetly ducked back toward the phone. He'd been one of the few white kids left on White Plains Road after the neighborhood turned black. Kent coiled up for action.

There was a moment of silence. Finally one of the youths slapped a dollar bill on the floor.

"C'mon man! Rock the house! We'll pay to hear you play!" he exclaimed. "We're the Beatmaster Crew."

Sid struck up the Good Times/Rapper's Delight bass line. The Beatmaster Crew got on the mike and started rapping. "To the beat/To the beat/To the beat that makes you wanna freak/Yes, yes, y'all/Yes, yes, y'all." Kent broke out a pint of whiskey and they passed it around.

"Man, y'all were rockin'. That's why we stopped in," said the main rapper, Original Man. The other two were MC Bambu and Roc-Star.

The white guys mumbled thanks for the compliment, but inwardly their emotion was utter and complete disbelief. Black and Puerto Rican dudes getting off on *Ted Nugent*? Kraftwerk was weird enough, but at least that was sort of disco.

Kent popped a blank tape in his box. They jammed

for half an hour, three rappers and four rockers, running through Sid's inventory of R&B basslines—Taana Gardner's "Heartbeat," ESG's "Moody," P-Funk's "Tear the Roof Off the Sucker," Rick James' "Super Freak." Kent pumping out Stax-Volt and James Brown rhythm licks, François on tambourine, Tommy thumping big and simple on the kick and snare. Kent took a break to roll another one, then played the Ventures' "Apache"—a slow Western instrumental that was a favorite of Bronx DJs.

"Man, that was great," said Original Man. "What was that?"

The tape ran out. One of the crew's hangers-on picked up Kent's box and headed for the door.

"What the fuck—" Kent was pissed.

"Hey, what the fuck you doin'?" It was Bambu. The kid handed it back.

"All right, you three can stay, but the rest have to leave." Kent. "We'll do another tape."

Original Man, Bambu, and Roc-Star stayed. Kent popped another cassette in the rescued box. Original asked the name of the band. The Bad Words, said François. Why? "Ya know how when you're a kid and you say 'fuck' your parents always go 'That's a *bad word*'? It's like outlaw words, forbidden words, illegal words. And words that come from deep inside your heart, words that have power, words that say the things they don't want you to say, like that kind of bad, like they say Shaft is a baaaaad—"

"Shut your mouth!" Tommy interrupted. They all cracked up.

"I know where he got his name," Sid said, pointing at Bambu toking on the joint.

"I'm the Original Man because the black man is

the original man. Not meanin' to disrespect you, but we were here first, know what I mean? And because we're not imitatin', we're unique, we're doin' our own shit. Always originatin', never imitatin'."

Sid blew out a cumulonimbus of smoke, affected a stentorian, slightly English voice. "Zinjanthropus *boisei*. This species of human lived in Africa 1,818,000 years before Christ."

"Yo, like you know the way them punk-rock dudes dance?" Bambu. "What is that about? Like bangin' into each other and shit?"

"It's not about fuckin' people up." François. Punk-rock missionary, possessed with the righteousness of his cause. "It's about gettin' our aggressions out, and like we agree that we're going to tolerate gettin' banged into so we can all get into the music. Like if somebody falls down, people gonna help him up, because these are our brothers and sisters out there."

"I don't know about that," Sid tried to get a word in. "It used to be a lot cooler."

"Man, you do that shit in the Bronx, you might not live," Bambu. He and Original cracked up. "You got to be real polite, bro. People are touch-y. They got short fuses."

Roc-Star came out of the bathroom. "Yo, what the *fuck* you got on your wall?"

"It's Sid's girlfriend's art project. She's working in a new medium." Kent's clipped sarcasm was thick and condescending. Sid wasn't sure if Roc-Star was picking up on it, but he didn't say anything more than "Shit is bugged out, man."

What it was was the week before, Kent had gotten pissed off when the toilet backed up. He'd blamed Sid and François' girlfriends, Sinead and Ellen, for the blockage, accusing them of conducting some kind of witchy lesbian-feminist pagan power ritual involving menstrual blood. Well, Sinead had once done a triptych of minimalist red-on-black paintings utilizing hers, and Ellen was a Goth, adorned with all manner of crosses, stars of David and pentagrams as necklaces, noserings and earrings. Kent had scrawled, "Don't Put Your Goddamn Tampons in the Toilet" on the wall, and Sinead and Ellen had hung theirs up in retaliation, with the legends "Mine Are Fucking Blessed by the Goddess" and "We Need Them to Make Transylvania Tea." They were now a dark pine-needle shade of green.

In a way, Sid was grateful to Kent for getting him off the hook. He plugged in an envelope filter, a green automatic wah-wah box. "Yo, let's play some more."

Kent pushed the Record button. They ran over a lot of the same riffs and grooves, but this set was looser, more comfortable. Tommy and Kent tried to turn the cowbell-and-guitar intro to "Honky Tonk Women" into a breakbeat, but the rappers couldn't find the handle. "Planet Rock" fared better, Kent doing the synth lick on guitar and François making space noises on Sid's pawnshop Moog. Sid hit a discofied C-B-E groove, sort of like a garage version of Cheryl Lynn's "Got to Be Real." The bass seemed to be resonating perfectly, clear and rich. He locked in perfectly with Tommy, holding back beats for his snare to crack through, diving back in with fat low-end runs, sliding up and down the E string, the envelope filter adding funky duck overtones. The rappers were freestyling, trading verses and tags. Tommy's kick drum boomed like a 16-story project building that had just learned how to dance. "I'm the

R-O-C, the superstar/With the fly girls comin' from near and far." It was awesome how they kept the flow going, spitting out word for word to the beat. "I'm MC Bambu and I get you high/Rolling up on the rhythm like a stick of Thai/I don't do stickups and I don't do crime/I'm cold gettin' paid for the deffest rhymes." Now Original came in with the lead, and the other two joined in on the response.

The Boogie Down Bronx is the place to be
But we come to bring the rhymes down to
  Avenue B
Black, Chinese, Puerto Rican and white
We're down to rock the party to the early light

Fadeout. Tommy was sweaty, winded. He was the only one in the band with a job. At eight o'clock tomorrow morning he'd be lugging sheetrock. Roc-Star came out of the bathroom. Kent handed Original one of the tapes. "Nice playin' with ya." "Keep it real, y'all."

The tape self-destructed in Tommy's van a few weeks later, devoured by the car stereo on the way back from a party at Ellen's house in Long Island City. The Beatmaster Crew's sole legacy was Roc-Star's tag, inscribed on the bathroom wall in black Magic Marker in the angular scribble-scrabble of South Bronx calligraphy. The O was blacked in like a 12-inch, and the R looped around it like a tonearm. A shooting star arced out of it, with The Little Prince riding the top on the arc.

TONGUE FULL OF ACID, TONGUE FULL OF LOVE

My name is Vince Carozza and I'm from Massapequa, Long Island. Matzoh-Pizza, my mom calls it. After its ethnic makeup. Mine too. Hometown of Candy Darling nee James Slattery, not first, not last, and definitely not least in the pantheon of boys bearing the stigmata of Marilyn. So of course we have to do "Walk on the Wild Side." And wiseass motherfucker Jack's gotta sing it "Vincent came from Massapequa, Long Island/In the back room she was everybody's darling." Yeah I'm a slut. I take it up the ass. I fuck men. And women. I leave the cat alone. I like the indiscriminateness of it all, like there are no barriers to my lust, no pleasures I won't explore, indulge, embrace. I like cruising, the idea that I can will a man into fucking me just by eye contact, the cornucopia of cock, the constellation of cum. When I fuck I feel like I'm tapping into the ancient heavenly dynamo, the cosmic inferno of the sky above and the raw rhythms of the animals below, wispy wiry rock'n'roll boys with poetry in their eyes, cocks round and hard and silky like lacquered rock maple arcing cum, and round-hipped redhaired girls, their pussies dripping like the tangiest and most exquisitely textured navel orange, screaming and calling on the gods to satisfy them. To consume human flesh, drink it in with every sense I have, eye and ear and taste and touch and smell and sight and sound, and not destroy it. And wiseass motherfucker Jack can't deal with it, he's got all his sad petty and pathetic little rules about Being A Man he's gotta live by, like when Jeannie took me to this swingers party and there's eight of us there, up all night and she and two of the women are going at it on the rug like maniacs, and I'm sitting there on the couch with their husbands just watching and not talking, no connection, no nothing, just this fuckin' narrow pathway of allowed rituals and practices. And he's one of them, he can't deal with the violators of the code, like I got fuckin' sunflowers, orange and black Mexican exotic beauties and giant yellow ones from the Kansas prairies, and he's gotta fuckin' destroy it, like nothing so pretty should be allowed to exist, everything's gotta be concrete and gunmetal, he shoots out all these little poison-pen remarks. I hate the fuckin' creep, but he's in the band, and we're starting to happen, we got one or two or three gigs every week, we can't tear it up, like destroy the foundation, and Lenny's his drinkin' buddy so they're allies. Lenny thinks the world's all a big fuckin' joke.

I miss Jeannie, she dumped me two months ago. I've been drinking a lot since then, I can't get it up to go out looking much. Like sticking my dick out on the inspection block after being immersed in ice water.

And then this week I get hit with the double-headed hammer. First I get laid off from work. Fuckin' Reaganomics. Budget cuts. No more processing Medicaid claim forms for me. Which I was getting sick of, I'd been there a year, dingy back office in downtown Brooklyn, it was getting boring. I was the office punk-rocker, one of the few whites on the job. City jobs are a lot less picky about your lifestyle than private companies. They always seem to want you to fit some Corporate Profile even to be a fuckin' file clerk. City just cares that you can show up and do the job. I'd saved up enough to buy a Strat, then liquidated half my last paycheck on a lavender Ibanez chorus box. Except for that, I was looking forward to 39 weeks of collecting unemployment. More time to play. Government subsidy for the arts.

We're at the Deuce in New Rochelle that night, two sets, $150. We get back to the city at 4:30. We finish loading back in and Al the drummer announces he's quitting. Taillights of his van disappear down Avenue B. Cancels all gigs for the foreseeable future till we find a new one.

I stay fucked up for the next six days. Gin and juice for a dollar a round in Lana's on Avenue A. "Baliums" from Tompkins Square. Old English 800 from the bodega. Couple Tuinals from the things that creepeth upon 14th Street. Herb bearing seed from the Dulce Candy Shop on Ninth Street. I don't really like pot, it makes me paranoid, like everybody's putting out these sinister overtones I don't comprehend, but liquor kills the paranoia. Play records obsessively, play guitar along with them, crank up the practice amp and blast my rage, the neighbors start banging a broom on the ceiling. I got a couple decent new riffs.

On the seventh day I rested. I was almost broke. My unemployment hadn't come through yet. We had our first practice since Al quit, try to write some new songs. I put out my new riffs and Lenny and Jack shoot them down right away. I bring out this sort of Tom Verlainish thing, a loose, jammy riff, and Jack goes, "That sounds like the fucking Grateful Dead." Then it's a two-chord one, and I get, "Bor-ing. Bor-ing," from both of them. Then Lenny comes out with this lame-o white-blues thing and Jack laps it up. The message is getting clear.

I don't want to knock Lenny out of the spotlight, he's the lead singer, but he doesn't want to share it, not one ray, not one stray photon. What am I supposed to do, get on stage and not have any presence? And Jack knows I'm better than he is, and bass players are replaceable, so he's got to solidify his alliances and cut down his rivals. We used to like playing together. I didn't know he was so fuckin' psycho when I joined the band. Obviously. You think my taste is that bad, I deliberately go out and pick people who are fucked up?

Preemptive strike. They're putting me on the bus to Brian Jonestown with a box of swimming-pool chlorine and lime Kool-Aid.

In my building I grab the guitar case with both hands to get it up another flight. There's a kid about nine bouncing a blue spaldeen on the stairs, it's Nelson Ruiz from the third floor. "You Mick Jagger from the Beatles?" he pops. He extracts about half a grin. "I see that Kool-Aid smile," he chirps.

I don't feel sociable, but I don't wanna go home and stare at the fuckin' walls. So I go out to the C-Section around 2. Hang out a bit, it's kind of empty, the band on's generic hardcore, nurse a drink, say hi to a couple people. Next band on is some guy who once played with some guy who once played with Johnny Thunders.

Shaping up like a boring night. I'm too broke and too brittle to get drunk. And then she walks in and the world turns. Girl Lori I know from the band, she's a stripper, must've just gotten off work.

How're you doing, she says. Not too good, I say, Al quit, so we're fucked till we get a new drummer. Oh, I'm sorry to hear that, she says. She's the voice of concern, solicitude incarnate. And she's cute, medium height, skinny, short black hair buzzed close on the back and sides, a sharp nose. I'm infatuated, zoning out on what she's actually saying, then it comes from out of the blue, "Do you think we're all going to be here six months from now?"

"What?" I say.

"Do you think there's going to be a nuclear war? Like Reagan really believes in this crazy end-of-the-world shit, like the Russians are the evil kingdoms of Gog and Magog, the ones the Christian soldiers fight at Armageddon, and he doesn't care if we all get incinerated if it fulfills the prophecy of the apocalypse, and the only things surviving are cockroaches. They'll be blind from the flash and the radiation, but they'll still be crawling around."

Her eyes are a little bugged, she's got that toxic-smolders look, obsessing on the things we leave buried in the undercurrents to keep from screaming. "I don't know," I sort of drawl. "I guess when it comes there's nothing I can do about it, I just want to be as fucked up as I can and having sex with as many people as possible. And Jet Boy's probably going to be poking around in the rubble looking for a clean set of gimmicks."

She laughs. Jet Boy was a 35-year-old junkie who made his living copping for scenesters afraid of going to Avenue B. He had long beaten the actuarial tables on the Minor Neighborhood Celebrity Death Watch.

It's hard to talk in the club, we're screaming in each other's ears and constantly going "What? What?" Eventually she asks me if I want to come over.

Walking down Avenue B she's going on about a bomb drill in third grade. You remember them? No. "Oh, right, you're younger than me. I wouldn't do it. I said this is stupid. I got sent to the principal's office." I can hear her giving an explicit description of exactly what would happen to PS 235 in a nuclear explosion, speaking in the chillingly guileless tones of an eight-year-old describing destruction: "People in Manhattan would be boiled alive and there'd be nothing left of them but shadows, and there would be a big ball of fire that would burn up all of Queens. This is stupid, you just want us to think nuclear war is safe."

A grimy-bellbottomed junkie walks by and interjects, "Yeah, bro, time to put your head between your legs and kiss your ass goodbye." He's one of those 35-going-on-50 types, the junkie's taffy-pull rasp overlaying the street Nuyorican in his voice.

She lives on 4th between A and B. On the way home she stops off at the corner spot to cop, we're on line with the strung-out whores and thieves of the late watch. Climb the stairs. Snort the dope. The bitter taste creeps down the back of my throat and fills me with benevolence. My head's spinning in a slow dance of golden lights, we're curled up on her couch together. She gives me this look that translates as *Why don't you kiss me, you fool*, so I do. You know you have a face like a penis, she says, I think it's so sexy.

I'm surprised I can get it up, but I do, and I'm slow in coming, it's like there's a wall in my dick and neck and shoulders, like a sound barrier blocking release, but the seawall cracks and I'm in that magic moment, a loaded boxcar cut loose and rolling, and then it's like the ocean gushing into the lowlands. We're curled up together afterwards and I want to absorb her, to be absorbed into her, but I'm drifting away into viscousness.

Next morning we're pleasantly woozy, warm, it takes two to make coffee, we're all over each other. "You know I like somebody when I can stand to be with them in the morning," she says, "there's so many guys I've been with where I just think What the fuck got into me last night, I just want them out of here." Pause and there's implications. "But not you," she amends. Eye twinkle. This time we really fuck, getting comfortable, initial jitters gone, learning each other's rhythms and ecstatic neural pathways. It's rainy and miserable out but it's cozy inside, we stay under the blankets in the leaden light. I don't want to leave but she's got work and I've got practice.

She walks me over. "Who's that" Jack says.

"Her name's Lori."

"It's that stripper chick who hangs out at C-Section," Lenny says.

"How many dollar bills did ya put in her G-string?" Jack probes. It's supposed to be a joke but there's just enough spin on it so it comes in like a punch, but not hard enough to be obvious.

"Actually she said I had a face like a penis," I say.

"She wants to ride his schnozz," goes Lenny. He

99

makes it sound like Brooklynese pidgin for penis. Then again, Lenny can make almost any noun sound like Brooklynese pidgin for penis.

I stay home that night, Saturday. I see her again Sunday. I start bitching about the state of the band and she's telling me I should look for something else, do side projects.

We're walking down Avenue A and who should we encounter but Jimmy, a little singer-songwriter who looks like a younger Marvin Gaye. He's a fling of mine from a couple years ago. He had crushed-velvet skin and the beginnings of dreadlocks, I loved to run my hands through them. We shared an obsession if not always taste, we used to stay up all night smoking weed, chain-playing records. Pot made him loquacious, a raconteur, and me gruntingly, nervously inarticulate, it wasn't a good combination. We stayed friends but ran in different circles.

He asks me who I'm playing with and I tell him, and we need a drummer. "Well, if you're not doing anything next weekend," he says, "I'm doing a demo, and it would be truly terrific to have you on it."

His stuff's kind of like discofied Lou Reed, acerbic and witty personal observations over a heavy dance beat, a bit too idiosyncratic for either camp. And he wants me to play rhythm guitar on it. I say yeah and we agree to get together Thursday.

"See what I mean?" Lori smiles after he leaves.

"He's an old boyfriend, sort of," I say. I'm never sure what the etiquette of introducing exes is.

"Maybe that's why I like you," she goes. "Straight men can be so cold, like there's things they just never get."

"Gay men can be pretty fuckin' cold too. Like the

100

ones that give you the prissy dismissal, you know, like the red rope doesn't part for the likes of you."

"Everybody's cold when they're dumping you. That's not what I'm talking about. When I was first getting into rock'n'roll I thought musicians were the coolest people in the world, they were smart and enlightened and creative, the whole bit, and do it all with perfect style, just being there, open to any scene, the perfect line at the perfect moment. And you know what I found out? They're not. You wouldn't believe how fucking boring they are, they're into the whole me-Tarzan-you-Jane shit, they're as stiff as some British upper-class twit, you know, 'Well, that's just *not done*,' all these stupid rules and taboos that keep them from being open, being vulnerable. Sometimes you need to get fucked to understand what it feels like."

"Jimmy used to tell me people who fucked played better together, they knew each other's rhythms."

She doesn't look amused. What I didn't know I was hinting sinks in. "Uh—not that I'm planning on it this week."

She laughs. "You aren't one of these people who says, 'I fall in love with the person, not the body'? I hate that."

"No, I love bodies, I don't always like people." Pause. "But not you."

So we're talking about sex some more, I don't fall in love with men very well, it's like I'm always out looking for the next one, it's like a perennial bar scene. I don't really trust them to get close, I'm not into setting up house either. I don't really trust anyone, no matter how hard I fall there's a place inside where it's like *and no one comes in, no one*, like in the Black Flag song. She starts going on about work. "When I first

101

started dancing, it was like, 'Oh my God, all these people are looking at me naked, they're seeing every lump and flaw in my body, my stomach's too fat, my tits are too small.' I had to have three drinks before I could do it. And then it was like being a star, like all these men are getting off looking at me, they're paying money for it, they're getting hard and *they can't have it.*"

She laughs slightly at the last bit. I nod, I don't want to interrupt, and I don't really know what to say, other than the sight of her in a G-string would put me somewhere beyond corundum.

"But you know, some nights I hate them, I just want to take a gun and slowly pan it around the room like a movie camera, half of them are probably fantasizing about raping me. I'm just a commodity to them. I think that's why dancers and musicians end up together a lot, we're both commodities, we're putting ourselves out on stage naked and hoping somebody thinks we're hot enough to pay for it."

"Yeah, I know," I say. "Being a rock star's like being a porn star, you got all these ritual moves you're supposed to do, all that fuckin' MTV hair-band shit, 'Hello, Cleveland, are you ready to rock!' I mean, you're supposed to get people off at gigs, but it's like some of them are just getting off on the image they think they're supposed to get off on, they get pissed at you if you don't feed them what they're trained to like."

"I don't mind it with some of them, they're just lonely, they're like mercy fucks to me, but I hate playing the game, walking around with a fucking painted-on smile, acting like they're God's gift to womanhood because they wave a few dollars at me."

102

She lights a cigarette, blows the smoke out. "Ah, fuck it, being a secretary was the same shit in a different package. And I make a lot more money, and I don't have to wear office clothes, or fight off the boss wanting a blowjob. 'Oh, Lori, could you come into my office for a minute?' Clubowners are a lot easier to fend off, you can always go somewhere else."

We go back to her house, do more dope, she's painting her toenails, cotton balls between them, while I play guitar, twisted tritones, jagged clumps of razor chords. She's got some kind of nihilistic dissonant music on and it's like for the first time in my life I viscerally understand it, stuff that always sounded like bad chemical depression, now I get it, it's about being able to feel your pain without being hurt by it, to know it's there but far away, it can't touch you, and it's got a softer letdown than alcohol. The chorus makes it crystal clean, sheer metallic shimmer.

Tuesday afternoon we're trying to recruit a new drummer, we go over to Frank from the Blue Tarantulas' house on 13th Street. They broke up last year when everybody else was a junkie and his girlfriend got pregnant again. She's at work and he's home with the kids, tiny two-room walkup on the fourth floor. He's a big guy, dyed black hair starting to grow long again, bulbous features, a bit of a gut developing, sips on a beer while he changes the baby and tries to keep the two-year-old from demolishing the place. "Dylan! Get outta there," he croaks, kid is under the sink about to pour a whole can of Ajax on the kitchen floor. There's bright yellow and blue plastic kid stuff everywhere, one of those plastic big-wheel trikes like the kid in *The Shining* had.

Lenny takes the lead for the visiting delegation.

"We'd be honored to have someone of your talent be our drummer, man, you're one of the best musicians on the scene, we need somebody with experience like you, we haven't forgotten about you. You're perfect for us."

He talks like this is a mission from God, but Frank's got his hands full. "Yeah I'd love to, but y'know… like Amy's workin' full-time, I can't go off and leave her with both kids all the time, you know how it is."

Lenny tries humor. "Hey, we'll just put Dylan in the drum case, he can be our roadie." Then he goes for the glamour tack, mixed with desperation and guilt-tripping. "We're starting to happen, we're getting good gigs, we got some label interest, but if we can't get a drummer fast, it's all going to fall by the wayside. You know you want it, you're too good not to be out there."

"Yeah, I know," Frank says wistfully. "But, y'know if we make it, then I'm gonna be out on the road all the time, and where's that gonna leave Amy? No offense, but I just can't do it." The baby starts crying, and Dylan starts begging "Dad-dy! Bah-ble." He needs to be like some multi-armed Hindu god to handle this onslaught, heating up a bottle for the baby, pouring one full of apple juice for Dylan. Jack gives Lenny a fuck-it look. We get ready to leave, say thanks anyway.

Except for Jack. As we're squeezing out the door he turns, draws a bead for a parting shot. "You're a fucking pussy-whipped asshole, you're not a musician anymore."

"Fuck you, Jack," Frankie screams back. And little Dylan's waving his toy hammer and going "Fuk oo, Ak."

Out in the hall, Lenny jumps down his throat. "What the fuck did you do that for? Cursing him out in front of his kid?"

Jack hates backing down, even when he knows he's completely wrong. "You two are wimps, none of you want to stick up for the band, you don't want to do the dirty work. You gotta confront people when they're fucking you over."

"That was totally uncalled for. What do we have to gain from it?"

"You gonna make him wanna play with us by calling him an asshole?" I chime in.

"Fuck you two faggots," he says. It comes out. Now the only cylindrical object that's ever spurted exciting liquids into Lenny's mouth is a beer bottle, but reality is not the point here. Time to drag out the ancient drag-queen riposte, "I'm more man than you'll ever be and more woman than you'll ever get," I spit at him. Hackneyed as hippies and rednecks, but effective as a spike-heeled kick in the balls. And I leave.

Now I don't know what to do. The fucking band is obviously falling apart and I'm broke. I got $7.43 in my pocket. 75 cents go for a tall beer at the bodega on Avenue B and now I have to think, shit is churning, it's too chaotic for words. I settle down a bit, call Lori. She invites me over.

I don't even know if I have a band anymore, I moan. She's not in a good mood either. She had a bad night at work last night, they sent her home after four hours because there was nobody in the club, and it's the beginning of the month. Rent's paid and we're broke, got $10 between us. Cop one bag and she talks me into shooting it, says it's not going to be enough to get us both off otherwise. Swabs alcohol onto my arm, no subacute bacterial endocarditis here.

I don't have works, I say.

"You can use mine," she says. "You don't look like you've got any diseases."

So I do it. And this time I don't like it so much, I'm queasy like a kid who ate too much candy, like you're getting away with saying fuck you to everybody who hectored and nagged you about it, and then you realize it doesn't even feel that good after the first few rushes. I believe that things you do mutate you in the long run, music mutates you as every note you play or feel inscribes itself on your nerves, every ravage, every thrill, like vibrations subtly aligning the molecules of ash or alder or mahogany. And sex inscribes itself too, every orgasm an explosion of benevolence to every cell, the ghost of its electricity purrs in your moves and your face. And kindness, and callousness, and cruelty. And I don't like the way dope mutates people, the emaciated whores who cop on my block, desperation and decay reducing them to a ghoulish, pathetic caricature of sexiness. The writers, pale blood-drained skin preserved in formaldehyde. The street veterans, face turned to vulture beak and hands to talons by the constant prowl for car-stereo carrion. So I'm not liking this. I feel like there's an unknown poison lurking inside me. It's like drinking when your head starts to rotate and you wish you never touched it, never again until next week.

But really I'm not gonna do it anymore. Lori compliments me but I think she's disappointed, she wants a partner to get high with, an ally, a comrade, someone who's not of the life yet. She's encouraging me to do other stuff musically. "Those two don't want to do your songs, you shouldn't have to put up with Jack's shit, you can do better, you're really talented, you should start your own band." I don't know. I talk about Jimmy. She's not into what his music sounds like but tells me to do it anyway.

Jimmy calls on Thursday morning. He's gotta cancel the session, he's had this weird sore throat for the last week. And swollen glands.

He's gonna call back when his voice gets better.

NIGHT SHIFT

Monday, April 2, 1984—
I checked the headlights and rooflights on the cab, checked the back seat to make sure it wasn't loose, adjusted the mirrors, and made sure the numbers on the meter matched the ones on the trip card left from the day shift. Then I clipped the picture of Marvin Gaye out of the *Daily News*, edged it in black with Magic Marker, and taped it to the partition behind where my head would be before pulling out onto 21st Street.

I made the first left onto Seventh Avenue. I didn't carry a radio with me, unlike some drivers—most notably a titanic-Afroed Panamanian loner who blasted Latin disco on a box the size of a Fender Twin Reverb. People often asked me why, like the skinny blonde "working girl" waiting for her pimp to return from some mission or other at 37th Street and 11th Avenue. "I love music," she said. I figured at best it would go flying into the dashboard when I made

109

short stops, and most fares probably wouldn't like my taste. I'd gotten fired from my last office job for playing a tape of John Coltrane's *A Love Supreme* in my cubicle. "Can you not listen to something more pleasant?" an Anglo-Pakistani clerk had asked, and a secretary with a harsh Queens accent had complained about "screechy saxophone shit." They told the temp agency I had a bad attitude. At worst a tape player would be bait for thieves or drown out their plotting. My first day on the job I'd gotten stuck in traffic on Fifth Avenue and overheard a fare I'd picked up on Times Square tell his teenage girlfriend, "If this motherfucker doesn't hurry up, I'm a rip him off." I made sure I dropped them off in front of plenty of witnesses, even if it was a crowd of Rivington Street junkies. $4.90 fare, 10-cent tip.

But old Marvin songs kept running through my head. "What's Going On" was the fall of 1971, all the teenage rebellion I grew up with crunching into nihilistic despair, my old pot-smoking friends turning from the weed to scag and Seconals. "Let's Get It On" was a house party somewhere on Long Island in the winter of '74, a luded-out lapsed-JAP named Jacqui dancing slowly into my arms. "Got to Give It Up" was hitching to Rockaway Beach in the summer of '77, cruising over the Cross Bay Bridge in a gorgeous old late-'40s Hudson. "Here, My Dear" was the end of my first marriage. "Sexual Healing" was the beginning of my second.

That one was all over now except for the paperwork. I had a six-month-old son who was probably squalling for a bottle or a diaper change as I shuttled and jockeyed the potholes of midtown Manhattan. An artistic-looking white guy with a portfolio going

110

from Sixth and 20th to Penn Station. A thirtyish black executive-secretary type going from there to 46th and Park. Two corporate lawyers going to 78th and Lexington. Back downtown empty until 59th Street.

At 4:55 I dropped two late-twenties German tourists off in front of the Carlton Arms Hotel, 24th and Third. Two black guys jumped into the back seat.

"Brooklyn. Fulton and Nostrand," one of them said.

Bedford-Stuyvesant. Fuck, I thought. It wasn't a racial thing, it was going deep into Brooklyn in rush hour. Once I had picked up two Haitian women at 27th and Broadway, loaded 14—count 'em, 14—shopping bags into the back seat and trunk, spent half an hour fighting my way over the Williamsburg Bridge to drop them off by a red-brick building on Marcy Avenue with the meter at $7.60—and received eight dollars and two dimes as my reward. Late at night I'd welcome fares to Brooklyn or anywhere in the outer boroughs—running up the meter on the trip out and zipping back beat hell out of waiting on line 20 minutes outside of Danceteria for a three-dollar fare, some coked-out yuppie going to Heartbreak—but this meant spending half an hour coming back empty. In traffic. The only consolation of rush-hour driving normally was that the cab would be perpetually occupied while you sat in near-gridlock, carbon monoxide seducing your red blood cells.

I clicked the meter on and made the right onto Third Avenue. "I want you to meet my nephew," the older of the two said. He was short, about 40, had gray-streaked hair, and wore a brown leather bush jacket, tinted round wire-rimmed glasses, and faded designer jeans. "Best nephew in the world." The younger man was about 24, at least a head taller, and was wearing an oversize blue denim jacket and a white sweatshirt.

Traffic on the Bowery was glued all the way down from Houston. An oil truck blocked two lanes between Rivington and Delancey. The sky had turned gray and it was starting to drizzle.

It took 10 more minutes to get as far as Grand Street. "Driving for Williams" was the cabbie's expression for working off the bills, and at three blocks in 10 minutes the meter wasn't producing much in the way of Williams fodder. My personal Williams started with ninety dollars a week rent and sixty in child support. I heard a knock on the partition.

"Wanna do some coke?" the uncle asked.

I looked into the back seat. The two were snorting street coke, digging into an inch-wide wax-paper bag with a gold spoon. "No, but thanks for the offer," I said. Cab-driving was nerve-wracking enough without the added stimulus. I didn't even drink coffee on the job most of the time, although that had more to do with the logistics of pissing in Midtown than with my nerves. The impossibility of finding a parking space at rush hour was inevitably directly proportional to the intensity of bladder pressure. The Koch administration had busted three cabbies for indecent exposure in the taxi lot at LaGuardia Airport, where a thin strip of dirt at the back of the line had the highest concentration of organic nitrogen of any patch of soil in the city. And procaine, ephedrine, amphetamine, and baby laxative were probably worse things to put in my body than deli diuretic.

"Suit yourself," he said, digging into the bag for another line.

I finally made the left onto the Manhattan Bridge. The upper deck was a perpetual construction site, concrete barriers crudely shunting traffic into a single lane, wet brown sand strewn over the roadway.

I heard arguing coming from the back seat. "You don't know a god-damn thing," the nephew said.

"If you don't shut up I'm gonna do like Marvin Gaye's father," I heard the uncle say.

I got nervous, but didn't hear any sounds of mayhem coming from the back seat as we passed by the nursing homes and vacant lots of lower Fort Greene. I dropped them off in front of the light at Nostrand. The fare was $8.10.

"Thanks a lot, my man. Keep the change," said the uncle, handing me a ten and shutting the door.

As I made the right onto Nostrand, a goateed, fortyish man in a golden-brown leather jacket was standing across the street. "Make me want to holler, throw up both my hands," he half-sang, half-shouted at passers-by. "Make me want to holler, the way they do my life."

I headed back towards the city on Atlantic and Flatbush. *Why can't we brothers protect one another* was going through my head. Not a Marvin song—Curtis Mayfield—but the sentiment fit. I had a beautiful old guitar in my room, a red Gibson semi-hollowbody like Mayfield's guitar player on the *Curtis/Live!* album. I couldn't remember the last time I played it for more than 15 minutes. At Cadman Plaza I picked up a couple going to the West Village. The Waverly Theater, Sixth and Third. Not a total loss to come back not completely empty, I thought.

The sky was clearer as I crossed the bridge, the setting sun backlighting the buildings with a pale, moist glow.

113

OPENING TASTE

Out of New Jersey through the valley of bad smells. Interstatia, land of boring highways, landscaped to death, an isolated tunnel through nondescript fields and forests, passing by an occasional God's Golf Ball tower. Only when the landscape is powerful enough, mountainous or urban, does it break the monotony.

The New Jersey Turnpike around Linden, Elizabeth and Newark is almost universally considered one of the ugliest places in the United States. But the industrial wasteland has its own beauty, giant, alien, grotesque and functional. Coming back stoned at night from a gig down the shore, patina of grease oozing out of my pores from the last McDonald's French fries I will ever eat, one refinery looks like an Art Deco ocean liner. Another is a fantastic unhuman city of lights, a pearlescent machine civilization, shimmering iridescently in the scatter of night raindrops on the windshield. The whole morass is bisected by

115

the highway, the nation's grimy aorta.

Its ugliness comes from its gruesome side effects rather than its esthetics. It's the legendary place of bad smells, a smorgasbord of burning rubber, gasoline, hydrogen sulfide, methane, and something uncannily resembling manmade catpiss. Toxic chemicals assaulting the body, causing cells to go berserk with greed. But it's not bad-looking if you've developed the taste.

Baltimore—an old city, narrow alleyways, the genuine 18th-century and the gentrified pseudo-colonial. There's a giant statue of George Washington, several stories high on an aircraft-spotlit pedestal, that from a certain angle—eagerly pointed out by our new friends—looks like it has a hardon worthy of a gorilla.

Show is canceled due to police harassment of the club. Don't get so smug about Czechoslovakian rehearsal-studio pre-censorship and remember Victor Jara's fingers. Some people have no heritage but TV cop shows and will give up anything for security.

We set up a house party, play with Kent on acoustic, Brian drumming on a bass case, me playing through a fuzzed-out battery amp. We collect $16 for gas money. Then we get a cynic's-eye tour of downtown, the new seaport theme park, glass elevators. Pipe City here we come. Two conduits for every boy. The boa constrictor and its owner pass out. Boys with unchanged voices flex their opening tastes of freedom and punk haircuts. Woman in a black dress and spiderweb combat boots tells me tales of her bagperson brother in New York and walking naked down oceanside highways.

Out of the city through another silent ghetto.

Breakfast in an International House of Pancakes in an ocean of parking lots. Crass calls to cut-rate luxury eclipse the bucolic dreams that brought people out there, leaving behind a succession of low-key traffic jams.

Off the highway in North Carolina. Deserted small towns at crossroads, roadside factories, whites in neat red-brick bungalows, blacks in weatherbeaten wood ones. Temples of country-style superfly, the Cool Pool Room, the E.T. (Extended Time) Disco, "I'm From the Big Apple, But I Love Franklinton, N.C." Greyhound bus to New York in the opposite direction.

In Raleigh, a railroad-motif hero shop brings relief and sustenance. Show here was canceled two days before we left, but Tanya says this is where the punks hang out—a barefoot girl in a black dress, an olive-skinned Stegosaurus mohawk, a genial cartoonist. We've got an instant place to stay, a house party to play, cold beer and ice water, and a cheese, sprouts, tomato and mayo sandwich. There's a sodden, saddened wino with the face of one who's seen too many ghouls in the mirror. Play another quasi-acoustic set in a small house on the outskirts, pass the hat for $12 gas money. It reminds me of suburban house parties.

Crash on the floor at Will's, a garden apartment gone hardcore style, white wall-to-wall carpeting, air-conditioning, lingerie, cans of Bud and distortion boxes strewn everywhere. The story is he pulled off some kind of scam and is living large for a few months. There's no furniture, but the rugs are thick.

In Chapel Hill we get a place to crash with an academic type who takes us all out to dinner, but only about 20 people show up for the gig. The show is in

117

between summer sessions at UNC. There's a woman I'm flirting with pretty intensely after the show, but I'm holding back. I'm supposed to be reconciling with my ex, Nancy Brownstone, mother of 18-month-old Coleman Younger Hawkins Brownstone Berkowitz. (The Coleman Younger was from her Jesse James obsession, the Hawkins was my, "well, if you're going to name him Coleman, let's get a musician in there.") Tanya's too tired to drive back to Will's, and I'm the only other one with a license, so that settles it.

Fifth day on the road, en route to Athens, rolling through the Piedmont with dub, early Stones, rockabilly, Hendrix and the Wipers. Kent's mix tape. A lot of it's the kind of stuff that would've been too predictable to bring myself, but it's perfect.

Rainstorm in northeast Georgia—two-tone world of gray and green. Clapboards and satellite dishes.

Post-insomniac morning in a driveway in Winterville, ten miles outside of town. Set last night was pretty good, grinding the graveyard groove on the slow things. Once again, we hit a college town in between summer classes and end up playing to 20 people. One was a woman who sat down by herself with a pitcher of beer, and the only question was which one of us she was going home with. "Well, it's a dark and dirty job, but someone has to do it," Kent says, and steams in. I talk to her after he's established his claim and she's nicer than he deserves. Fucker whispers he's just doing it for a place to crash. The rest of us settle for trying to get drunk enough to sleep in the van.

I failed, but no hangover. On the other hand, my back hurts from moving equipment, my armpits are ripe enough to attract flies, and a fiscal crisis is looming. We haven't made more than $25 a night yet.

In this placid-looking structure—a brick ranch house in three shades of tan, suburbs invading the country style—lurks the other group Tanya roadies for, one of the most perverse bands in America. No one's home. We can see an eight-track recorder through the window. Tanya says they all do tons of acid, jam out and record everything for three weeks. Makes me wonder if there's more than pictures of Jesus and Reagan going on in all the other houses out here. Probably not. Athens and the Triangle in North Carolina seem like oases.

Get to Atlanta a day early. The club there says we can sleep on the stage after the show, which is the Enemies, a Vancouver band we've opened for a couple times. It's an old warehouse by the train tracks. Lots of skinheads in the scene, which is centered around a squat across the street. The loudest one calls himself Johnny Moron. The first band on is all women, from San Francisco, and the skins aren't used to it. "Take your clothes off," they're all yelling.

"We'd like you to, except your dicks aren't big enough to be seen in public," the lead singer answers. They dedicate a song to Johnny Moron, then say, in a syrupy kindergarten-teacher tone, "but you're probably too fucking stupid to understand it, right Johnny?"

The Enemies rip. They're fucking amazing, probably the best live band in the world, muscular anarchist punk-boy rock, ever-pounding drums and walls of guitars. Meanwhile the skins are trying to tip over the women's van with them in it. The Canadians are all big, so they intervene.

I'm broke the next morning. I know Kent has money, so I hit him up for the $20 he owes me for the

119

band phone bill. He says I'm anal-retentive and a cheap prick. Then he turns up at the show with a dime of pot and a pint of Jack Daniel's. You can guess the rest. He's out of time on every song, breaks three strings on his guitar, borrows my Tele—it *was* in tune—and tells me it's a piece of shit. At least we get paid $50, which means a full greasy-spoon breakfast of eggs, coffee and fried okra.

Out of Atlanta. I am increasingly convinced that suburban sprawls are the ugliest places in America. Not even grotesque enough to be interesting. It's the same coming into Chattanooga. More of the same, just an endless parade of single-lane corporate franchises, agents of a larger entity, their petty sirens. Deep in the heart of Reagan country suburbia meets redneckdom and new money.

The children of these banally ugly suburbs regard the world they are growing up in and most swallow it blindly. What the corporations put on the plate is all there is to eat and it's good, so why imagine anything else?

But some of them want to scream, with the power to shatter glass, with the power to shatter complacency, to dive into the pit with the grace of a gymnast and the anarchic desperation of a suicide. Loud enough to wake the mentally dead.

Most of what they produce is just ugly, redundant and self-destructive. What can we do not to be ugly, redundant and self-destructive?

Dinner in a diner with an amazing jukebox—Z.Z. Hill, B.B. King, Al Green, Ann Peebles, "Just Enough to Keep Me Hanging On." Chattanooga is the best show of the tour. We're on and the kids are desperate. There's teenage punks from Dalton, Georgia, Cleveland, Tennessee and even monkey-trial town Dayton. The misfits, loose nuts and partial plates find each other with some joy.

House party afterwards. Kent scams on the one available woman. Me and Brian stay up all night drinking and talking philosophy with a woman who's in between bouts of born-againism. She's got big white scars on her wrists.

Long drive home. At a rest stop northeast of Knoxville Kent is sitting at a picnic table rolling a joint. It's obvious what he's doing even hundreds of feet away.

"If the cops come we're fuckin' leavin' him here," François whispers.

"Deal." I concur. They don't.

Tanya's the only one who stayed sober last night, and she's on a macho trip about doing the whole 850 miles by herself. Barreling through the Great Smokies, the Blue Ridge and Shenandoah, deserted mountain freeway. I talk her out of the driver's seat for a bit, but the batteries on the box fade just as I crank up my Mötörhead tape. No "Ace of Spades"?! My energy level dips precipitously. Tanya gets her way.

In northern Virginia the accents change, and our newly acquired "What time y'all want us to go on?" drops away immediately. South of Harrisburg we pull into a gas station and the car next to us is blasting The Real Roxanne. We're almost home.

Five hours later we're down on the industrial bayou and the Holland Tunnel becomes portal to St. Marks Place. There's a woman shooting up in the doorway next to the studio while we're unloading. On the way over to Nancy's squat a somewhat bohemian-looking balding man is trying to talk a scarred-

121

veined prostitute out of her price. Be it ever so decadent there's no place like home.

6:45 AM. Little Coleman is standing in his crib glowing. I play with him for half an hour and pass out cold.

Kent quits a week later.

THE KINDNESS
OF STRANGERS

Out of Jersey once again. Through some mysterious monster technojungle. Atmospheric murk casting its dull blurry glow over miles of cybernetic rabbit warrens and factory spew.

We've got two new members in tow, both dysfunctional rich kids. Roach Wein on rhythm guitar, formerly of the Killer Bees, an oilman's son from Dallas. Yes, they have Jews in Dallas. He's total Sunbelt hardcore boy, short brown hair, white T-shirts and a fucked-up elbow from a skateboard crash. I connect to him through tribal loyalties and a million old punk-rock jukebox favorites. Julia Streicher from Minneapolis on lead, daughter of a 3M executive, recovering from a four-month affair with dope and the boyfriend who turned her on to it. She's ultra-thin with stringy blond hair and wears the kind of short skirts and black stockings that could pass for either well-dressed punk or avant-garde corporate. I connect to her when she plays "It's All Over Now" at her audition, hitting the crunching punctuation on the out-chorus, "because I used to love her—*ka-rom krong*!—but it's all over now."

We record two new songs with them to add to the nine we did with Kent, whose presence in the studio is not missed. The album comes out the second week in January on Sabotage Records from San Francisco. They hook us up with booking.

Two days in West Philly. Everybody at the show is real young. They thrash to everything. Saturday in a codeine cloud with a bad migraine, wrapped in a sleeping bag and winter-afternoon grays. The people we're crashing with are paying something like $900 for an entire eight-bedroom, three-story house. Night is back at the hall for a party, a dub and groove marathon. We do a short set building into an Arabic trance groove. The bass player from one of the opening bands is a fat black guy who makes me want to go home and practice for hours. I dream that I smoked a ton of pot and couldn't find my way back to bed.

Out of Philly. Railroad tracks wind around narrow river valleys. Houses clustered on hillsides. The road rolls and pitches up to the edge of the Allegheny plateau. Cross the frozen Susquehanna and get a dose of leftover Three Mile Island radiation. Cruise south across snowy farmfields into Maryland.

West Virginia is beautiful, or at least the bit of mountains we saw before it got dark. It's severely hilly and isolated, frame houses with hairpin driveways, contort yourself trying to fit under the eaves to piss. The woman who runs the club is cool, it used to be a stop on the Underground Railroad. We play for dinner and gas money and stay in an attic with Lizzie, a wire-rimmed bundle of nervous energy who talks about "maintaining" a lot. Six of us fit on the floor. She's got a kid so I connect with her on that. She says Morgantown is a spiritual power spot because the Monongahela River is the only one in the world that flows north. I'm skeptical, but can't think of any others. Later I look it up and find the Nile and a whole bunch in Siberia.

In Columbus we play a Monday night in a gay disco, open to all-ages punk on the deadest night of the week. Los Hijos de Sam from Barcelona open, Lorca the guitarist attacking his Telecaster with measured aggression, jagged passion. But what comes out of the band as a whole is pure generic hardcore, distinguished mainly by Mierda the lead singer's incredibly guttural voice. He bellows like he's singing from the bottom of a cauldron of medieval snot, caked with 300 years of Gothic cathedral crypt dust. He's barechested, covered with scars and snaky, looping barbed-wire tattoos, a pierced lower lip.

There's only about 25 people left when we go on. The sound is a sea of tin and no one's dancing, but we rip anyway. I hang back by the drums, concentrating on Brian, crank up the low end and we lock in like a locomotive, our underdrive shaking the rails, people finally get up and into it. For an encore we do—François' idea—Jethro Tull's "Locomotive Breath," Roach chunking metallic crunch-rhythms and Julia scorching out high notes where the flute solo would be, François preaching the sacrilegious lyrics.

There's a party back at the house we're crashing at. This is not the first time in my life other people's beer has provided a significant portion of my daily caloric intake. We made $70 and per diem is down to

$5. We bond with Los Hijos. I stay up until 5 talking to Lorca, he's a serious anarchist and Zappaphile, asking me, "How do you translate 'ram it up your poop chute'?"

Next day we head over to Gilead College, a ghost town, abandoned dorms like a vacant hotel. Academic bohemia '80s style, punks coexisting with hippies and lesbians in a half-deserted oasis in serious Middle America. Really nice people here.

We open for Crackpot from San Diego. The back of their van proclaims "WE SUFFERED FOR OUR MUSIC—NOW IT'S YOUR TURN." They play slow, dense, grinding, an amphetamine-crash soundtrack. They're all drunk as shit, so drunk they look simian, and we blow them away.

Outside we discover real white people—not Jewish or Italian like in New York but ones out of Norman Rockwell or TV. America looks in the mirror and likes what it sees. Not bad people here in Reagan Country. Not cold-blooded advocates of eviscerating Central American nurses in the name of anti-Communism, but willing to not dig too deeply into investigative journalism. What they don't know won't disturb them.

I streak my hair green with help from Maureen from Massachusetts. She lives upstairs. She's blond and brown and green and has a triangle shaved in the back of her head with an eye tattoo. We talk about liking industrial landscapes better than suburban shit.

Derangement of the senses like Rimbaud said. I want my brains scrambled and exploding, nerve endings firing away and chattering like teletypes, churning out dumpsters full of word salad, newspaper montages and elbow-shaped pieces of excelsior

126

inscribed with talismanic words.

Flint is chaos city. The van breaks down on the exit ramp. Push it into a gas station and call the hall. Steve the drummer from Mindless Violence gives me a ride over. He works in the GM plant. "Yeah, I work 9 to 5, but I don't mind cause I'm a rad union man." Dinner is one can of V-8 and four of beer. Michigan is a rock'n'roll state, the sound of car factories and metal cranking, Chevys and Gibsons, Fenders and Fords. The hall is full of kids bouncing off the walls and waiting. Opening band is fucking terrible one-beat generic amateur hardcore. Mindless Violence are great. Me and François are up in the frontlines shouting along with them.

We go on real late. Running wild trying to blow out all the fuckups. One of those gigs where it feels like they let you out of a cage for 45 minutes, out of the bonds of everyday existence, exploitation, your own being. Julia's amp blows up, fried-speaker smell on stage. Slip a spare in. The stage is rickety as fuck and when I come down from a jump my stack falls over. One channel's out so I play on the other. We rip anyway. Bodies are flying all over the place. The stage is 18 inches high and kids are still diving. And we make $450, the high for the tour.

The van goes out again after the show. Drunk and tired, curl up on top of my speaker cabinet and pass out, using Brian's trap case for a pillow. As much sleep as I can get under the lights. Tanya punches out some creep who was inviting her to come sniff his farts for two hours.

The outskirts of Flint are one of the ugliest places I've ever seen, rectangles upon rectangles of suburban crap covered with gray slush. I'm avoiding corporate food as much as possible on this tour. Here it's hard. We stay in Ruth's attic. She's a 37-year-old divorcee, veteran of the radical rock'n'roll dope days around 1969—FREE JOHN SINCLAIR! TOTAL ASSAULT ON THE CULTURE! KICK OUT THE JAMS, MOTH-ERFUCKER! Now she works in a factory. Looks spiritually battered but still warm on the inside—well she must be if she put up with us for three days. Two daughters, 12 and 13, misfits in junior high. House is party central, always somebody over, horror movies on TV, cracking up to the Meatmen's bits about Ann-Margret's winking-pink birthday cake and Elvis' veined blood bomber. Someday biolinguists are going to discover the exact link between beer, testosterone and the creation of inventive terms for sexual body parts and vomiting.

Meanwhile we're all cracking up with crises. Two amps and the van down, 800 miles from home, there's six inches of snow on the ground and we're supposed to be in Detroit tonight. Janet the booking agent is playing psychiatric nurse on the phone from San Francisco, telling us the album's doing really well in California, getting added by college stations in Boston, Olympia, and Cleveland. And *Revolution Pop!* zine called it "long-awaited... the best we've heard so far this year."

Somehow we make Detroit. Jesse the 19-year-old promoter borrows a car, drives us and guitars down and we borrow gear from the other bands. Jesse is a motherfucking saint. We have always depended on the kindness of strangers. I play through a DI box, no amp. It's a cavernous old ballroom on the southwest side, no alcohol, just tons of Jolt Cola—"all the sugar and twice the caffeine." Crowd is still a little dead. I hang out with a girl named Nina from Ann Arbor. Me and François want to see Detroit real bad. Detroit Rock City, the Home of High Energy, Motown, the MC5, the Stooges, and the only place in America whose reputation is worse than New York's—so Nina's friend Mary drives us around. We don't see very much. She's from one of the suburbs, nervous about late-night ventures into the inner city. We get ridiculously lost somewhere like Dearborn, in a snowy maze of affluent rectangles. All we get to see is Renaissance Center glass and a Greektown coffee shop after the bars close.

The whole city is virtually abandoned, Jesse says. The rich whites took the money and ran after the '67 riot, and the decline of the auto industry did the rest. Some other guy says whites looted and fought cops too. Ruth says there are dozens of abandoned mansions there, infinitely explorable and possibly squattable.

I have a migraine for the next two days. Tanya's wrist is broken from punching the creep. She flies back to New York. Muskegon is canceled due to van crisis and snow. By Monday the van and amps are resurrected and we're westbound on I-94.

Wisconsin has the cheapest beer in the USA. Madison is crisis city #2. James, a friend of Julia's, is flying out to be our roadie; Rat, a friend of Roach's, is taking the bus out. Julia gets in a fender-bender in a university parking lot and the van gets towed. While we're waiting for it we hang out in the student union and harass Young Republicans for the Rape of Nicaragua.

The show here is pretty good. The crowd likes us but is pretty cerebral. There's a metal band opening and the stage is really small. Me and Roach decide to jump off at precisely the same moment and crash into each other. Very Spinal Tap.

There's a gay bar downstairs and a pile of safe-sex flyers in the hall. "Don't come in his mouth. Don't let him come in yours," it reads, with crossed-out circles over drawings of the appropriate sex acts. "Jacking off is good clean fun and spreads nothing but joy." We take one back to the van and start singing it. "Young man—Don't let him come in your mouth/I said Young man—Don't let him come in your ass/You can jerk off—and it's good clean fun/And spreads nothing but joy." François does the horn blats and Julia the letter-signs as we sail into the chorus. "It's no fun to get A-I-D-S."

We're here for two days. We stay at Louanne's apartment. She's six feet tall, has a six-inch full-color your-father-got-drunk-and-fucked-a-peacock Mohawk, and is more muscular than anyone in the band. All this and brains too. Three of the boys immediately develop crushes on her. We're sleeping three in the bed and her Mohawk keeps poking me in the face.

Afternoon off and I hang out with Julia browsing used bookstores. Used bookstores are a sign of civilization, they mean people are literate even if they can't afford more than two bucks for a book.

She's the only other one in the band who likes to read, except for Brian who's heavily into science fiction. We bond swapping paperbacks. I bond with her and Roach musically for totally opposite reasons. He knows every single song on the first four Ramones albums, he's got it engraved like a skate-crash scar. She knows the universe didn't begin with "Blitzkrieg Bop." Brian I can play anything with, throw any groove or riff at him and he'll come back with something better, plus he's the sanest one in the band most of the time. François is the one who puts the face on it, the vortex, he does what I can't do, persona and vocals, and I do what he can't do, music and hooks, we got our own little symbionese liberation guitar army. Rat's a runty 18-year-old longhair from Queens, a bit in awe of all these "rock stars."

I go out for Nepalese food with Julia and Rat. This is extremely rare—a decent vegetarian meal in the Midwest, and for under $4 too.

Everybody in the band's got their own food quirks. Roach believes he's going to get ptomaine from anything that doesn't have a brand name on it— his idea of health food is the salad bar at Wendy's. Julia's almost totally macrobiotic, how she finds anything to eat on the road at all bewilders me, she carries a tiny pot, brown rice, and dried adzuki beans. Brian's got redneck phobia, he thinks stepping into any coffeeshop west of the Appalachians or south of DC could end up like *Easy Rider* or *Deliverance*. Rat is nominally a vegetarian, but he seems to live on 7-11 Slurpees. I'm a vegetarian too, unanimously banned from eating at Taco Hell because we're traveling in a small enclosed space. François is the least quirky, a rare occurrence. He'll eat anything as long as it isn't too corporate, too spicy, or too rabbit-food.

We seem to be attracting lots of very intelligent rock'n'roll misfits. Good sign. The next night I go back to the club—it's 25-cent beer night—and meet Nadine. At this point I've been away from home long enough for her casual allusion to blonde pubic hair to cause serious turgor in my veined blood bomber. She's 21, from a rock'n'roll (Zeppelin, Pink Floyd) family with racist parents (no black-music records allowed in the house). She ran away at 16 and discovered rap, reggae and R&B. I spend most of my $10 per diem on the jukebox, playing Temptations, James Brown and Archie Bell and the Drells cuts she's never heard before. It makes me feel old, but it's some kind of connection. She tells me about this long story she wrote about a society where musicians are banned from listening to any music but their own, to protect them from contaminating influences, and only authorized listeners are allowed. Violators are maimed.

Back at Louanne's François is pissed about the amount of metalthrash people played all day. "We need allies, not alloys," he's ranting. Can't say I'm innocent—me and Roach were bugging all the State Street record stores about when the new Metallica is coming out.

Up north to the nation's icebox. Green Bay. It's fuckin' arctic up here. The rivers are frozen solid. It's flat, sparse forests, farmlands and factories and 8 fucking degrees out. We're getting used to it. We're playing in a VFW hall. The PA is a piece of shit and no one is over 20 but Bill the promoter. Julia is ready to dismember me for playing too loud after her amp blows up again. Fuck it, you're supposed to feel the bass, not bury it. The more crazed I get when I play, the more signal it puts out. I've only got my amp turned up to fucking 3. After half a set of wackness I settle back by Brian and the drums and we crank. There's an androgynous longhaired boy up front and I'm dancing with him and he's screaming PLAY IT, MOTHERFUCKER, PLAY IT! We bring up Jason Sickness from *Bubonic Reducer* zine for the encore, a morass of covers, "Pipeline," the Stooges' "Dirt,"

"Holiday in Cambodia," the Subhumans' "Slave to My Dick," "Sonic Reducer," and "Blitzkrieg Bop." Jason's a goateed neo-beatnik type who spews out genius scatological rants in infinitesimal type, scamming the Xerox machine on his job to print it.

I'm so sweaty I load out in a T-shirt and don't feel the cold. Underage shows are paradise for Roach, so he's not much help. François is always representing and Julia weighs like 95 pounds, so me and Brian end up the beasts of burden. Bill takes us to his place for reefer, conversation, and warm beds. He looks like the quintessential middle-aged Midwesterner, but he's cool. A lot of people in the scene talk shit about him cause he's gay, like the only reason he puts on shows is to scam on young boys. They should be fucking grateful to him. We got paid $300 and everyone gets their own bed.

Breakfast in Oshkosh at the Country Kitchen— all you can eat for $3.99. We look like the Fat Boys video.

Rolling towards Chicago with rockabilly on the box. In Chicago the gas-station bathrooms are out of order for us. Posters for politicians everywhere.

James Dean Is Still Dead
I can still find happiness even in a really fuckin' shitty mood by sitting barefoot in the back of the van on a warm springlike day with a Black Flag live tape churning out of the box, cranked up to 8. Henry Rollins screaming black coffee and death, Greg Ginn grinding and ripping on a clear Lucite guitar.

Two days ago, we were in Green Bay and it was 8 degrees out. Today, we're in Champaign, Illinois and it's 55 and sunny. I'm still in a bad mood. Last

133

night's gig was more fratboy bash than punk-rock houseparty. They were even moshing to the reggae and slow psychedelic-drone stuff we played. And the woman I was in intense conversation with found her purse had been ripped off and disappeared. Well, at least my girlfriend back on 11th Street won't have anything to be pissed off about. I'm trying to preserve whatever it is we have. I've been good on this tour.

Later I go off on a rant about drug-testing—what's next, compulsory anal swabs to see if you're at risk for AIDS?—and wander around downtown Champaign in a daze, getting gawked at by bland-oids. I have discreet green streaks in my hair, which is relatively staid-looking by Lower East Side standards, but marks me as a demented freak out here in the heartland. STOP STARING AT ME!

I come back to the house and crawl across acres of beer-soaked carpet. Chicago tonight is canceled. It was a benefit for some leftist organization, but we were supposed to get $150. James is from Indiana, so he's going to use his local connections to try to scam us up something.

James comes through. He's got us a show. So three hours later, we all pile out of the van in what passes for a bohemian neighborhood on the north side of Indianapolis. A guitar store, a used-record shop, and an old movie palace called the Vogue, which is where we're playing. No money, but all we can drink for free.

Our band is divided into overlapping factions on three crucial issues on the road: vegetarians vs. non-vegetarians, drinkers vs. non-drinkers, and the faithful vs. the slutty. Of course the lines aren't always clear, especially on the last issue. All of us are coupled off back home, but only Brian is completely without sin. Brian's the type of guy who works the phrase "my girlfriend" into the conversation within five minutes after he meets a woman. Naturally, his girlfriend is the most jealous. But tonight, we're all fucked up and frustrated, and the promoter's buying—no small consideration on a $10 per diem. So everybody gets drunk—even François, who normally is more likely to be pontificating about how Budweiser symbolizes all the disgusting bigotry and complacency of Reagan America, and Julia, the health fanatic.

We've been playing mostly all-ages punk shows, so it's a relief that there are actually women over 21 here. Unlike Roach, I can't sustain a conversation with two 15-year-olds about the relative merits of Captain Crunch and Lucky Charms for more than 30 seconds. The types who gravitate to me after the show are usually guys wanting to talk equipment—guitar talk is like car talk, I got a '71 Fender Precision with a DiMarzio humbucker running into a 300-watt Peavey Mark III head and a two-15" bottom—or strange, precocious girls, like the 14-year-old in Green Bay who told me "You're old enough to be my father if you were sleazy in junior high school." I end up downing vodka-and-grapefruit at a table with several, hanging mainly with one who used to be a dancer in New York, but moved back when, she says, "I lost my obsession."

We're supposed to go on at midnight. We're all obliterated by then. "Gentlemen, start your amplifiers," says Jack Rubin, the promoter, and the Marshalls start to rev. Julia's still putzing around setting the time on her digital delay, so we take up the dead air with a contest: Who—me, Jack, or Roach—has the biggest nose? The winner gets an all-expenses-paid trip to

135

London to compete with Pete Townshend and a chance to reclaim the world nasal-length championship for the sons of Israel. I come in third. The applause meter puts the hometown favorite all over the top.

I don't remember the set at all, but I guess we did more of the slow songs cause we weren't playing to mosh-crazed kids. I think we were pretty good, though. We're supposed to sleep at Jack's house, but he wants to take us to an after-hours club first. In Indianapolis that means it's open from 2 to 3. There's a big bleached blonde cooing "I just love Jewish guys" over me and Roach. We're starting to act canine. Jack is jumping around with his dick out. It's significantly longer than his nose. "I'm not staying at his house," Julia says. "He looks like he's got at least two hours left in him."

James says we can stay on his parents' farm, somewhere near Fort Wayne. It's at least two hours away. We get in the van. I pass out.

I wake up. The van is stopped. We're in a field somewhere in the middle of nowhere, the full moon lighting up the snow. People are getting out of the van. I fumble for my glasses. We're in a fuckin' graveyard. I try to focus my eyes. There's nothing around but a few bare trees and thousands of tombstones. The one we're parked next to says:

JAMES BYRON DEAN
FEBRUARY 8, 1931—SEPTEMBER 30, 1955

Yes, the remains of the mutant king, the angst-ridden icon cooling his demons with a bottle of milk on his forehead, are approximately six feet beneath us, salvaged from the ruins of a Porsche gone over the cliff on an eternal chicken run. It's easier to be an

136

eternal rebel if you don't have to live to middle age, said Jimmy Keniston, the guitarist in my first real band, whose real name was James Dean Keniston and was therefore obsessed. Jimmy didn't know this when he said it, but he'd never reach middle age. There was a virus we had never heard of lurking in the dick of a future lover. François, who is distinctly prone to fits of pretentious fuckery, of course has to prostrate himself in front of the grave, letting out his best Method tortured-teenager yowl: "YOU'RE TEARING ME APART!" Then everybody sees ghosts and gets superstitious and splits.

It's light out by the time we ooze up the dirt road to the farmhouse, nestled next to a creek poisoned by fertilizer runoff.

James' mother cooks us pancakes. We head east for Ohio and I-75 southbound. I'm driving, badly hung over, got a large cup of bad 7-11 coffee. Rat's riding shotgun blasting Metallica, relentless double-kick-drum battery, he's bouncing up and down, playing air guitar, air drums, clattering the beat on the dashboard, knocks my coffee over. "FUUUCCCKKK!" I scream scalded, fishtailing through the midmorning traffic, nearly sideswiping a van full of sheetrock and a Greyhound bus, regain control, pull off at the next exit for more bad coffee and settle our nerves. Get back on the highway with calmer music—Bruce Springsteen's *Nebraska*. Rat is freaking out, "GET IT OFF! I CAN'T STAND THAT FUCKIN' FAKE SOUTHERN ACCENT!" I tell him to chill.

I can't stay pissed at him. He's the only one in the band family who can keep up with Coleman, chasing him around the living room, teaching him to say "Mo-dahed" and "Tallica." "Why don't you bring Cole-

137

man on tour?" he asks. "Yeah, what am I gonna do, change diapers on stage and throw them into the audience?" We get into Dayton around 3:30, crashing in this rambling semi-derelict maze of a ranch house at the edge of the ghetto, get showers before the show.

We're opening for this country-punk band named the Rebel Kind, Los Hijos de Sam on first. I don't remember how we play, I got two hours sleep and have an intense migraine. Two songs into the Rebel Kind's set I go out to the van and pass out cold.

I get awakened by François and Los Hijos shaking the van, then by Kevin their roadie telling a crying teenage girl he can't drive her home, 25 miles isn't "just out of town." There's a post-gig party we get to just as they're running out of beer. I smoke some pot, courtesy of a woman who's so high she seems like she lost 40 points of IQ. At one point she leans over and asks Julia, "Do you speak English?" Anyone who says anything more complicated than "Yes" gets the same routine. "Do you speak English? Does ANYONE here speak English?" I don't know whether it's the prospect of putting up with her babble or nagging doubts about the ethics of seducing someone so wasted, but she gets turned down by three guys in the entourage.

One of them is Carlos, Los Hijos' bass player. He's the proverbial tall, dark and handsome, with dark-brown shoulder-length ringlets. He's got a girl-friend at home, disappointing many. We talk music—he comes out of psychedelia and glam, the Stooges, Dolls, and Hawkwind.

Brian throws up blood, he's been complaining about stomach pains all night. We take him to the emergency room and they hold him for observation, gig tomorrow or no gig tomorrow.

It's the biggest show of the tour—we're opening for the Enemies from Vancouver, Los Hijos on the bill too. Gonzalo their drummer says he'll do the set with us.

The next morning I go out for juice when we stop for gas and the caravan drives off. Stranded in downtown Dayton with 21 dollars, six pills, and a half-gallon of grapefruit juice. I track them all down at Brian's hospital room. Mierda jokes about "we see Sid on milk carton." Rat and Roach are both severely hung over, pale, clammy, and woozy.

Cincinnati is a puritanical city. You gotta go across the river to do your sinning, and that's where we're playing, in Newport, Kentucky, an aging vice satellite of topless bars, liquor stores, and pawnshops full of guns. Frank Sinatra played here in the '40s when it was a mob hangout. For food there's a choice of a redneck-infested White Castle or not-quite-canine Mexican food at restaurant prices.

Without Brian we have to teach Gonzalo, who speaks almost no English, seven songs in a 27-minute soundcheck. Roach insists on trying "Peace in the Pit" without the stops. François and I demur. "Why won't it work?" he insists.

"BECAUSE THE FUCKING SONG'S NOT WRITTEN THAT WAY!" I explode.

"You New Yorkers are so tense," says the soundman. "Down here we do things a lot slower." Julia thinks we're behaving in a highly unprofessional manner. An hour later we're sharing a beer, jamming on my baby amp in the dressing room, so I guess things are cool.

The Enemies' manager gives Gonzalo two lines of crystal meth, coming off like we're overworking him by making him do two sets. This feels patroniz-ing-Svengali, like dosing a sick child star with mor-phine so she can get through a day's filming, like he can't do two sets without it. Speed's a vindictive drug, it exacts its pound of flesh much more than dope, it's like running a 200-watt amp through a 100-watt speaker.

I'm doing the show completely straight. Alcohol is good for abandon but can lead to enervation and sloppiness if not timed right, and I'm the one who drives the band, and energy is our avatar, thou shalt have no other gods before it.

We pull it off. Carlos and Mierda lean over the drums, one on each side, coaching Gonzalo and trans-lating our instructions. "Thrash song." "Reggae." About half the songs get transmogrified rhythms, but it works out OK with no disasters. We rip through "Create and Destroy," the simplest of ours, and "Sonic Reducer," the cover he knows best, to end the set, and get tons of compliments. LosHijos season their thrash with funk and dissonance, Lorca's guitar convoluted screams. The Enemies have just driven up from Tal-lahassee and are tired as fuck, but they're probably congenitally incapable of doing a bad set. They encore with the Subhumans' "Fuck You," the Vancouver punk national anthem, when Joey Shithead from D.O.A. becomes prime minister it will replace "Oh Canada," and the crowd erupts into a forest of middle fingers on the chorus, "We don't care what you say—FUCK YOU!"

The guy who wrote the song is doing five years in jail for conspiring to blow up an unfinished nuclear power plant.

The Enemies and Los Hijos are leaving for Mem-

140

phis right after the show. Lorca is waxing sentimental when we say good-bye, "We are musicians, we are rebels, we are brothers, that matters more than what piece of soil we come from." A bit florid, but I appreciate the sentiment. It's true.

We crash in Cincinnati, at this kid Jason's mother's house, a large and well-fixtured loft downtown that rents for the extortionate sum of $350. The New Yorkers are jealous. I'm up till 7 with Aileen, Jason's skinny magenta-haired girlfriend, talking about books. François is going on about scene politics, and she says she can like both Kerouac and Truman Capote even though they slagged each other ruthlessly in the '50s. Presence of a brain is definitely indicated. She's got hippie roots under the peacepunk costume, she grew up "hearing my parents' Jefferson Airplane records in my playpen."

Pick Brian up at the hospital in Dayton, he's OK but he probably has an ulcer. Drive across Ohio to Cleveland, enter the city by night, lit by flaming smokestacks. The club's down by the river. The singer for the second band says he's classically trained, but they sound like just another hardcore band. We're solid—probably the most solid show of the tour—but the crowd doesn't really get going till we encore with "Sonic Reducer." Saluting Clevo's homeboys. The promoter's a hippie who underpays us, $120 instead of $150. Then he wants a hug and says we can crash at his house. The bass player for the first band is flirting with me, says we can stay at her house too. She's the slightly plump blackhaired Mediterranean type I have definitely been known to go for, and she wants to take me to after-hours R&B clubs tonight and the art museum tomorrow. We've got two days to get to

141

Hartford and everybody wants to spend one of them at home, so I'm rescued from temptation.

Three days later the tour comes to an ignominious end in a motel room in Lee, Massachusetts. The van is dead. Really dead this time. Muerto. Kaput. XXX. A useless piece of shit. A hunk of junk fit only for a conflagration in the parking lot.

Night in the Berkshires. The landscape is not vernal verdance or an autumnal riot of earthtoned iridescence but a nightmarish hellscape of navy, dirty gray, and black. Ominous clifflike shapes loom over the highway, darker than the night, alternating with unseen abysses. Freezing rain inundates the van. The dying fire of the headlights is too weak to illuminate the fog.

The first record I listen to when I get home is *Back to the World* by Curtis Mayfield. "Soldier boy ain't got no job." One gig Saturday night and then nothing for four weeks. Being back sucks. There's no heat or hot water for four days. The landlord's trying to empty out the building, get rid of all us low-rent people, punks and Puerto Ricans and 76-year-old Ukrainians. I rant a lot about "a rat-plague of real-estate parasites" and "scum with a poisoned soul." Seeing what they've done to my city hits a lot harder when you've been away.

I bring my amp in to the shop and the guy says I've been playing on a shattered circuit board since Flint, it's a miracle it lasted this long.

VAN RATS RULE

Nancy gets herself dolled up for this gig. It's a day out for her, she usually doesn't get to see the band anymore. Spends half an hour doing her makeup, alchemy with lipstick and glitter to produce a metallic shade of purple. Leather jacket, Harley-Davidson T-shirt with the sleeves cut off, skin-tight black stretch pants, lurid green streak in her copper-orange dyed hair. On top of all this she's lugging the huge dirty-pink diaper bag for Coleman. The net effect is Punk Rock Mom.

I get Coleman and my bass, the unwieldy Fender rectangle, and we go downstairs and down the block to the studio. Coleman's jumping up and down and going "Tudio! Tudio!" I let him bang on Brian's drums while we're waiting for Rabbit and Rat and the band to come by.

Load the gear in Rabbit's van and head up First Avenue. The gig's in a park somewhere around 155th Street. It's a free concert and "Stop Killer Cops" rally for Ewart Michaels, a Jamaican cabdriver killed by a cop on Second Avenue two months ago. The story is he was pulling over to park just past Fifth Street and cut off a cop coming out of the Ninth Precinct. Witnesses said the cop, in plainclothes, jumped up to the driver's side of the cab, pulled a gun, and shouted, "Hey, asshole, open the fuckin' window." Michaels tried to pull out and received one bullet in his left occipital and one in his left temple. He was D.O.A. at Beth Israel and no charges were filed against the cop, who's telling a shiny-object story. The Red Guards are putting on the show and I don't like them, but we've never played in Harlem before and we're on the bill with Conscious X and Winston Smith. Plus Michaels' aunt and uncle live down the block from François' parents, so he's acting like they killed his cousin.

Everyone's black or Latin except for the Red Guards and the white bands on the bill. Roach and Julia are freaked out about being in Harlem, they've never been up here before. I haven't been up here very much either, saw P-Funk at the Apollo once. Nancy's from the Grand Concourse, so it's no big deal to her. She used to come over all the time to see blaxploitation movies back in the day. The park is on the Washington Heights border, so the color line's not so intense, the Dominicans blur it. The kids running around don't look any different from the kids Coleman plays with in Tompkins Square, rowdy five-year-olds in two-tone jeans and sneakers, kids bouncing on see-saws, careening down the spiral slides, whirring through on plastic tricycles. Red Guards are running around with flyers and clipboards. One of them interviews me, asks Why are you here. Hey man, it's a good cause. Dumbass rock'n'roller attitude. I get the feeling

144

she expected me to say "Because we dare to struggle against all forms of oppression under the glorious vanguard leadership of the Red Guards." Coleman's having a good time running around.

Couple punk bands go on, then some young rappers, neighborhood girl sings a Whitney Houston ballad a cappella, interspersed with speakers while they're changing gear, then us. It's in the low fifties, so we're all kind of stiff. Everything sounds rushed. We're not burning, so we try to compensate with speed. The rap interlude in "Tropical War" is thus devoid of funk. The punk stuff actually goes over better. We close with "Rise Up" and it finally starts to gel.

Winston Smith does a solo piece on one of those Steinberger headless guitars, a goat's head soup of Hendrixisms, James Brown licks and dissonance. He's really tall, thin, with almost waist-length dreads, round shades. Conscious X comes on next. He's just got his first album out, *Black-on-Black Rhyme*, does pieces called "Word Sound" and "Crack Vile" and a remake of "The Revolution Will Not Be Televised." He's from the Melrose projects just across the river, so he's got the biggest following, several dozen who crowd around the stage. They know all his songs. When he calls out "Name your poison" they all shout back "CRACK VILE!"

After his set a Red Guard speaker is on and I'm backstage with François, getting into a whole art-and-politics colloquy. He and Conscious are the hardline message types, they also connect on wordplay. A Spanglish-talking kid in a red sweatshirt comes up to me, asks "Why do you try to play our music?"

"Because we like it, and we figured we're coming

145

up here, we should play something people might be into."

"No," he says, "we like yours, it's something different, all that rock stuff. You don't have to imitate ours."

I know what I want to say, but I don't think of it until later. If I went to Puerto Rico, I'd look like a stupid schmuck if I went around pretending I was raised in Loiza Aldea and my mother's name is Maria Gonzalez, but I'd go over a lot better if I knew some Spanish. And I like rice and beans and cafe con leche a fuck of a lot more than I like McDonald's. Know what I'm saying?

Back in the circle Conscious, wearing a red T-shirt with his name on it in iron-on Gothic lettering, is passing a joint. I take a hit, François demurs, he's on an antidrug kick and doesn't want to interrupt his spiel, "Music isn't worth shit if it doesn't have something to say," he's going on. "It doesn't have a point, it's just decadence. You have to make people conscious of their oppression, inspire them to fight back."

"Nah," says Fat Freddy, the DJ playing in between sets. "I do a party, people don't care about the message. They gotta deal with that shit six and one-half days a week, they don't want to be reminded of it, they want to feel like they're somebody fly. They want to step out, know what I mean? They get on the dance floor and they wanna hear something funky, they don't want to hear somebody preach." Freddy's gesticulating with the joint before passing it, he's got a gut like the world's biggest pumpkin.

"I'm not a preacher, I'm a teacher," expostulates Conscious. "You got 30 minutes up on that stage, and I'm gonna use it to communicate, to educate, to make

146

people conscious. So many of our brothers are just deaf, dumb and blind, and I'm not gonna play into that, just talk about, you know, gold chains. Why use words if you ain't gonna communicate?"

"I'm trying to communicate," says Winston. "I don't necessarily want to be so *overt*." He talks really slow, measured, with a slight Jamaican accent, or at least the Brit inflections of an educated Afro-Caribbean.

"Uh... I think if you're not gonna communicate, you oughta shut the fuck up." My contribution. It cracks everyone up.

Nancy's hanging out talking baby stuff to a girl about 18 in a scarlet track suit with big gold earrings and hair pulled flat against her scalp. She's holding a baby, looking as much Hip-Hop Mom as Nancy looks Punk Rock Mom. The baby is Kuumba, her and Conscious' six-month-old daughter. Nancy brings Coleman over. "It's your turn," she says.

I know what that code means. I take Coleman over to the red-brick bunker of a bathroom. Inside, it's dim and everything's concrete and they've taken the doors off the stalls, presumably to deter cruising and shooting up. The result of this brilliant municipal policy is that now any little boy who doesn't want to shit in his pants has to go to the bathroom wide out in the open where any lurking pervert can see. At least there's still a toilet seat cover, so there's a level surface. I get Coleman's denim jacket off, unbutton his overalls. Conscious' pot is stronger than I think and is creeping up hard. There's a yellowish-purple haze from the lightbulbs, visual reverb on everything. Coleman's diaper is full of virtually undigested peanuts. This is not an esthetically pleasing experience. At least

147

it's not all smeary and stuck to his ass. Thank the powers that be for small favors. Coleman is squirming and I try to talk him down long enough to wipe him clean and dust him dry. It'll be a long time before I eat peanuts again.

Three days later we leave on tour. Nancy's pissed that I'm going to be leaving her alone with Coleman for two months. "I'm going back to school, trying to make something out of myself so I can provide for our baby, and you're still farting around like an over-grown teenager." Well, what the fuck did you expect from me? "That band is never going to make any money." The night before we leave I'm all romantic, last fuck before we leave. She turns her back. The motion is as final as a portcullis slamming down. When I wake up in the morning she's already gone, taken Coleman to the babysitter.

Load up the van that afternoon, my sunburst Fender and black Rickenbacker basses, amp, and cabinets; Roach's Marshall stack and Ibanez and Flying V guitars; Julia's Les Paul and Kramer, her Roland amp and effects rack; Brian's drums, blue-sparkle Ludwigs, kick drum, floor tom, rack toms, and trap case; and backpacks and duffle bags for six people, the five of us and Louanne the roadie. Drive through the newly walled highways of New Jersey to Bethlehem, Pennsylvania, play an aging hotel bar there, crash in the empty rooms upstairs. Next morning we get breakfast at a greasy spoon, drive through the Pennsylvania hills into Maryland, west into the Appalachians as the sun goes down. It's dark when we get to Morgantown for soundcheck and pizza.

We go on at 9:30 to an audience where no one's

over 17 but the promoter. It's depressing, all peer pressure and lack of roots. The sound sucks but we go over well. I'm sitting at the bar afterwards and a little wire-rimmed figure pops up next to me, it's Lizzie, she's grinning. I remember our conversation about north-flowing rivers. Monongahela doesn't exactly roll off my tongue like venison, but I tell her I looked it up and there's a whole bunch in Siberia, the Ob, the Lena, the Yenisei, and a whole bunch more in Alaska and the Northwest Territory. I think she's impressed somebody paid attention to her ideas. She throws her arms around me and kisses me.

We go back to her place, she's wiry, muscular and voluptuous under her flannel shirt, I thought she was just a skinny little thing. I eat her pussy until she comes a couple times, then we fuck. Second time she's on top, I'm having a hard time coming, she flips us over in one smooth athletic move and voom!

Next morning we take the scenic route through Appalachia, two-lane blacktop with hairpin turns unblessed by guardrails, steep and rapid descents beckoning. Villages sit astride narrow ridges, small clusters of silent houses, not a person in sight for miles. The rest of the band bitches at me for not taking the Interstate.

Fuck that. Interstates are boring. They just get you where you're going with a minimum of interest, you don't see the country till you get off.

Athens, Ohio gig is competent but rote, and severely acrimonious. I get really pissed at François for talking too much on stage. It's like having to stop every two minutes in the middle of sex to listen to a public-service announcement on condom use.

"Man, it totally fucks up the pacing of the set," I

tell him. "We can't get anything going if you're gonna fuckin' talk for two minutes before every song."

"You don't understand," he says, slight whine. "You guys can hide behind your guitars. When I'm on stage it's like I'm fuckin' naked up there, I got nothing but my voice and my body. It's like doing open-heart surgery on myself. You don't want anybody stickin' their hands in there. You don't know the pressure I'm under."

This doesn't settle anything. I know he's the one fronting the band, I just wish he wouldn't act like he's fuckin' lecturing the crowd. So I get drunk, wanting to feel something, some connection to some kind of music, anything. I'm in somebody's dorm room, playing the Pagans, "What's This Shit Called Love"— *anything baby would be better than nothing*—Joy Division cranked to the point of speaker despair. The music is the thread connecting me to sanity, a thin fucking thread. Joy Division doing "Sister Ray," Hendrix doing "Gloria," the two and three-chord wonders of the world. I WANT MADNESS AND ANIMAL VITALITY, LIKE LUST THROB, LIKE WE ARE ON A GOOD NIGHT—NOT THE IRON CLAW OF THE VOID.

I wake up thinking alcohol is the perfect puritan's drug. Its addled poetics, rabid theatrics, bludgeonous passion, and canine sluttishness are all duly and dearly paid for within one-half of the diurnal cycle. Somewhere down the hall somebody's playing Stevie Ray Vaughan, overplaying slow blues into the land of triple-time wanking, and my head is screaming at him to shut up.

Two days of chilling follow. So far this tour is ahead of the last one for intelligent conversation and edible meals. There's actually decent pizza in town, hippie-vegetarian calzones. Other than a Brooklyn expatriate's place somewhere in rural North Carolina, it's the only good pizza I've ever had outside of New York, Chicago, and San Francisco.

In East Lansing we play in a basement to 50 people, bisected by the oil burner, and rip. The kind of naked amps, people in your face show we love to do. It's one of those gigs that feels like everyone there is part of a secret society, part of some unique dionysiac rites, experience and innocence admit you to the elite. Laurie the hippie goat farmer's there, couple guys from Jesus Christ Cocksucker, Ted Gein. Laurie and two women from the Jesus Christ Cocksucker family circle, engaged in a discussion of birth traumas, turn to me and say in near-unison, "And how do *you* feel about circumcision?"

"I don't remember," I say, with all the gravitas of a corrupt politician trapped on the witness stand. Roach comes to my rescue, singing "Circumcised" to the tune of Suicidal Tendencies' "Institutionalized."

Flint is canceled—skinheads trashed the hall during a Shoot Bush First/Jesus Christ Cocksucker show last month—so we're stuck here another day. Serious claustrophobia develops. Waiting, killing time, waiting. Spend an hour puttering around pawnshops and used-record stores in Lansing's red-light district, where renegade farmgirls finance Fieros amidst flaking yellow paint. There's a mutant Gibson in the pawnshop, an orange-red quadrilateral. The used-record stores are full of Lawrence Welk albums. I'm in a bit of culture shock. I miss Jews and Puerto Ricans. Girls out here really look like the cornfed silicone dolls in *Playboy*, the Midwest princesses who go to

151

Fort Lauderdale for spring break. I bet their boyfriends would love to know about the sexual practices of the Spartan army. College students take the football team very seriously. Ted Gein points out all the places riot cops get stationed on football weekends. He's the resident misfit. There's another guy in the house who's from Long Island, he went to my high school. They have armed guards in the halls now, "to cope with the drug problem."

I probably would've gotten shot.

In a perfect police state the only crime you need is a bad attitude.

Detroit is different from cities I'm used to. It's built to auto scale, low-rise, the main streets multilane boulevards. It reminds me of East New York, populated by demented drivers and nocturnal trios of Fila-shod youths, full of shattered one-story buildings, abandoned gas stations, and that Michigan institution, the party store. "Billy Jack Walking Tall Party Store." Beer, wine, rolling papers, potato chips. Last week a 14-year-old boy was murdered by another for refusing to give up his purple silk shirt. Yesterday a 15-year-old got shot for revenge on a fight. His friends went and ripped up the suspect's house. Nearby is Vandyke Avenue, origin of the Van in Martha and the Vandellas. We're playing on Michigan Avenue on the southwest side. Two blocks from the hall is a topless bar called Baby Love with a Diana Ross lookalike on the marquee.

The show here is marred by a squabble between the two promoters, resulting in no promotion. but the 50 who showed know us and love us, and we rip like we usually rip. The Flint crew is down, Jesse and 3/5 of Mindless Violence, Nina from Ann Arbor and her friend Mary, most of Destruction and Artificial Apathy. Jackie from Destruction is telling me how her nine-month-old son likes to howl along with construction-site noises. He should be their next lead singer, they're into industrial noise.

The gig's kind of skin-heavy, but they're not hardline homophobes or hair-trigger-temper psychos, they talk more like white kids who got beat up one too many times in the Detroit public schools. They seem open to the "assholes come in all colors, so don't judge" line.

Afterwards we vegetate for a day at Mary's parents' mansion in Ann Arbor, they're in the Caribbean, she's telling Brian about the time she tried to hang herself with an American flag. We go see *Blue Velvet*, Dennis Hopper as malevolent macho personified. Roach will spend the rest of the tour holding a bandanna over his nose and mouth and hissing in a rising scream, "DON'T YOU FUCKIN' LOOK AT ME!"

One more night at Nina's. She's 16, got ex-beatnik parents, they smoke herb, play bongos, and recite poetry on Friday nights. Her mother's dying of breast cancer, rendered temporarily coherent by the mercy of morphine. Warmth and intelligence radiate from the ashes. In the morning Nina cooks a mountain of blueberry pancakes and we gorge.

The opening band in Kalamazoo plays new-wave copies and goes on way too long. We're sandwiched between them and the Dead Flowers from L.A., like us a punk band with pretentious overtones, they're almost political Goth. We work hard, impress the Dead Flowers, and leave most of the audience cold. They do too. It's new-wave night in a college town, and they just want to drink and pick each other up.

We stay with a local metalthrash band. Julia gloms onto their bass player and indulges her thing for longhaired boys. She doesn't come out of his room until it's time to leave for Louisville. For the rest of us it's another day in Michigan, two blocks from a minimal and overpriced grocery. Somebody's got a hollowbody guitar, a beautiful old red Guild with a whammy bar, and I spend the day writing minor-key dirges.

Keg party that night. Roach chases young girls to a soundtrack of speedmetal and generic hardcore. I drink a Kool-Aid pitcher of beer out of boredom. I have a severe headache the next day, befouling a beautiful drive through Indiana, sun over fields, creeks, and changing leaves.

Ennui and resentment the prevailing mood, primarily due to cancellations. The few shows we've gotten to do are as diamonds in a sea of putrefying fecate. Too many rainy days sitting around other people's houses with nothing to do and no money to do it with.

The Louisville club is a serious dive with the most fetid toilet I've ever seen anywhere with indoor plumbing. I'm not kidding, it's so gross I have to piss from six feet away, eventually falling short. It makes the bathrooms at CBGB's look like you could eat off the floor. Decent sound system, we play two good sets to a handful of local musicians, get paid $75. Louanne goes out for coffee and gets in a fight with a redneck, comes back bloody. The cops won't do anything because we're leaving town.

We head back to Gilead College, crash there before tomorrow's show. Maureen from Massachusetts and Chad do a sort of post-nuclear-apocalypse

154

domestic scene to open for us, but we're not as epic as we want to be. It's cold in the black-painted auditorium, muscles cramped, strings brittle, and I break the E strings on both my basses. We burn in spots, but don't ignite the crowd, they look like Mount Rushmore. Everyone's intelligent and affectionate anyway, and we get paid $400.

4 AM and I'm in a motel room on the outskirts of town. Pistachio walls, pink bathroom, K-Mart TV, magenta and pale-green neon lights outside. It looks like someone's 1951 Miami Beach vision. I'm all alone, it's warm and it's great.

Indianapolis is a flat, rectangular city. We pass by Kurt Vonnegut's high school on the way to the hall. We played well, but not many people show up, it's a matinee, us and Death Before Dishonor and two other bands, so the promoter gives us the "hey-man-you-gotta-support-the-scene" line when it's time to get paid. We blow up, Julia the most vehement, he guaranteed us $200 if we didn't book any other shows in Indiana. He says, "OK, if I pay you, then I'm not paying the other bands, and I'll tell them they're not getting paid because you didn't want to give them any money."

Fucking promoters. Their dictionary reads "**Guarantee** (n): A bullshit number you dangle in front of the band to sucker them into playing, subject to drastic reductions according to how much money the show brings in and your whims."

"And you're not staying at my house," he snips as we load out. One of the opening bands is from West Lafayette, they say we can do a house party there tonight.

We eat greasy grilled-cheese sandwiches at the

Triple XXX Drive-In, billed as the oldest drive-in restaurant in America, get shut down by the cops at one house party, wind up jamming in the basement at another, this kind of brick barbecue pit in the concrete floor, me and François and a bunch of locals. Roach and the guys from DBD are upstairs hitting on the local girls, college-freshman types.

Fuck yeah, we're rolling now, party with whoever's willing as long as they aren't obvious trouble—you learn to suss that drunken-smolder aura—or annoying hustle. Dude named Deshawn is playing guitar, he's got a Strat and an Afro and sunglasses like some '68 militant, wah-wahing out on "Papa Was a Rolling Stone." I kick in with the three-note bassline. The song's applicability to my current situation does not go unnoticed.

Coleman's probably asleep now, dreaming whatever two-year-olds dream about, what kind of concepts go through their heads when they've only got a few dozen words to define them? That's why he gets so pissed off, he knows what he wants, but he can't say it, so he screams. I wanna be around for him, but I don't want to give up playing for it. It would be like cutting my dick off. I don't want to end up a dilettante in a shitty underpaid day job, too weird to fit their world and no time or energy for mine. But somebody's gotta pay constant attention to the kid, and that devolves on Nancy. We hardly ever go out together any more, if we want to go see a show it's like 50 bucks with the babysitter, it's easier to do it separately.

It's been a long time since I met her, love at first sight the night Joey Rush and the Users did their live album. We opened for them and I was in the frontlines next to her during their set. A lot of bad blood has flowed under the bridge since then. Too much.

What did she think she was getting into? Musicians are irresponsible. I'm not as bad as most, but the gig requires being away from home. A lot.

My position is indefensible.

Fuck it, all I can do is play my heart out and burn through the contradictions. I gargle with the 40 a few more times and we stay up till 5, jamming on metal-funk and alcoholically mangling an endless medley of protopunk classics like "Heroes," "I'm Eighteen" and "Walk on the Wild Side." It's the most fun I've had all tour.

I wake up the next morning wondering where the fuck I am. Slowly consciousness dawns, we're on the ground floor of a giant garden-apartment complex, we're staying at this kid's house while his father's out of town. His father's a middle-aged swinger, got a waterbed and lots of chrome and glass in his bedroom, coked-out decor. Not a single book.

Julia is pissed, she stayed home last night with a yeast infection, spewing invective at the rest of us, Brian came home early and got the worst of it. I drive her to the emergency room and she's at it all the way there.

Champaign is canceled, so we've got a night of recuperation. There's a food co-op in town, an oasis in Wendy's land, so we eat rice and vegetables, watch the Red Sox obliterate the Mets. Alana the woman I met in Champaign last year comes by later.

We drop Julia off in Chicago, she's got a friend there, she's still sick and angry. Once again all I see of Chicago is gas stations, pissing underneath a poster of the Democratic candidate for alderman in the 39th

Ward. We head out to Iowa on US 20. Out here the land begins to open up, miles and miles of deserted prairie, browning cornfields, and weathered silos. It reeks of cowshit. Cross the Mississippi at Dubuque. No more civilization for 90 miles. We get lost west of Waterloo, wind up at a dead end in the middle of a dark cornfield. We finally find the club in the middle of an S-curved street in town.

It's like a scene from *Spinal Tap*. There are exactly ten people in the club, not counting the bartender, and the atmosphere is morose. We drove 400 miles for this. Roach and I go out back and start giggling uncontrollably. Laughing Sickness opens for us, they play hypnotic drones with oil-drum percussion, distinctive among opening bands. I like them, hang out with Linda their bass player, she's a fat blonde with a cat tattooed on her arm. There are only three paying customers when we go on, but we get into it, we take requests, and the sight of one of them drinking a Heineken directly under a Pabst Blue Ribbon neon sign is irresistible to those of us who've seen *Blue Velvet*. François grabs the guy's beer, points it up at the sign, and declaims, "Heineken? Fuck that shit! Pabst Blue Ribbon!"

Naturally there's an argument about money. The guarantee is $125, we talk the promoter up from $25 to $75. We sleep crammed into Linda's one-room apartment. She has to lock the door and stuff towels under it to smoke pot. I share her single bed, not fucking or coming on to her, just whispering and being mildly affectionate.

Heading back over the Mississippi the leaves are turning on the bluffs. "Pure poetry," says François as a train passes slowly along the waterfront. Chicago tonight is canceled, so we head to Madison where Louanne has friends. Julia will meet us in Milwaukee. Night off in Madison and we go out dancing. The DJ's abysmal, sparks the latest in a spate of tirades against prefab synthemusic. It's a semi-gay club, and I wind up dancing with a skinhead. Long way from the queerbashing crazy baldheads of the Lower East Side. After closing time we go out looking for a party, somebody tells us to follow them. When we pull over Run-DMC's "King of Rock" comes on the car radio and we're all into it, Louanne's pounding drums on the dashboard and we're all screaming along, "And I won't stop rockin' till I RETIRE!" We get so obsessed we lose the people we're supposed to be following.

Milwaukee's the next night, and I call Mitchell the booking agent to see how the West Coast dates are going. He's got us as far as L.A., and then he's got us four shows in three weeks to get us back, and he's not putting any more work into it. "I'm sick of dealing with all these fly-by-night punk promoters," he says. "This is not a level I want to work at, they're just not reliable, and I can't work with them any more."

"Well, how the fuck are we supposed to get back from L.A.?"

"I got you four shows on the way."

Fuck him, he's not getting his 10%. I send my share—$65—home to Nancy.

The dressing room's got the traditional showbiz rows of lightbulbs around the mirrors, but it's not a time for personal esthetics. Roach and Julia want to cancel the tour.

"We're not making any money," she says.

"And I'm sick of sleeping on people's floors. Why can't we stay in motels, at least a couple nights a week?" he says.

"Why don't we just cut our losses and go back out when it's practical?" she says.

"No way. Absolutely no fuckin' way," I say.

Brian seems neutral, which is surprising, considering that he calls his girlfriend every single night. Their phone bill must be more than he's making. François hasn't said anything.

"It's not a good investment," Julia says. "Not in terms of our time, not in terms of our career. Why don't we wait until after the next album, when we have something to promote?"

It's not a fucking investment, you stupid bitch, it's a fucking way of life. "I've been in this band for six fuckin' years trying to get to California," I say. "Either we do it now or we break up the band. After all the fuckin' canceled tours we've had, we'd be fuckin' totally insane to volunteer to do it."

"Yeah," François finally chimes in, "if we cancel the tour now, every club in the country's gonna think we're totally unreliable."

That settles it. Except Julia doubles over in pain at the end of soundcheck, and Louanne drives her to the emergency room. We won't see her again until San Francisco.

After this the gig is kind of anticlimactic. We do OK, but it's a hardcore crowd. A huge U opens up down front for the pit, and it's completely dead, vacant except for the usual pair of big guys with their arms folded. Nothing happens until three or four songs into the set, and then it's like 20 guys slamming away all night. A fuckin' narrow-minded cult, you could fart into the mike and they'd mosh if you did it fast enough.

160

We crash with two women and a metalthrash bassist somewhere on the east side. Naturally Roach is hitting on the women. We head out to the all-night supermarket to get broccoli, tomato sauce and Creamettes elbows for a 4 AM dinner. A band travels on its stomach. It's an eerie place, half-darkened and vast compared to the cramped bodegas of Loisaida, a cavernous cornucopia, towering banks of pasta, appliances, cans, cereals, and spatulas under cardboard overpasses, populated only by the night-packout and floorwax crew, puttering around in the dim light. One floorwaxer has an electronic dance duo, he's from New York and thinks I'm the road manager. At the entrance security guards hand out black crayons and tell everyone to mark prices on everything they buy. Later it's explained that the UPC computer's down.

Wake up the next afternoon to the bassist jamming with his drummer, load up the van and head to Oshkosh.

The hall there is a low-ceilinged lariat-decor roadhouse. It looks like Bob Wills should have played there. The PA is abysmal but the show's intense, one of the most emotional we've done. Finally two shows in a row and we're on and smoking, it's like a teenage punk-gospel rally, François has the audience's hearts in his palms, me and Brian play slow and pulsing like the undertow in the Jordan River, hypnotic for "Land's End," then we get militant for a grand finale of "Tropical War," "Rise Up," and "Create and Destroy." Triple encore of punk-classic covers, and we get decent money without an argument. Kelley the promoter's a 16-year-old with purple hair, we crash at her father's garden apartment. He's divorced, a foreman in a

161

refrigerator factory, wants us to talk her out of drop-ping out of school. Turns out Roach already did.

In Green Bay we play in a boxing club, the ring the stage. It's in a rundown older section between a '30s-vintage movie theatre and a couple porno shops. The clubowners are both black, one looks like a jheri-curled, grizzled bluesman, the other like a middle-weight Muhammad Ali. He's an aspiring rapper, poses for pictures with me and François. The show is note-perfect and complete chaos. Waves of bodies crash like human surf against the walls, the stage, the edge of the pit. We dodge them as they jump on stage, then swan-dive into the moil, then we rip loose. François is thrashing around on the floor, flinging his body into the crowd like a kamikaze. Someone shreds a bag of fiberglass, someone else holds up a lit lighter and a newspaper with Reagan's picture on it, François sets it, waves it around like a torch, then shreds it with his hands and throws the burning scraps out, me and Roach are bouncing off the ropes, leaping around.

Afterwards we're drained, drenched, say hi to Jason Sickness and Bill the promoter, who's mysteri-ously attired in a platinum-blonde wig. The 14-year-old who told me "You're old enough to be my father if you were sleazy in junior high" last winter is there, introduces me to her friend Corrina. She's small, ragged corona of sandy-brown hair, wearing a black thermal shirt and ripped jeans, she talks about going to demonstrations in Madison and at the nuclear-missile site in Iowa, she's a vegetarian. Why do I always attract vegetarians? Is it some subliminal cue? We end up making out, but I'm untimely ripped out of her embrace by the news that we have to leave for Omaha now.

162

"How old is she?" Roach leers as we lug his Marshall bottom out.

"Eighteen?" I say.

"Yeah, surrre. Her friend told me she was 15," he informs me with glee.

Get in the van and sleep through the rest of Wisconsin.

Omaha is where the Midwest shades into the West—the streets are wider and the buildings lower, the skies bigger, carrying intimations of the plains beyond, a lot of Indians among the winos at 24th and Leavenworth, between the thrift shops and the 11-Worth Cafe. Mothers and old people seem weatherbeaten and worn, but the club crowd is the usual hardcore-kid to adult-rocker spectrum, a bit older than we've been getting. Play a solid if not crazed set, crash on someone's floor and couch, and next morning head out on the prairie.

The country on US 275 is quietly beautiful, grasslands of green and purplish-brown, gentle hills with thickets of low cottonwoods by the creeks in the valleys. Last trees for 500 miles. Further on the land becomes drier, brown rows of dead corn marked with signs advertising seed brands, on into the sand dunes, giant hills.

Reach the Indian reservation in South Dakota just after sundown. It looks like a depressing place, like all there is to do is get fucked up on the cheapest booze there is, Mad Dog or Night Train or Midnight Dragon.

Night falls and there's more stars than I've ever seen in my life, the Milky Way dusts the heavens. The Mets win the World Series and we pull over to celebrate, we're running around by the side of the road screaming like banshees. Not a single car goes by for

20 minutes.

Burning up the white lines. America's endless conveyor belts, dual strips bulldozed through the landscapes, field and forest and city, the green signs above, all blurring at night, EXIT 25 UTOPIA PARKWAY EXIT 428 DEATH, rolling to the mechanical polyrhythms, points click, spark plugs explode, pistons push, gears grind, tires hiss on the road, capstans turn cassette, encoded metal blares reconstituted guitars, drums mesh with the engine. Engine whine cancels out the low end, the result is a dog's ear view of many of our favorite recordings.

Contort, curl, stretch, try to get comfortable, wall of black-tolexed gear behind us, guitar cases, drums, speaker cabinets, cheap trunks protect the amp heads, we can't afford anvil cases. Daytime there's prairie, forest, cornfield, suburb; nighttime, there's nothing but the signs and the lights, trucks blast by, dusty semis flash through the night. We're somewhere in South Dakota or Wyoming, Coeur d'Alene or Spokane, dazed under sudden onslaught of fluorescent lights, circadian rhythms lost in the nocturnal world of gas stations and truckstops—who pumps? Who pisses? Who's loitering in the souvenir shop, trying to see which of the $4.99 cassettes might be worthy box fare? Willie Nelson? Red Sovine's Truckers' Favorites?

All-night convenience stores, each with the same 98 items, cupcakes, pork rinds, beef sticks, beer, soda, the only ones with a recognizable link to something that actually grows are the waxed-to-death apples and small bags of salt peanuts. And bad coffee, stale, acidic and too hot. We drink it by the pint anyway. Sleep and drive, sleep and drive.

. Morning begins acrimoniously in a motel some-

164

where in central Washington. We're supposed to be in Vancouver tonight, then two shows in Seattle. But François has no ID to cross the Canadian border, the problem we've been dreading all tour. His birth certificate is supposedly in the mail to the Sabotage Records office in San Francisco. It gets worse. One of the Seattle shows is canceled—the club booker says Mitchell never confirmed it—and the promoter of the other one neglected to tell the people running the hall that we were coming.

The people who live in the hall say it's cool if we stash our gear there. It's an abandoned church inhabited by Johnny Thunders wannabes. They say they'll set up a houseparty Friday night. Someone lends us a birth certificate, and we head north, hoping François can pass for 19 and not get tripped up on biographical details. After all the trepidation the border is absurdly easy, the guard's a young Japanese dude who totally swallows our benefit-party story. "You're not getting paid for this, are you, eh?" "Of course not!"

By the time we get there the veins in my head are in a Vulcan Death Grip. Codeine is legal over the counter in Canada and the club is a block away from where my friend Lisa lives. She puts out a zine called *Electric Sheep*, I met her selling T-shirts at an Enemies show in New York last year. Three 222 pills and a half-hour with her and I feel great. The show is ragged but right, the bass amp I borrow is all fuzz and no bottom, but we've got our welcoming committee.

I go over to Lisa's to smoke a joint after the show. It's Welfare Wednesday, the day the monthly checks come in, and the city's awhirl, neon beer signs and porn-theatre marquees flashing, dozens of people strolling and stumbling on the sidewalks. Lisa says

165

Vancouver has the most feminist go-go dancers in North America, because it was the only gig a lot of punk-anarchist women could get. "It's getting fucked up here," she tells me. "We're getting evicted, they're doing the Expo here to bring in development. Now I understand what you were ranting about gentrification, eh? You know the Dils' song 'Class War'?"

"Yeah," I say. "The D.O.A. version." If I didn't know the *War on 45* EP, they'd have a legitimate reason to turn us back at the border, for shameful ignorance of Canadian culture.

"Well, I used to think that was just bullshit posing, boys playing at soldiers, but now I walk around singing it, these fucking bastards can come in and kick us out of our home just because they've got money. I see them drive by in their limos and I want to fucking smash them up."

"What are you gonna do?"

"I don't know. I think I'm going to move to Portland or San Francisco, if I can get into the States. Or I might go up to the mountains, work on my book. There's a lot of community up there, and there's a lot of pot-growing, you can get work trimming buds, it pays $25 an hour."

Hippie dreams, the back-to-the-land thing, it never dies. But I like the hippie-punk hybrids I've been running into, they've absorbed the idealism and longevity without the stupid sappy shit and the classic-rock stagnation.

She's working on a novel, it's environmental sci-fi, she's not sure if it's going to be apocalyptic or utopian. "Did you ever see a clear-cut?" she asks me. I say no, I'm a city boy. "It's like a rural slum," she says. "It's like your neighborhood with all the thrashed

166

buildings, but it's trees, eh? It's really sad."

I'm flipping through her albums, they're out in wire milkcrates on the floor, and dig out the Velvet Underground third album, the quiet one with "What Goes On" and "Pale Blue Eyes." "And you're telling me you're not homesick?" she gibes.

Later on we catch up with the band at a house-party in the East End, there's a 20-foot sculpture of empty beer cans on the lawn, most people are falling-down drunk and there's a strong undercurrent of junk in the dazed barstool occupants. Kevin the Enemies' roadie cooks us a mountainous egg-and-potato omelette.

The American border presents more problems than the Canadian. The guards tally up our collective appearance. Louanne's Stegosaurus Mohawk. François' well-decorated leather jacket and stringy brown hair colored orange, chartreuse, and black with shaved temples—and they haven't seen his tattoos yet. In a surfeit of teenage Satan-worshipping he got a pentagram and 666 on his right arm and a skull on his left. They've since been modified to more mature and ecumenical motifs, the pentagram decked with vines and tendrils, the 6s filled in with yin-yang symbols, and the skull has Keith Haring radiance. Me in a ripped-up leather and jeans, long black hair streaked strawberry-blond and fading blue; Brian with shoulder-length hair; and Roach in a "Rambone" T-shirt, a grease-painted guerrilla wearing nothing but a steel helmet and cartridge belts and wielding a 14"-caliber rod. Plus we've driven 2,300 miles in the last five days. "OK, we got five of these things here," they tell the boss, and put us in a bare yellow room with hard plastic chairs. They won't let us go to the bathroom—we could be flushing our drugs.

François still has no ID. We're trying to talk them into letting us in if he can recite the entire lineup of the '69 Mets. "Leading off, the center fielder, Tommie Agee; batting second, the second baseman, Ken Boswell; batting third, the left fielder, Cleon Jones...." Next he goes into the pitching rotation. "Tom Seaver, Jerry Koosman, Gary Gentry, Nolan Ryan, Don Cardwell." Ladies and gentlemen of the jury, I ask you: Would any young man who did not grow up in the United States of America know that *Don Cardwell* was the fifth starter for the 1969 New York Mets? Would any illegal alien know that *Bobby Pfeil* was the third-string third baseman?

This might have worked for some German-accent World War II straggler trying to convince the military police he really was from Milwaukee, but not for us. The guards are neither moved nor amused. "How can you cross a border without any ID?" they demand. It's the same question we've wanted him to answer all tour, but we won't say that. Finally they call his mother in the Bronx collect, and the computer doesn't turn up any warrants on us, so they let us in.

We couldn't get a show in Portland, so we've got a night off in Seattle before the party. There hasn't been a punk show in Portland for a year, skinheads started shit at every venue there. In the skinhead bestiary Lower East Side skins are homophobic, but not racist—it doesn't take much brains to figure that lone gay men walking up Avenue A make easier victims than Puerto Ricans who might have 20 cousins in the Avenue D projects. San Francisco skins are the psychos, the ones who'll bite your nose off if you look at them wrong. Portland's where they have the

Nazis, they just beat an Ethiopian to death at a bus stop.

We're in serious junk territory here, lots of conspiratorial mutterings. Carl the guy in charge of the house has a band called Cottonshot. He's got the junkie-glam image perfect, long stringy hair and a black suit jacket with narrow silver lapels, a whole coterie surrounding him. Me and Brian jam with him and John his bass player, I'm playing guitar. He's slightly haughty, but impressed that I know almost the entire Dolls/Heartbreakers repertoire. They've got the look and they've got the drugs, way easier than it comes to us, but they don't have the heart, the burn, the roots—it doesn't come out right, it still sounds like malls and MTV instead of some after-hours basement, all hype and no love, all cool and no desperation, no humor.

Carl's telling us he had a $400-a-day habit, supported it by dealing. Once somebody gets that deep into dope you write their obituary and fill in the date later. He's got the aura that someday he's going to be found naked and dead, his dick limp for the last six months and now forever, all the color drained from his slack flesh except the lividity, a bottlecap full of bloody cottons by his side.

None of us have ever made $400 in a week. We could make three albums for what this motherfucker spent on dope in one month.

Cottonshot opens for us the next night to about 75 people. By the time we go on there's about 30 left. At least fuckin' hippies and Deadheads time their drug abuse, they want to be peaking when the band's on instead of passed out in some unknown cranny. The cops shut us down halfway through the set, telling us they'll confiscate the equipment if we play one more note.

Louanne and Brian are already putting the drums back in the cases.

Two longhairs about 19 or 20 come over, they've both got that teenage-burnout flannel-shirt-and-ripped-jeans look. One of them's redwood-tall, he's like 6' 8". "That was awesome, man," he tells me. "You're a fuckin' great bass player." I mumble thanks, and he starts asking me about gear. His friend's this scrawny little dude, easily two heads shorter, fucked up out of his mind on Vicodin. They've got our album, they're starting a band, they came all the way from some tiny redneck town outside Olympia and got to see five songs.

"Fuckin' pigs, man," the Vicodin kid whines, his head rolling, if it wasn't connected to his neck it would drop and clunk like a lofted bowling ball. "Fuckin' pointless to live like this." He looks like he spends about 90% of his waking hours thinking about slitting his wrists, saved only by the belief that actually picking up the razor and making an incision would be even more pointless. His friend seems like his lifeline, his translator to the outside world.

But then he opens his mouth and says, "But you know, like, they can't stop us from wanting to do it—EVER." He gets a big green-eyed goofy infectious grin, half like he's embarrassed to have such a positive sentiment and half like it's the only thing keeping him alive.

Yeah they can, I think, but I'm not gonna tell him. He knows it well enough. They leave me with a five-song demo.

I'm glad the cops didn't search the room we're

sleeping in, because there's a garbage bag full of pot there. I use it for a pillow. They'd never notice if I nicked a nickel for the road, but I'm so pissed off I don't even think about it.

In Oregon we were supposed to have a hall show in Grants Pass, but Nick the promoter says Mitchell never confirmed it. He says he'll hook us up a party, so we go driving out on about eight miles of dark country road. Finally we come to a hippie barn dance. The adults are serious crunchy granola, the teenagers are all punks, moshing it up like puppies to the first band. We do one fast song, then I ease us down into a reggae groove, barefoot women in long skirts spinning and swirling on the dance floor, a goat wandering around. This is still too much for the host, who pulls the plug because we're not mellow enough.

We spend the next day at Nick's house, the five of us and two sisters, 15-year-old Star and 14-year-old Moon. Nick sets up a party in an abandoned farmhouse, running the gear off an extension cord from the house next door. We pass the hat and make $42 and feel appreciated. I cook spaghetti after the show while Star passes me joints of some very fresh and intense sinsemilla. There's about five of us stretched out in sleeping bags on the floor, I'm playing on headphones through a digital delay, revved-up and hypnotic, burbling triplet rhythms off the echoes, seeing lights, the extremes of the color spectrum shooting at me in instant synapses, little overtones of explosion reverb, the echoes falling away like bowling pins into space. Then a more definite shape takes form in the darkness, Moon's head bobbing over Roach's torso.

Sacramento is canceled, no surprise. Star and Moon ditch school to hang out with us the next day.

171

Roach calls his girlfriend in New York and swears eternal fidelity. François takes forever to get up and going, and it's dark by the time we get to the redwoods on 101, wending through the dank fir forests of the Siskiyous. We drive all night through the Humboldt. Roach and Louanne are sleeping, me and François and Brian are bonding over memories of one-hit wonders. Somewhere near Garberville we get pulled over.

"Where's the fuckin' pot?" the lead cop snarls.

"We don't have any," I say.

"You're a fuckin' liar. You expect me to believe that? We find anything, you assholes are gonna be away for a long fuckin' time, and your van is ours, you hear me, you fuckin' piece of shit?"

Oh yeah, the dim realization forms. We're on band time, everything revolves around getting to the next gig, and I haven't bought anything bigger than a dime in years, so I'm not thinking. We're a beat-up van with New York plates at 1 in the morning in the middle of harvest season. "Officer, you're wasting your time," François tries to be persuasive. "We don't do drugs—"

"Shut the fuck up. Did I tell you you could speak, asshole?"

There's six of them, some in camouflage fatigues with "CAMP Potbusters" baseball caps. They make us empty out the entire van, all the gear, all our bags. Louanne's groggy, irritated. "Do you fuck all of them?" one cop asks her. "Do you gang-bang her?" he asks me.

"No," I say meekly, like I'm back in 8th grade, cornered in the locker room by some jock asshole twice my size who's demanding to know if I'm a fuckin' faggot, if I like to suck cock. And the coach says boys will be boys, and queer commie-doper losers need to be shown their place. Why I can understand kids who bring weapons to school.

They leave all our stuff scattered by the side of the road. It takes us an hour to repack it by flashlight. "Holy shit," mutters Brian. "What kind of war do they have going on out here?" That's about it for dialogue.

If they want to outlaw a fuckin' plant, why don't they pick poison ivy?

We're pissed off, so we take it out literally when we come to a rest area. We piss all over the floor, and François scrawls "FUCK POLICE PIGS DIE" all over the walls, signing it BAD WORDS PUNK ROCK NYC with a garland of anarchy symbols. "Anarcho-urination!" he exults.

We get to San Francisco at eight in the morning, caught in rush hour with bloodshot, sandpapery eyes. We spend two days recuperating at our old roadie Truck's house in the Fillmore, then another at the *Revolution Pop!* house in the Mission, eating burritos the size of my biceps—$3 at Pancho Villa's on 16th off Valencia—and checking out Eric and Gina the publishers' cornucopia of punk 45s.

San Francisco is the biggest gig of the tour. We're opening for 900 Dead Assholes at Cerv/Eza, an abandoned brewery somewhere in the southeastern industrial flats. "Pissing people off since 1978" is their slogan. They had their first practice the day after the People's Temple version of the Electric Kool-Aid Acid Test. Their first album, a year and a half later, was called *White Nights in Satin*, the cover featuring lead singer Napalm McDonald standing next to a police car in a white bridal gown, one sultry leg up on the

173

hood like Marlene Dietrich at the piano, holding a Molotov cocktail in one hand like the Statue of Liberty and a Twinkie in the other. Napalm says his name represents "two American icons."

The hall holds 2,000 people, and we rise to the occasion. Four fast ones in a row to set it off, it's great to have Julia back, we've got an amazing wall of sound and there's bodies flying everywhere, a huge pit, kids leaping up on stage and plunging into it. Normally playing bass is more sexual for me, a low loin-pumping groove, but tonight my mood is violence, sonic attack, maple-necked revenge on every asshole who ever pulled a petty or not-so-petty power trip on us, like the tables are turned, motherfuckers! I got your heads lashed to the speakers and you're going to feel every fuckin' note LOUD. We simmer down for "Land's End" and Bob Marley's "Burning and Looting," then scorch through four more, closing with "Create and Destroy" and "Rise Up." We're totally out of our heads but every note's in place, people are so into it they're not even moshing any more, just staring at us awestruck.

We get two encores and Napalm is gushing, "I didn't know you were that good…I mean, I knew you were good, but I didn't know you were that unbelievable." Backstage is packed, people from other bands, girlfriends, Sabotage and RP, everybody's got some kind of affiliation, but it's more about celebrating than networking, everybody's pouring out congratulations. "My life is complete," says Rachel from the record company. My brother Aaron's never seen us before, he's impressed too. Brian's girlfriend, Anita, flies in, they've got a hotel room. Roach has six still-sort-of-cold beers secreted in Brian's trap case. We drink them

174

during 9DA's set, watching them from the side of the stage. Brian's back behind the drum monitors, entranced, he and Anita are all over each other.

A reporter from *San Francisco Sound* music weekly buttonholes Napalm after the show. "Why does your band have such an offensive name?" he asks.

Napalm is quick on the uptake, he's been asked this a million times before. "Because if people are stupid and blindly obedient enough to kill themselves on orders from some guru, then they're stupid and blindly obedient enough to kill anyone, to kill you or me. It could be in Jonestown, in the Manson Family, or the US Army, it's the same thing, it's the same mentality. We use the name to show our contempt for that kind of mentality. Idiots are dangerous. We want to shock people into consciousness, to make them think for themselves, not just do what they're told."

Reality sets back in the next morning, we have to figure out what to do about the rest of the tour. We've got gigs in Santa Cruz and L.A., and then we'll rely on Napalm and the Sabotage people to get us another show in San Francisco and Death Before Dishonor to get us some in the Midwest. We'll make it home with food and gas money.

We've already lost two good gigs in L.A. First we were supposed to open for Ian Slater and the Eternal Curse, an English Goth-blues band, at the Western Ballroom, but Ian got busted shopping on Avenue D after one date into the tour. Then we were supposed to open for '70s veterans the Lice, but they broke up again the day before their reunion tour. So we wind up playing a tiny hole in the wall in Fullerton, to an audience consisting entirely of members, relatives, and girlfriends of the opening band. The lead singer's got a room in Hollywood, so we sleep on his floor until sunrise, when we have to leave before his landlady finds out.

7:30 in the morning and we have to laugh. We're the archetypal showbiz failures, wandering the streets of Hollywood with no money and no place to go, still in our stage clothes from last night, ragged, black-clad creatures luxuriating rootlessly in the suburban sun.

So far L.A. reminds me of Queens with palm trees, wide boulevards where gas stations and 7-11s mix with office towers and porn shops. We wind up in front of a big guitar supermarket on Sunset Boulevard, it's 9:45, so we wait around till it opens at 10. I'm checking out all the gear we can't afford, buy picks and strings. It's early, it's dead. Julia's flirting with one of the sales guys, a poodlehaired lite-metal type. Me and François come over. The guy looks at François' "Impeach Reagan" button. He screws up his face in a simulacrum of deep thought and goes, "Like... Dude... What's Reagan got to do with peaches?"

I guess there is some truth to the stereotype. Nancy's theory is that excessive exposure to sunlight impairs higher intellectual functions. It sounds crackpot, but she did live here for three years.

"I used to get stopped by the cops all the time," she tells me when I call. "They thought I was a prostitute. They'd always say, 'What are you doing WALK-ING?'"

I finally talk everyone into going to the beach, so we're off to Venice. It's the first time in 30 years of life I've gone swimming in the Pacific. The synagogues and boardwalk remind me of Brighton Beach, except that there are lower buildings and fewer old people. Conga drummers play under the palm trees, hippie

176

borderline-wino types, and the mountains to the north are solarized by the smog.

I fantasize about living here as a home-studio owl, spending days on the beach and recording sound-tracks for obscure, surreal, and trashy movies at night. We watch the sunset and I get accosted by a brown-haired, thirtyish woman who informs me she's just escaped from a mental hospital. "People in California are... sexy," she says, touching the inside of my wrist. "But New Yorkers are... REAL."

It might be the most intelligent conversation I have here.

Not counting Nancy's old roommate Consuelo, who's back in town and says we can stay for two nights. We head over to Silverlake and overrun her shower. She says there's a party at the Soundboard Lounge on Sunset Boulevard with some bands she knows, we can probably do a short set.

So we schlep the instruments down there, Brian's reluctant, he wants to chill in front of Consuelo's VCR. He's sitting in the van drawing while François and Julia and Roach socialize. I can't connect with anyone. "Got any blow?" one asks. "Do you want to buy some coke?" On a $10 per diem? Are you fuckin' kidding? I can barely afford this one beer I'm nursing. "Got any krell?" Depression descends like a slow black mud-slide, lava-like in its inexorable weight. Then this big, chunky semi-surfer type in a tank top and baggy white shorts gloms on to me, starts pitching his record pool. "Only a thousand bucks and 400 albums, and we get your records delivered to all the top alternative radio stations in the country." He's wired up and I'm stuck in this corner, a captive audience. "We've worked with the Red Rags, Less, Brian Steele, Circuit C, Sexx,"

177

he goes on. I've only heard of two of these bands, and they have nothing in common with us besides being human. Red Rags are well-scrubbed red-leather-and-bandannas new wave, starting to catch heat for their name, its supposed "gang associations." The world of the Bloods and Crips is almost as far from theirs as the Andromeda galaxy. Sexx is sex-and-drugs-and-image hard rock, in the Motley Crue vein. They probably get laid more, do more drugs, and use more hair dye than five bands like us, but they suck. Their music's about as sexy as silicone tits. Like the serpent offering Eve a plastic apple.

"How do you know these stations will actually play us?" I finally ask.

"Well, you've got to take risks to achieve success, you've got to pay to play in the major leagues. The American Dream is out there if you go for it, it's all good," he perorates, blond hair flopping over one eye. "Buy some blow?"

After two hours of hovering we get on stage, only to find the bass amp being rolled off. "Who told all these bands they could play?" the clubowner is shrieking.

I miss Nancy and Coleman.

Everyone sleeps forever the next morning except for me and Louanne, so we drive around, miles of boulevards lined with low, dusty, yellowish buildings, older rundown neighborhoods greeting Asian and Latin immigrants, KIM'S ENVIOS PUPUSAS PHO PATAPONG FLATS FIXED OAXACA TAQUERIA, iceplants by the roadsides, brown, barren hills with tan-tufted prairie grass, orange and lemon groves, palm trees and gnarled, stunted evergreens, twisted Y-shaped bushes. Louanne wants to

178

see cholos, so we drive through the downtown—its proportion to the metropolis size is like that of a Stegosaurus' brain, if a regular city's is like a mammal's—and over the Sixth Street Bridge onto Whittier Boulevard in East L.A. The smog is dense and a smoky brown. The *L.A. Times* rates today's air quality "satisfactory." I'd hate to see a Stage II pollution alert.

We load up the van and head north on I-5, up through the desert, back to San Francisco.

Rachel from Sabotage gets us a gig at an old punk club in the porn district. We're opening for Divine Love, Billy Devine's new band, they're mutating from political punk to bluesy, psychedelic roar. He's a fat Louisiana queen who sounds like Janis Joplin, he's one of the few punk vocalists who can actually sing, they're amazing. It's a good bill. We're sloppy but inspired, almost as good as last week.

We leave for Chicago at sunset. It takes us four hours to get past the suburbs, so it's midnight by the time we reach Reno. I drive all night, stopping every hour or so for coffee while François pisses change into the slot machines. Barreling east at 90 mph in the wee hours, the only thing on the road for miles and miles. I'm charcoal by the time we reach the Utah line.

In Salt Lake City the used bookstore keeps *Playboy* and *National Lampoon* in the back room with the porn. Brian's getting skittish, we have to go to three coffeeshops before we find one sufficiently redneck-free.

Utah, Wyoming, Nebraska, Iowa roll by in a slow blur, sleep and drive, sleep and drive, huddle under sleeping bags in the back of the van to keep warm. We hit the wintry grid of the Chicago suburbs and the lights on the snow beckon us, we're only 800 miles from home.

We play a party to an all-male cast at Death Before Dishonor's house in the western suburbs, then head for Columbus. I've got a migraine, I'm eating codeine all day and night, listening to Coltrane on Julia's Walkman.

Columbus is an armed camp, riot cops lined up on both sides of the street to control the drunken hordes of disappointed Ohio State fans. I go out for Chinese food with Julia and jocks hassle her about her "loser boyfriend." We're playing in what was once a black club, they play Clarence Carter's "Strokin'" on the PA, asking everyone "When was the last time you made love?" We're getting wistful. My perception's all warped like melted candlewax, but we rip. My amp blows on the last song. I borrow DBD's for the encore. We stay at a house full of jockish, preppy girls. Roach gets lucky.

"Safe sex," he brags the next morning, "is anything more than 200 miles from New York."

Our last show is in Kent, populated by hippie-punk hybrids. The waitresses at the diner across the street have shaved temples and long flowing skirts, they come to the show. I borrow an amp from a kid in the first band, give him a signed album in exchange. We go out on a grand note.

François buys a truckers' compilation tape in Pennsylvania and finally prevails on us to put it on in New Jersey, Red Sovine's maudlin ghost-of-Highway-309 stories and Dave Dudley's "Six Days on the Road." Past Paterson I-80 swings north, then we swoop into Fort Lee. Our hometown's coming in sight.

We have the van for one more week, so I take

Nancy out to the New Jersey corporate swamps to see Hard Roxy at the Byrne Arena.

She knows their lead singer Eric White—nee Weissenthal—a bit; hung out with him once in 1979 at an after-hours club called the Box. One of her girl-friends was having a short fling with him. Able to afford all the drugs he could take, Eric was thoroughly raddled yet considered a prime catch on the glam-girl scene. He and guitarist Billy Manzano are a toxic-twins duo in the tradition of Jagger and Richards, Tyler and Perry, Johansen and Thunders. Born in Providence, raised in the bars of a hundred mill towns and suburbs, and hitting full-blown decadence in places like this, giant concrete ovals in the suburban jumble.

This is their first tour since coming out of rehab, and they sound like they're awake again. But like most shows this size, it's more spectacle than rock'n'roll. The lasers get more applause than the band.

After the show I walk down to the side of the stage, concentrate, and muse.

My band is good enough to play this stage.

If we work hard, hit it right, and get inspired, we could get up here and do it. No lasers, no props, just energy and music.

I believe this.

That doesn't mean it's gonna happen.

181

CRASH

This has not been a good year for me.

We finally get to make another album, but everything's a mess. Brian announces he's quitting to get married right before we go in the studio. Nobody can understand that he might actually be in love, and that it might feel more permanent than this argument-ridden shoestring of a band, cult following or no cult following. *He's walking out on us.* I call him a motherfucking rat. "Deserting a sinking ship," he snaps back. He does his tracks and leaves.

The producer we have is Dimitri Rieder, who supposedly produced the Who in the '60s but didn't get credit for it, did a whole bunch of other English bands too. One rock critic calls him a "living legend." "Arrogant asshole" fits him far better, except that "asshole" is nowhere near a potent enough word to signify his true vileness. Our lexicon of invective is pathetically limited when the strongest epithets are body parts we all touch daily and sex acts we do as

183

often as we can—well, with one obvious exception. "I had records in the English Top Ten before you had hair on your prick" is his attitude.

I'm too paralyzed or desperate or stupid to follow my instincts. He ends up running the album way over budget with all sorts of stupid overdubs—it's coming out of our royalties—butchers the mix so you can't hear the guts of the band or the hook of the song on a single track, and gets away with all this by playing every schism in the band for all it's worth. He picks Julia as Protege and me as Scapegoat.

The aftermath is that Julia decides she's the new musical director of the band. She's constantly telling me my playing sucks, I should take lessons. This is hard to take from anyone, especially her. I played CBGB's in three different bands before she learned how to play an E chord. She's got a gig doing freelance PR for Mobil, writing ad copy about what great environmentalists they are. I call her a sellout, writing fucking propaganda. "I'm just using the skills I have to make a living," she says.

Actually Julia is not much for confrontation; going behind people's backs is far more efficient. I don't know what she's feeding François, but he's pissed off at me over a lot of things I never said. I'm not getting along with him anyway either. We haven't written any new songs in months. Every lyric he brings in is heavily political, with at least eight verses and no chorus, except for an anti-crack song that actually includes a "Just Say No" chorus.

"That sucks," I say. Real diplomatic.

"It's supposed to be ironic," he says.

"We don't even know anyone who does crack," I say back. Yeah, coke, dope, alcohol, we all know

184

casualties, but crack's about the only drug rock'n'roll people don't do. Meanwhile, I bring in an album's worth of riffs and song ideas and he finds about two he remotely likes. "Simpleminded shit, been there, done that."

And now we have to find a new drummer. Plus Napalm McDonald, the guy who runs the label, gets busted. 900 Dead Assholes are doing a show in Phoenix and some rent-a-cops there are beating the shit out of kids trying to stage-dive, so he says "Hey, leave those fuckin' kids alone." They bust him for obscenity, impairing the morals of minors, and inciting to riot, and drag in the band and the road crew too, all the way down to the girl at the T-shirt stand. Eight people. They've got a fucking maniac prosecutor down there. I think he was about to get indicted on some land deal, so he's trying to be Crusader Against Corruption of Our Youth. They've got this organization PUCK down there too, Phoenix United in Concern for Kids, that's had a hard-on for Napalm since the '85 tour. They were trying to get a law passed barring kids under 18 from coming to rock'n'roll shows without a parent, except for really safe major-label shit, and they were picketing 9DA's show. Napalm comes out wearing a suit and tie, the roadies unfurl a PHoenix United in Concern for Kids banner, and he starts preaching:

"We must erect a stiff barrier against the filth and pornography that is defiling our society and endangering our youth.

We must take the staff of righteousness firmly in hand and arouse ourselves to moral indignation.

And we must keep our fervor up until the fruit of our efforts spurts forth like a mighty stream."

The group later changes its name to *Parents* United

185

in Concern for Kids.

We find a drummer pretty fast, a Czech dude named Vaclav Pilicek. He's been in America for three years. The first time we played with him was the day Daylight Saving Time went into effect and he was an hour late. "I am very sorry," he tells us. "Government moved time and I do not know about it." He's got an amazing sense of time, can play all these odd Zappaesque meters like 5/6/7, even if sometimes he plays like he's counting "one-and-two-and-three-and" in his head. In Czechoslovakia, he says, bands have to get their lyrics checked out by a state censor before they can get into a rehearsal studio. High price to pay for free medical care. Here you can pay $10 an hour to scream "I want to fuck Ronald Reagan up the ass with a Molotov cocktail" over 45 minutes of howling feedback and the only person who'd care is the studio owner who's scared the feedback's going to blow his amps. Unless you're big enough to be a threat—which is why Napalm McDonald is facing a year in jail for saying "fuck" onstage in Phoenix.

I've got problems at home too. Nancy's pissed at me for being utterly useless as a breadwinner six months out of the year. Plus she's never been in a band, she was mainly into the scene just to hang out, and that wears pretty thin once you hit 30. I get to have the ecstasy of playing and I don't give a fuck if there's plaster falling off the walls, which there is plenty of in our apartment. My girlfriend crying in the shower stall is something I hadn't planned on. I actually got a decent temp job this year, three midnight shifts a week at $15 an hour, but things are too far gone for that to mean much. We never walked down the aisle to Suicide's "Cheree"—*oh I love you, my black leather*

186

lady—and the way we're getting along that day is receding farther and farther into the nonexistent future.

Oh yeah, there's now a crackhouse in the building. The rent-controlled and rent-stabilized tenants haven't moved out fast enough for the landlord's liking, so Apartment 3C has been rented out under the table. Well, at least I don't have boils. And there aren't giant frogs jumping around our kitchen peeing on the floor. Although it is inhabited by a large number of creatures approximately the same size and shape as locusts. "Don't pick that up," I tell Coleman when we find a used needle in the hall. "You could get AIDS."

I see the landlord—"real-estate mogul Leonard Kaplan"—on the news with the Mayor and Nancy Reagan one night. "Daddy, why are you yelling bad words at the TV?" Coleman wants to know. We go on rent strike again.

We're supposed to do another big tour in September, but Julia never told us that Vaclav would lose his job and thus his green card if he takes two months off from work. So we have to teach yet another drummer a set and a half worth of the old warhorses in order to do the tour. We borrow this guy Tim O'Hara from the Worthless. Nice guy with a weird style of playing, like only his arms move, his torso stays absolutely still.

I'm out drinking five nights in a row before we leave. The last gig we have is the fourth of them, in a tiny basement on 5th and A. It's only 15 feet to the bar and I have an 18-foot guitar cord. Large quantities of cheap tequila make things much more palatable. Julia, François and Roach all get pissed at me for set-list deviationism when I try to start a two-chord jam, A minor and F. We have an album to promote, we have to play the songs people know. I just want to play something fucking different for a change.

Nancy leaves me a note before we leave. *Whatever you do on the road, just use a condom.* First stop is Buffalo. We make the gig half an hour before we go on. Two sets, we rock, the promoter gives us a case of Labatt's and me and Roach dive in.

Next morning I'm wandering around with a blinding migraine, looking for a coffeeshop. We're playing Toronto tonight, a $500 gig. More important is I want the fucking pain to stop. Out of pills, I throw up on the sidewalk on Elmwood Avenue. I'm buying aspirin-and-codeines the minute we get over the border.

We get turned back at the border, fucking working papers not in order, the promoter never bothered to get them set up. I hate borders. WHY THE FUCK SHOULD WE HAVE TO GO THROUGH ALL THIS CORDON OF SHIT JUST TO CROSS A FUCKING IMAGINARY LINE ON THE MAP?

This day deserves to be consigned to oblivion. But I don't drink.

Crashing at an outpost of intellectual bohemia, two girls from Gilead College in grad school at Buffalo. As usual Roach is the first one up, me second. Some territory is virgin and logistics are too subject to the cruel vagaries for touring to be predictable, but some perennials are re-emerging: the first cup of pancreas-rotting truckstop coffee, scamming house parties when gigs fall through, François not believing in suitcases or getting up while it's still light out, and the van eating up the white lines like some amp-laden Pac-Man juggernaut. Western New York is beautiful and dreary like some 1810 landscape painting, the Niagara River roiling black beneath endless serene waves of pine green and gray.

Another day in town, a house party. It's oddly disconnected—we're playing in the kitchen and the pit is in the living room. Julia comes up to me after the set. "You totally fucked up the bridge on "Rise Up," and you're playing too loud," she says. She walks away before I can say anything back. The best part is we throw together a fuck band afterwards, playing extremely noisy punk-funk-jazz with me on guitar, Roach on drums, Joseph the roadie on bass, and a horn section of Tim on alto sax and François on this trumpet he got for 50 bucks. We call it Flatulence.

Afterwards I get invited to party with some thirt-yish geriatric punks, two couples, smoke pot, listen to old Dead Boys albums, watch videos while the couples kiss and moan. I haven't had a drink in two days.

Collective paroxysm of relief as the Canadian border guards buy our story and we cross over unscathed.

Somehow El Gran Combo seems out of place on the box amidst the goldenrod and cornfields of Ontario. But what the fuck, it's a bit of Loisaida, going to the bodega on 11th and B for milk and juice for the *niño* and *cerveza para mamí y papí*.

London show is small, but Canadian punks and metalheads love it, and the opening band is great. Band factions coalesce—me, Roach and Tim sleeping in the house, François, Julia, and Joseph in the van. Next morning I visit a drugstore and buy 500 aspirin-and-codeines, enough painkillers for the next six months. They're called 222s in Vancouver, they're 318s here. Cross the border at Port Huron and eat bad Mexican food, crash in Flint.

Ann Arbor show is kind of lackluster, we played well enough but the crowd doesn't get into it until the end. Kelley from Oshkosh shows up and I go back to East Lansing with her, we crash at the house we're playing tomorrow and talk about suicidal ideation and other cheerful subjects. Everyone else stays in Flint.

East Lansing houseparty is your basic college-town alcoholic pothead bohemian blowout—they're getting evicted, they don't care about the place getting trashed. Whole bunch of people I know here from the last couple tours, Laurie the hippie goat farmer, Ted Gein. Things get organized and I start drinking. No sign of the band so I get nervous, try to pull together a fuck band out of Seth from Jesus Christ Cocksucker and this dude from the Oral Majority with a beard and long robe who looks like a cross between Christ and Iggy. "What covers do you know? What covers do you know?"

They show up about 15 minutes before time. Set is great but François is snotty and pissed at me and Roach for being drunk and bumming beer from the audience after we drank the last one on stage. It interrupts his preaching, "This song is about people in South Africa who are being oppressed right now, while you people in America are just apathetic, you're drinking your Budweiser." OK, OK, you're on the right side but I don't want to hear a fucking moral lecture before every song. And *we're* drinking Haffen-reffer Private Stock, 90 cents a quart at finer conven-ience stores throughout the upper Midwest. I'm also only speaking to Julia when absolutely necessary, which is usually too much. Flatulence plays after-wards, but I can't get into playing with Joseph's jazz-fusion licks. My mood is slop. I come back when Roach and some locals inaugurate a metallic trashfest of covers—"Louie Louie" into "Wango Tango" and so on. The purplehaired woman I've been flirting with disappears. Everyone goes home. I sleep alone.

Hang out in East Lansing another day—it's getting to be like a small town, there's quite a few people saying hello to me on the street, including the purplehaired woman, we hang out a bit that night but she has to disappear, the vibe feels like unspecified drug business. Everyone smokes pot here, this feels heavier, more secretive.

In Flint at Lisa and Mona's house Tim cooks up a massive garlic, oil, and vegetables spaghetti dinner. We play in a large barn, Jesus Christ Cocksucker opening. They're falling apart, their bass player and drummer quit, they play just Seth and Joe, guitar and vocals. Joe doesn't sing much, he talks about his wife walking out on him after he came home from a gig with $12. We're functional, go over well enough, but I'm really fucking bored with playing the same set again.

Detroit falls through because both the Pope and the Aggro Boys from London are in town. Lisa and Mona set up a house party to compensate. Clean out the basement, hang black crepe and blue lights, and we rock. Basement gigs give us much more freedom to stretch out. "Burning Sand" turns into a long psychedelic-punk trance, "Walk This Way" creeps in twice and "Rapper's Delight" once, and somehow we open "Tropical War" with an instrumental version of Johnny Thunders' "Sad Vacation." Mona waves a candle. It makes me feel like we're U2, all these kids sitting on the floor, swaying side to side. It's amazing

191

we can play so well when we hate each other so much. There's only room for two people up by the mikes, so Julia sets up her effects boxes there instead of back by her amp. She gets really pissed whenever me or Roach goes up front, so she starts blocking us out. Once we catch on we start doing it back.

Steve the rad union man from Mindless Violence is there—his kid's now 16 months, GM shut down the Flint plant, he's got enough seniority to keep his job, but they transferred him to Pontiac. "It sucks man, I got an hour commute each way, I got no time to play anymore." I start talking to this gorgeous gray-eyed woman, she used to be a model, wants to be a writer, I met her last time we were through here.

"I finally caught you in a good mood," she laughs.

It doesn't last for long. Lisa interviews us for Black Vinyl, the L.A. zine, in the living room. "Who writes your music?" she asks. "Like how is a song born? Like where did 'Rise Up' come from?"

This is the first time in five years someone has asked us a specific question about the music, not about scene politics or "What are your influences?" "I wrote it on guitar," I say. "I was unemployed one morning, I went down to the studio, and it just came out. It's kind of like 'Holiday in Cambodia' back-wards, but it goes up instead of down, so it sounds kind of like an uprising."

This line is unlikely to ever see print. François is squatting in front of the tape recorder singing the chorus. "WE WON'T BELIEVE THEIR LIES! WE DON'T WANT TO DIE!" He takes over. "We're about bringing the message to the people that you should believe in yourself, we're telling people to fight op-pression, not be into sex and drugs."

192

"Yeah, but I like sex and drugs," I say. "You can make a political point in a song, but you gotta get people off too, they need pleasure."

"What if their pleasure's beating people up?" he demands. "People in clubs, they're not thinking, they're just getting drunk and trying to pick each other up. We're missionaries, we're troubadours, we're traveling the countryside spreading the word, every gig is like a political rally, where we show our solidarity with the oppressed peoples of the world."

"But you know, there's a lot the left and punk should learn from Wall Street," Julia pipes in. "There's nothing revolutionary about being inefficient. We've got a new musical direction, people shouldn't cringe when they hear the words marketing plan. You have to be organized, you have to make the tough decisions. If someone's not making the grade, you can't be sentimental, you have to let them go."

"No, music is different, you can't just fire the drummer the minute they screw up a few times. Band chemistry takes a long time to build up, and we're supposed to be more human than them."

She shoots me a nasty look. François goes off on another monologue, and I go back downstairs to get drunk with Roach, which is what I should have been doing all along. Trying to save the world from bullshit doesn't pay.

Next morning I hear Julia in the spare bedroom teaching Joseph the basslines to "Rise Up" and "Desert Sand."

We drop the girl Roach picked up at her father's house in the North Flint ghetto, full of churches, rib joints, pawnshops, and burned-out record stores, and get on I-75 south. Michigan is Autoworld—Buick City

193

and the old Fisher Body plants, muscular overpasses in immaculately designed freeways, wide, swooping exit ramps with plenty of room for trucks.

Southbound through Ohio. Ride in silence. We've been this way before.

Julia wants to get brown rice. Where the fuck are we going to find brown rice at 7 o'clock on a Sunday night in rural Ohio? She's insistent. We pull off, a closed shopping mall. Try again at the next exit. The van blows a tire.

Me and Joseph walk a half mile to the nearest gas station, I call the club, tell them we're going to be late. We roll the tire the half mile back and change it.

It's almost 11 when we get to the club in Cincinnati and there's about 20 dispirited kids hanging out. The promoter says there were about 100, but most went home. He says we can go on anyway, and he'll give us 25 bucks plus passing the hat for gas money. Nobody wants to bother.

"It's your fault," Julia lights into me in the parking lot. "Why didn't you tell them we were going to be late?"

"I just fuckin' did," I hiss back, but she's walking away. *I hate this, I don't give a fuck if the band breaks up. Cancel the fucking tour, I just want to go home.*

At least we have a place to crash, with two girls named Jane and Marian. None of us have had dinner yet, so Jane borrows Marian's car to take us out. I slip into depressive reverie as she pulls out of the driveway. *This fucking sucks, what the fuck am I doing here out on the road with these assholes, why bother being fucking alive?*

The car smashes into a dumpster. A fucking Niagara of red red krovvy pours out of my nose. I'm lying on the asphalt with some girl holding my hand going "Can you see me? Can you see me?"

I don't remember how we get to the emergency room. They palpate my nose—it fucking hurts—tie an icepack on it, ask me the mental-orientation questions. "Do you know where you are?" "Count backwards from 100 by sevens." "Who's the president of the United States?"

"Reagan, that fucking asshole," I buzz through gouts of bloody snot.

Tour is over. I have a broken nose and a probable concussion; Roach has a torn muscle in his neck; and Tim has a broken wrist. Jane, who we thought had only had one beer, had one beer and five Valiums. She's OK. I'm not permanently disfigured, but I'm going to have a hard time breathing for a while. We recuperate for a day and then limp back to New York.

Six weeks later we're recovered enough to book 10 shows in the Northwest, San Francisco to Vancouver and back. Vaclav's got two weeks vacation, the record company advances us half the plane fare out. All we've got to bring is guitars, snare and cymbals. François and Julia have someone supposedly doing publicity for the tour who's lined up a van for us.

First gig is in Berkeley, a *Revolution Pop!* show. No one meets us at the airport, and no one can reach the van people. We end up paying 60 bucks to take a cab over to Berkeley.

We get paid $300. We're supposed to be crashing at the RP house, with a major argument on tap over why Eric and Gina gave our fabulous new album a bad review. Lisa from Vancouver is living down here now, and she and her boyfriend each grab one of my wrists. "You have a choice," Lisa says. "You can go back to the RP house and argue about scene politics with them, or you can come back to our house and have a drink with us."

I don't need much persuasion. They've got good pot too. Two beers later I'm sinking deep into the bathymetric levels of their couch, swimming with the mutant fishes in the lightless pressurized depths.

Next night we're opening for the Enemies yet once again, in the Alhambra, a big lush old derelict ballroom deep in the Mission District, near 24th and Potrero. It's a big crowd, around 700. François and Julia are outraged that we're third on a five-band bill instead of second. Such a lowly slot is inappropriate for an act of our stature. I don't give a fuck. I'm bone-and-soul fuckin' weary of all this petty-assed ego bullshit. Just get me on the stage and get me the fuck off. Well, I'm dressed up for the gig at least. I scored a silver velvet vest and a pair of silver-sparkle platform boots in a thrift shop on Valencia for $5. Halloween in San Francisco, am I supposed to go onstage in a fuckin' nondescript T-shirt and jeans like I'm going to the fucking laundromat? François and Julia seem to think so. Ain't no dot of luminescence supposed to outshine theirs, maybe they're conceiving giant bushel baskets to be lowered from the stage on wires like some backwoods version of a '70s Earth Wind & Fire arena show, only this time its purpose is not to make the band members look like starchild emissaries but to cover up the inferior ones.

They lose the argument with the promoter, so we go on third. I borrow Ron from the Enemies' bass amp, I don't think he's too happy about being asked three minutes before we're supposed to go on, like if he says no, he looks like a prick and holds up the show. I agree to write down his settings, plug in, get a sound. I'm ready. The crowd's hanging back from the stage, like they usually do when a pit's about to happen and they don't want to get hit. I hear a voice in my head. *Come in closer, this is the last time you're ever gonna see the Bad Words.*

Yeah, we play all right. I'm bored out of my fucking brain but we're competent. There's one girl up front, chubby with a flat pale face and bangs, around 18, in a homemade Bad Words T-shirt, a low-cut white thing hand-lettered in black marker, no bra, dancing and bouncing all through the set. The way she's looking at François I know she'd fuck him in two minutes and the way she's overweight I know his contempt could wither the Amazon rainforest. I'm out in the crowd after the set and she comes up to me and says, "That was great. You guys have so much spirit. I like your new album."

I'm sorry. Poor girl just uncorked a volcano of vitriol. "Yeah, we *were* a great band. That fucking album sucks, I hate that overproduced piece of shit." On and on till the break of dawn, I really shouldn't be subjecting this poor girl to this, she genuinely likes the band and I know that no matter how bad you think you suck people can still catch the essence of what you're doing and get off on it/be moved by it/whatever, but it's like she pressed the red button and now the rant runneth over.

"Wow," she says. "You sound like you're going to quit."

The thought hadn't crossed my mind yet.

After-show party somewhere way up by Haight Street. François and Julia grab a ride, leaving me,

Vaclav and Roach with the guitars, Vaclav's drum stuff, and François' bag of extra stage clothes. We leave the bag behind and crash on the floor of the RP house.

Two days off before Tuesday in Grants Pass, Oregon. Next morning I go over to my brother Aaron's for brunch, then over to North Oakland to crash at Vera's. Vera's boyfriend Jimmy is a blues piano player, a Texas psychedelic refugee, semi-name sideman with a lot of the '60s hippie bands, I was listening to his albums when I was 15 and 16. "Bring your bass," he says, "I got a gig tonight, I can get you to sit in."

I've got a mild hangover that's fast turning into an intense migraine, take three 318s before I get on the bus. Aaron and Ann live off Golden Gate Park, where the Haight hippie theme park starts shading into Richmond. They make me coffee and play with Pablo, the baby. I'm squirming and twitching and shuddering all through it, like a dead frog on a power line. Ann asks me what's going on, why are you so tense. She's for real, it's not one of those typical California-bullshit "You New Yorkers are so way tense" kind of things. A lot going on with the band, I tell her. I lie down for half an hour and Aaron gives me a ride to the Van Ness BART.

Vera and Jimmy live in a sea of tan 1940s tract houses. Jimmy's gig is at a club called the Crossroads, a few blocks away under about 14 giant strands of freeway and BART spaghetti. He's backing up a singer named Alesha Smalls. The club draws from both sides of the tracks, blacks from Oakland and whites from Berkeley. Not a "y'all not supposed to be here" ghetto dive; not full of yuppie fucks yelling "Yeah" in all the wrong places.

198

Jimmy walks in, says hi to everybody. "This is my friend Sid. He's a bass player from New York."

"You, my friend the New York bass player, are in the right place at the right time," says Earl the guitar player, a big bushy-sideburned cat, tobacco-sunburst hollowbody over a blue suit jacket and yellow ruffled shirt. Turns to Jimmy. "Miles appears to have vanished into the ozone layer." Miles being their bass player.

So I get a quick introduction to the rest of the band. Eli the drummer, a little skinny wisp with a mustache and an ice bucket, whiskey and soda set up on his floor tom; Ray, on harp, suntanned white dude who looks like a car mechanic on a night out in 1974, harp-case belts crisscrossing a brown and orange shirt like the cartridge belts models wear on war-chic photo shoots; and Alesha, in a sleeveless purple dress and matching shoes and red lipstick, an outfit that wouldn't be out of place in church if she covered up her shoulders. Jimmy's got white hair and a beard and looks a bit like a college professor with a drinking problem, like he could give a 45-minute lecture on the chemistry of hangovers with lots of been-there flavor. He's sober now. Vera's pregnant.

Alesha calls off the first song. Blues bar-band conventions. "Farther On Up the Road. Fast shuffle. In C. Start on the five." And we're off. Earl turns me down after the first song, shaking his head, but otherwise it's going amazingly well, considering I've never seen these people before and I'm heavily pillified. Z.Z. Hill's "Down Home Blues." In G. Keep it simple, stick to the roots, the eternal verities of the 1-4-5, two-note heartbeats, listen close to everybody else. Ann Peebles' "Breakin' Up Somebody's Home." A bit more

199

complicated. "In C, but it doesn't go to the five," says Jimmy. "And the chorus is F-E flat-F."

"There's a stop that goes to F and B flat. Watch me," says Earl, and he turns to show me the guitar neck when the changes are coming up. Musicians actually helping me out, watching my back. What a fucking novel concept.

Earl comes over after the end of the set. "Hey, thanks for coming down. You a lifesaver." To Jimmy: "Did you know Miles wasn't going to show up when you brought him down?"

Jimmy tells me, "Hey man, you should move out here, you could get some work."

"I can't. I got a kid in New York."

Earl says, "Well, bring your little rug rat out here then."

"I don't think his mother would be too into that."

I don't say how much this means to me. Fucking musicians actually giving me compliments, appreciating that I showed up, instead of the nonstop shit I've been getting from François and Julia. It's fuckin' unbelievable. And Jimmy's played with John Lee Hooker, Jack Casady, and some girl singer who got voted Ugliest Man On Campus by the fratboys at the University of Texas—he's got tapes with her from some folk club in Austin back in '65.

They're offering me free drinks, but mixing liquor and codeine is not a good idea unless I want to end up choking on my own vomit.

Settle in for the second set. Alesha does "I'm a Man" as "I'm a Woman"—"When I make love to you, I take my time." B.B. King's "The Thrill Is Gone." B minor, slow groove thing, pulse the bass soft but insistent, like making out when it's just starting to turn into sex.

> *The thrill is gone, the thrill is gone away from me*
> *The thrill is gone, baby, the thrill is gone away*
>   *from me*
> *Although I'll still live on, but so lonely I'll be*

Earl's lead is simple, short flurries of jabs setting up one-note cries. When he slides up to the E for the four chord it takes the top of my head off, one long bent scream, and all the pain and angst of the last eight months starts pouring out. Jimmy's piano solo is as final as death.

Third set a bunch of people come up to sit in, a sax player—I lend my bass to Earl and they do a Grover Washington-style "Inner City Blues"—a hippie blues-mama type with brown fluffy hair and a flowered dress for Jimmy Reed's "Baby What You Want Me to Do."

I click with her immediately. We hang out after the set. Her name's Vicki Martinez. "You've got a migraine? C'mon, try this," she grins. We go out to the back of the club, on a thin strip of asphalt between two dumpsters and a chain-link fence. She digs a lighter out of her denim jacket and we do what American musicians have done since time immemorial, or at least the 1920s.

"Yeah, this'll knock out your migraine," she laughs. "I use it for menstrual cramps. Just like my namesake."

"Whaddaya mean?"

"Queen Victoria. She used tincture of cannabis for cramps."

I have my own ideas about how to cure menstrual cramps. Topical medication, orally applied, also illegal in many states—several more if applied by a woman, despite Queen Victoria's misconceptions. I think she can read my mind, because her next line is "C'mon. You gotta meet my old man."

Oh yeah, and I get paid $25 too. Jimmy and Vera have a foldout couch. Between the codeine and the pot I get some sleep.

I wake up feeling OK, but I gotta go back to reality. It's a gray rainy day out, ride the BART past the shipyards and burned-out liquor stores of West Oakland. What ever happened to the days when me and François and Kent would haunt the nighttime streets of Lower Manhattan, blasting Joy Division out of Kent's box? *We fought for good, stood side by side.* Those days are gone. *Our vision touched the sky.* As far buried as the ninth level of ancient Nineveh. *I put my trust in you.* As dead as Ian Curtis.

It all comes down to religious differences.

Julia's is making it, she's in the underground as a career move, it's the only way to make a name for yourself as a neophyte, a small-timer. It's a lot less pathetic than the Sunset Strip pay-to-play scene, and a lot more open to women. I believe her when she says she hasn't done dope since she's been in the band, but she's still got the junkie's capacity for shameless, self-righteous lies, like how DARE you accuse me of stealing that money on the table, I was just putting it in my pocket for safekeeping, I was fucking protecting you from getting ripped off and this is how little you trust me? Couple that with ambition and you've got a deadly combination.

François is politics, that's the moral oil that sanctifies what would otherwise be a shamefully hedonistic and venal pursuit. A nightclub Savonarola, a self-styled saint in a world of whores. FRANÇOIS OF

LOISAIDA, KING OF THE PUNKS. And they parted his leather and cast lots.

Roach is the party boy, nothing must interfere with getting down, the Beer Can and the Amp and the Teenage Chicks.

Mine I guess is intensity; passion, fire, exorcism. Pleasure or pain, whatever burns brightest. Rock 'n' roll should sound like possession, like sex, pushing the groove to ecstasy and chaos in three minutes or less. Bare wires clinging to the frayed ends of sanity, searing the walls that lock you down. It could come from politics, but politics is not the heart of it, they're just the moral code for dealing with the world.

I expect too much from people. Maybe too little. Just help me make it through the rest of the tour, and if you can't save the band get me out without getting fucked over.

None of those prospects look particularly likely.

I PUT MY TRUST IN YOU.

Roach and Vaclav are at the Revolution Pop! house. We still don't have a van lined up. Eric and Gina said they'll rent us one, they don't care if we can't pay them back, RP can afford it, but François and Julia don't want to.

François calls at 3 AM.

"Hey, like me and Julia, we've been workin' all night to line up a van, we called Napalm, we got Truck usin' his connections—and, man, he knows everybody out here, you wouldn't believe it—we're really workin' on it, we've been knocking ourselves out."

"Why don't we just fuckin' let RP rent us one? They said it's no problem."

"I don't want to take their money. That's copping out. We'll find one tomorrow."

203

According to my Rand McNally Road Atlas it's 394 miles from San Francisco to Grants Pass. "Give me a fuckin' break. We got a six o'clock soundcheck in Grants Pass, and it's at least an eight-hour drive up there. We gotta leave at like fuckin' nine o'clock in the morning. Even if we rent a van it's gonna be hard."

"Yeah, well, we don't have to do soundcheck. It's more important that the singer be well rested."

"And we're gonna fuckin' get there like five minutes before we go on, fuckin' rush through everything, sound like fuckin' dogshit because we can't hear ourselves, no time to get a sound, get something to eat, chill out a bit before the show."

"You want your mommy to tuck you in afterwards too?"

"François, you keep talking to me like that and you're not going to have a band much longer."

"Yeah? I've got plenty of musicians who want to play with me, fuckin' serious musicians, people who could play jazz, classical, any kind of music, you name it. You know what Dimitri said about you? He said you were the worst bass player he ever heard."

"Fuck you. Go suck Dimitri's dick. Fuckin' last night I did a gig with this blues band in Oakland, with this dude who's played with Janis Joplin and John Lee Hooker and Jack Casady, and they said I should come out here and play."

"You would want to play with a bunch of fuckin' tired, pathetic, played-out fuckin' old hippies. You're fuckin' lucky we still let you play with us, because nobody else would want you."

"FUCK YOU, ASSHOLE! I QUIT!" Slam.

Phone rings again. Might as well pick it up before it wakes up everyone in the house. "NOBODY

FUCKIN' HANGS UP ON ME LIKE THAT! NO-
BODY FUCKIN' QUITS MY BAND!"

"I just did." Slam II, the sequel.

Roach stirs.

"What the fuck was that about?" he mumbles.

"I just quit the band." I give a one-paragraph
summary.

"Fuck it, I quit too then."

Next morning Julia calls, starts in right away.
"You quit the band just because you had a fight with
François? That's really immature. You can't do that in
the middle of a tour."

"People treat me like shit long enough and I don't
have to do anything for them."

Cooler heads eventually prevail and me and
Roach agree to at least finish up the tour, even though
Grants Pass is blown and we've still got no van to get
to Portland tomorrow and Olympia Thursday.

This time Vaclav is the problem. "Fock this," he
says. He says "fuck" like Al Pacino trying to play a
Marielito coke dealer with a Russian accent. "I'm not
wasting my vacation if the band's not going anywhere."

He flies back to New York the next night. I crash
on Aaron and Ann's couch and sleep more peacefully
than I have in the last eight months, ten hours of pure
uninterrupted.

Some aftermath. François won't come to the phone
when I call him. Julia acts like it's fuckin' Wall Street
and I've done a shamefully unprofessional thing by
quitting before the end of a project, denying them the
ability to get the last drops out before they downsized.
Fuck 'em.

One night I babysit for Pablo so Aaron and Ann

can go out and they've got a cheap nylon-string acoustic in the closet. After he goes to sleep I take it out and play a few tentative licks, just like the baby beginning to crawl.

RIOT GIRL

I t started with a phone call from L.T. Guarini. "Yo, Nicky." "Yeah." "I got a gig Saturday night at this new club, the Black Diamond. Down the block from CBGB's. Wanna do it? I'd be most pleasured."

Two days notice. Why not. Time for one practice. Nicky had played with him a bunch of times over the years, done three tracks on his album, and knew most of his stuff pretty solid, and it was usually pretty simple beats if he didn't. And L.T. needed him to avert disaster. L.T.'s gigs often teetered on the brink of disaster. Denise Morgan, his usual drummer, had been busted on Tuesday in a 7-11 on Long Island for shoplifting and possession of a syringe. He had wanted this 18-year-old Ricky he had a crush on to play bass, but the kid couldn't play anything he didn't know by solid rote and forgot half of that the minute he got nervous. Yes, there was always some melodrama going on. L.T. often felt like an unfulfilled promise.

But why not.

The Black Diamond was a hole in the wall on East First Street and Extra Place, around the corner from CBGB. Newly spiffed with a powder-blue and black paintjob and a small stage in the back, it was now adding overflow from CB's to its normal clientele of severely alcoholic artist types. You never knew whether the person next to you was going to start reciting Shakespeare or throw up.

The band was billed as the Ozone. L.T. had roped in some good musicians for the gig. His normal style was trashed-out R&B-rock in the style of the Dolls or the Heartbreakers; one of his proudest boasts was that he'd missed a chance to join Joey Rush and the Users in 1976 because he'd been doing his first stint in rehab. His one album, recorded in 1983, had a psychedelic-soul flavor, like Keith Richards in Memphis on acid. The concept for this show was trashy rock'n'roll meets free jazz. He had an old black dude playing tenor sax, a 46-year-old free-jazz player named Jeremiah Bryant. Jeremiah looked like a wino and talked like a philosophy professor with a downhome twist, going on about how free-improv jazz was the music that symbolized the existential dilemma of the 20th century, because the Heisenberg uncertainty principle had revealed the foundations of all matter to be very, very indeterminate—"'cause we realized we all standing on shaky ground." And Sid Berkowitz, ex-Bad Words bassist, on guitar. Sid's new girlfriend, a Colombian from New Jersey named Eva Ozuna, Eva Ozone for this gig, played bass. She was an unknown quantity with flaming copper-dyed hair.

L.T.'s state of mind was the other unknown quantity. His drinking and drug use had to be perfectly calibrated in order to deliver a coherent performance. Sober he froze up completely. More than one to three beers and he'd be a drooling, fucked-up mess—or take off all his clothes on stage, which was a lot more entertaining, if not necessarily a delightful visual experience for all concerned. Heroin was unpredictable. Pot turned his groove into a rut, made him think he could get away with playing the same two-chord lick all night. And he'd done most of the vocals for his album, probably his best singing ever, on mushrooms.

Nicky took a last preshow piss. L.T. and a beefy, pasty-faced dude in acid-washed jeans were snorting coke off the sink. "This is Brian. Want some?"

He demurred. On his way on stage he was seized from the side, felt leather and breasts pressing against his ribs. Renee Saldana. Five foot one, long straight jet-black dyed hair, little oval wire-rim glasses, wearing a black leather vest, purple leather miniskirt and black fishnets, a tattoo of a heart in intense anatomical detail peering out from her upper left breast. Incendiary. He'd met her at a gig a couple months back. They'd hit it off instantly, gone out drinking after the show, wound up making out on a bench in Tompkins Square Park at six in the morning. He'd invited her over and she'd informed him that she lived with her boyfriend. She'd given him her work number.

Nicky wondered what a stranger would make of the Ozone. Skinny old-school punk drummer, black hair/shades/shirt/jeans/sneakers, sleeveless T-shirt and oily olive skin; horn player in ragged dreadlocks and Salvation Army fatigues; a Neapolitan Mick Jagger wannabe up front, teased hair, eye makeup, a Les Paul goldtop and an electric-blue sharkskin suit; and a goofy-looking couple. Sid and Eva had worn matching outfits, wide-striped dayglo-green and black T-shirts and black jeans. They even had matching guitars, a sunburst-finish Strat and Jazz Bass. Fuckin' United Nations of rock'n'roll, two Italians, a Jew, a black and a Colombian. But they sounded good.

Open with "Street Party," an L.T. original, a Stax-Volt groove with dissonant guitar and horn over it, the sax mixed way too high like the soundman putting it up for a solo; into "Slut Boy," a rocker, the band on but the sound still wack—Nicky couldn't hear the vocals—the sound finally balanced for the third song, John Lee Hooker's "The Motor City's Burning," Jeremiah and Sid flaming away, L.T. singing, "My hometown's burning down to the ground, don't it feel like Vietnam." Spacing out for "Eternity," an ethereal dirt ballad; a reggaefied version of War's "Slippin' Into Darkness"; bring it back up with two rockers, "On the Floor" funkified, "All Alone" flat-out punk; close with Sam Cooke's "A Change Is Gonna Come," Jeremiah and Sid wailing the song into sonic chaos, L.T. screaming wordless over the top, Eva and Nicky battering away underneath until a perfect plummet back down to the verse. "It's been too hard living/ And I'm afraid of dying/I don't know what's up there/Beyond the sky...." Back up for the outchorus, then over.

"Wow, that sounded just like 'A Day in the Life,'" L.T. gushed, awestruck. "That was beautiful, that was the best." They got an encore, did the MC5's "Black to Comm," Sid starting the one-chord blues lick, L.T. and Eva picking it up like a train gathering steam, then Nicky set it off with a machinegun-clatter roll and the thing erupted, obliterating everything in its

210

path. Seven minutes of driving manic chaos, Jeremiah screaming and squawking, culminating in a milk-it-to-the-last-drop '60s-comeshot ending, Nicky flailing away at his cymbals, L.T. going "I love all of you, I love all of you," Jeremiah and Sid vying for the last blat.

Renee was up on stage almost before Nicky unscrewed his cymbals. "Can I stay at your house tonight? Phil kicked me out."

"What happened?'

Sid and Eva unplugging effects boxes, coiling cables around their hands, unplugging amps, placing guitars back in cases. Jeremiah swabbing out his horn. L.T. getting a pitcher of beer, accepting accolades.

"He came into the bedroom while I was getting dressed, he was like, Where the fuck you going dressed like that, who the fuck you going with, who're you fucking, I know you're fucking somebody. I told him to leave me the fuck alone and he threw a bottle at me. I booked."

Grabbed her purse, threw on a pair of black canvas sneakers. Raced down 86th Street, past the secretarial-clothes stores and Record Factory, into the R train. Too late, realized Phil could be following her, but the train was just pulling in, dived on. Got off at Ninth Street, found a coffeeshop to regroup and do her makeup in the bathroom, called home to see if Phil was there—he wasn't, if he was she would have hung up—bought a beer to calm down and drink on the subway. She took the F rest of the way into the city.

Commotion at the door. Panicky figure appears. "Sid! Nicky! Don't go home! The fuckin' cops are going berserk on Avenue A!"

Roach Wein. "Fuckin' cops going crazy beating the shit out of people! They fuckin' dragged people

211

out of Scurvy! They got François and Barry!"

"Aaah, if they whacked François upside that fuckin' swelled head of his, maybe I oughta make a donation to the Patrolmen's Benevolent Association." Sid, laconic and grumpy like an old man. François had been the lead singer in his old band, and their divorce had not been amicable. You did not want to get him started on the subject unless you were ready for a rant.

"Why don't you stay at my house," L.T. offered Nicky.

"Nah, I'll figure out a way."

No man alive was going to keep Nicky Squillici from getting one five-piece kit of green-sparkle Sonor drums, three K. Zildjian cymbals, and assorted stands and hardware into the sanctity of Apartment 2A, 200 East Seventh St. And braving a mob of bloodlust-crazed riot cops was less daunting than the prospect of schlepping his drums home from the Bronx on the 4 train tomorrow afternoon. It was also less daunting than the prospect of dealing with L.T.'s widowed mother. Nicky had had two phone encounters with her. Once he got a drunken crying jag about the plight of the homeless crippled children, once she hung up on him, telling him to "fuck off, ya rat bastid," she didn't want any filthy degenerate drug-addict perverts bothering her Lawrence. L.T. once said she had only been to Manhattan twice since coming to America as a war bride in 1946.

"I'll give you a ride." Brian the beefy guy. "We'll go the back way, and if anyone stops us, I'll tell 'em I'm on the job."

Offer accepted. Leans over to Renee, whispers in her ear. "Yeah, you could stay over, wanna come?" They piled into Brian's beat-up van, Brian and L.T.

212

doing another couple lines while Nicky, Sid and Eva stuffed gear in the back, Renee carrying the light things. Brian drove up to 14th Street, going over to Avenue B.

"Fuckin' cops just love to beat people up." Renee was on a rant. "They're nothing but a goon squad for the rich. They come down here and they think we're all just a bunch of freaks and weirdos and it's all fun and games."

"Yeah, I was out last night and they were prepared, it looked like fuckin' D-Day with the LST boats." Sid. "They had all these barricades set up, they had this fuckin' Winnebago command-center thing in the park. I was just out on Avenue A, drinkin' a beer."

"You fuck-n liberals are all the same." Brian. "Always the cops this, the cops that." Sputtering, his voice rising, almost screaming. "Why the fuck don't you go after the people who got real power? We're just the fuck-n guys in the middle. Why the fuck don't you fuck-n liberals complain to the scumbags who give us orders?"

There were no cops on Avenue B until a roadblock on the south side of 11th Street, five cops with shotguns manning it. Nicky helped Sid and Eva get their amps in their studio, a basement near the corner. Brian made a U-turn. They made a right on 12th Street, another down Avenue C.

"Sorry, I didn't know you were a cop." Renee.

"Well now you do."

"Everybody just chill out." L.T. "We had a great show, let's not spoil it. Keith Richards says any band anywhere on any given night can be the greatest rock'n'roll band in the world. Tonight we were it." The cocaine was inflating his normal delusions of grandeur a bit, but it had been a great show.

They stopped on Seventh and B, loading the drums into the hall. A crowd of people faced off against the cops on B, chanting "Die Yuppie Scum," trying to get to the Christodora luxury-condo building. They thanked Brian for the ride and closed the door, moving the drum pieces up the stairs one by one, the trap case last.

"Why the fuck didn't you tell me he was a cop?" Renee accused.

"Yeah, well, I thought you figured it out, like when he said, 'I'm on the job.'"

"Like I'm really supposed to think somebody's a cop when he's hangin' out in a club snorting coke. He looked like just some Brooklyn guy."

They rolled the trap case into a corner of Nicky's two-room apartment, piling the smaller drums on top of it. Nicky leaned down and kissed Renee. They swam in each other's spirits and saliva for what seemed like several minutes.

"Wanna go out, see what's going on, maybe get a drink?" she asked when they came up.

The scene on Avenue A was a little surreal, a Saturday-night party in a war zone. Riot cops, protesters, barhoppers. Helicopters overhead, malignant dragonflies. Spectral snipers on the rooftops. Longhaired rocker dudes in leather pants strutted arm-in-arm with bleached-blonde chicks in miniskirts and heels. There was a new crop of musicians coming up, more mainstream in their decadence than the militant misfits of the recent past. Periodically cops charged into the milling crowds, dragging somebody out and beating them to the ground. Protesters grouped and regrouped, chanting "No Police State" and "Big Sticks,

214

Little Dicks." Occasionally a bottle smashed on the street or clattered off a riot shield, the Ballantine XXX bottle the Lower East Side's version of the MX missile. A red jeep stopped in traffic, sound system blasting the mutant siren squeals of the summer's ubiquitous Public Enemy album. "Turn it up! Bring the noise."

Nicky and Renee wandered through the scene holding hands, trying to suss it out. Nobody really knew, just that there'd been a demonstration in the park and the cops had gone off. They walked down Avenue A, past Odessa, Ray's and Leshko's, crossing over by where A7 used to be. The old wino dude on the corner was half declaiming, half babbling, "Mekong Delta... Pleiku... Ia Drang Valley... Da Nang," cardboard "Homeless Veteran" sign at his feet. On the south side of Sixth they ran into Sid and Eva and a plump black woman, wearing one of those orange African-cloth hats and walking an Airedale.

"Yo, Nicky, Renee, this is Alice, Coleman's teacher."

"And she's not on 40 Valiums?" Nicky had seen Sid's little maniac in action at a Bad Words sound-check when he was three.

"No, he's a nice kid," she said. "Hey! What are you doing?" She turned to a couple crusties trying to uproot a sycamore sapling.

"Weapons. Fuck up the pigs."

"I planted that tree." Maternal ire. The Airedale barked. One cop walked up.

"Can't stay here. You scumbags have gotta move along." He rapped his nightstick against the sidewalk several times, perpendicular.

"And I'm supposed to be afraid of that?" Renee stepped back, planted her feet, crossed her arms over

215

her chest. "My fucking boyfriend broke my nose. What the fuck are you gonna do to top that?"

Sid tapped her on the shoulder. A phalanx of robocops was advancing down Avenue A, rapping their sticks on the sidewalk in goosestep rhythm, breaking ranks to run and swing.

The five split three ways, Sid and Eva running west, Nicky and Renee south, Alice and the dog east. The cop headed after Renee a few steps, then cut back to follow the pack, who had chosen to chase Alice. The sidewalk had a severe melanin deficiency that could only be cured by smashing some appropriately pigmented skin into it. Alice extracted her keys on the run and made it inside the iron gate of her building, slamming it shut. Nicky and Renee fled around the corner, ducked into a bar on Fifth Street.

"I need a cocktail," Renee said. "Shit that was scary. Did you know this was going to happen when you did 'Motor City's Burning'?" No. He had a double vodka-and-grapefruit, bought her a double vodka-and-cranberry. That was it for the gig money. The Fall's version of "White Lightning" was on the juke-box. Mighty mighty pleasing my pappy's corn squeezings. They decompressed, caressed and kissed, caressed and kissed some more. "Don't you two have a room?" some drunk asshole gibed.

Closing time closing in. They finished their drinks.

"Well, we can go back in the street," Renee postulated, "and get the shit kicked out of us by the cops, or we can go back to your place and fuck our brains out."

"Uh... I'd pick Door No. 2."

They slipped back home safely. Nicky clicked the deadbolt, set the police lock. Leaned over again, kissed

216

Renee. She stiffened up, her muscle fibers like high-way-guardrail cable. Another fucking asshole who's gonna fuck me and not give me the fucking time of day next time we see each other, she was thinking. She turned away, asked him for another drink. Nicky puttered about, mixing her a vodka with apple juice, rolling a joint, and riffling through his tapes. There was a reggae mix tape he was looking for, a '70s lovers' rock dub-style compilation he'd gotten on the street in Brooklyn. Renee paced the bare floor, chain-smoking menthols.

Nicky found the tape, put it on. U-Roy on the box, crooning, *Those other guys may put you down, you wear my crown.* He sat on the edge of the mattress, lit the joint, passed it to Renee. She gulped the rest of her drink, sat next to him. "Sorry about before. I was nervous. You're sweet." The liquor was spreading benevolence, maybe lack of judgment, who cares. She caressed his hair. A dub version of "Queen Majesty" came on, falsetto going *Could you really care for me?* They kissed some more, lying down, blue lightbulb reflecting off the floor. Her leather and lingerie and his cotton and denim dripped to the floor, time in slow rotation as they rubbed against each other. *I see love light in your arms.* As the sun came up over the East River projects Nicky was eating Renee's pussy in the gray twilight and she was coming, arching her hips off the mattress and writhing into his mouth, the sound of her moans blending with the bass-and-reverb heartbeat of the reggae, the chants of the protesters in the street, and the thunk of billy clubs on ribcages and skulls.

218

AFTERBURN BLUES

All right. I woke up this morning. That's how all blues songs begin isn't it? got the shades drawn but light still seeps through. onto the floor where i'm feeling around for my shoes. feeling around for my brain. do you know who you are and where you are? yes. do you know who the president of the united states is? yes, and who gives a shit about some fuck-n' politician anyway? find a clean tshirt. piss. white noise in the cascade mountains. fuckin' douglas firs, clean air and rednecks. what brought that into my head anyway? anyway, go downstairs to the bodega and get breakfast. coffee light and sweet buttered bagel daily news and 16-oz. bud. cigarettes. restore my chemical imbalance. sonny, you spent five bucks already and you didn't even get a real breakfast. whaddaya mean, i got protein, carbohydrates and intellectual stimulation. ain't your fuckin' sonny and i ain't sunny either. it's a nice fuckin' day out. go back upstairs and put on some old iggy. raw power.

219

the metallic KO bootleg. open up and bleed. yeah where he goes *who hates the stooges out there?* and half the audience claps. *well we don't hate you, we don't even care.* open up my coffee, pull the plastic off. cigarette. open up the paper. open up my beer, pull the intricate little aluminum thing out and snap! you have opened up a brave new world of rushing yellow rivers and foaming boise cascades. what was that girl from california telling me last night? you new yorkers are so closed off. people are like so much more open on the coast. fuck her. if you're so fuckin' open, all the garbage of the world falls in.

what the fuck did she say about me? i don't remember too well. oh yeah, she called me a cynical broken-down old musician. fuck her and her fuck-n' valley-girl shit again. what the fuck does she know? yeah, all those fuck-n' assholes talking about "edge" and "attitude" and and all those armchair slumming scum talking about how cool it is to be "living on the edge." yeah. so you go out to the edge. you have to. you do what you gotta do to get out there, you know what i mean? you gotta leave a bit of blood and guts and burning chaos up there on stage. otherwise you ain't givin' up nothing. otherwise you're just a fuckin' professional looking at his fuckin' watch to see how long is left in the set. yeah. if you wanna watch the clock, go work in a fuckin' office. i used to. i know my shit. command-q, i quit. control-x, i exited. i didn't take commands and i was out of control. yeah. so, anyway, you go out to the edge. And then you fall off. Yeah. And you crawl back and you're a fuckin' bag of battered bones with a bad liver and a broken heart. And then these people call you a fuckin' cripple. A fuckin' pathetic old burnout geek casualty. Fuck you,

220

I died for your sins. I gave it up like a fuckin' Buddhist monk with a can of gasoline. Spirit ascending to Nirvana in a whorl of black smoke and mirrors. Peace in Vietnam, dude. They roast marshmallows and hotdogs, melted charred sweet goo and meat cylinders seared to a tasty crisp. Yummy. Eeeyew.

I'm coming back. I know I'm coming back.

take an inventory of the contents of this room. my box & four milkcrates full of tapes my mattress my shirts hanging in the corner on a purloined garment district rack a tobacco sunburst Les Paul Junior and a red Epiphone that looks sorta like a Strat a Fender Champ amp three distortion boxes and a digital delay/chorus pedal that eats enough batteries to pollute Tokyo Bay unto the tenth generation. these are my worldly goods after 15 years of rock'n'roll. my records & Marshall are in my parents' basement.

I can still play. yeah, well whoever said I couldn't? that's another story. yeah but when I go on auditions I don't get called back. they all seem like hopeless amateurs or hopeless mercenaries anyway. they don't know what they're in for or they're just in it to get signed. they talk about their marketing program and target demographics. fuck that shit. yeah, these guys look cool, but they probably hired a fuckin' image consultant with mom and dad's money. they look like fuckin' dress for success. yeah they probably think I'm too old, well it ain't what you got it's how you use it. i can swivel when they all shrivel. I forgot more than they'll ever know. you gotta knowhow to move the crowd. you gotta have just the right mix of crudity and finesse.

I gotta have another beer.

I'm not an alcoholic. I can stop drinking any time

I want to.

I don't want to.

Sometimes I wish there was a drug I could take that would make me unconscious for 48 hours, make me thank god that I'm not aware, you know where that comes from. I hate fuckin' dope though. I did it once when I was 17 and puked my guts out for four hours.

I know I was good enough. Put a band on the road and have them do thirty gigs in thirty days and we'd be the fuckin' most on-and-smoking hot thing that ever graced a stage. That's if they don't hate every note of every song in the set and every molecule of air each other breathes. I coulda been a contender. Yeah, I could've had a shot at the Garden. Instead I got a one-way ticket to Palookaville. Fuck that pathos shit. I don't want your pity. No, no, it was you, Charlie, you were supposed to look out for me, you were supposed to be my bass player, my brother, my glimmer twin.

Charlie Parker Renehan. That was his real name. I mean is his real name. I'm not kidding. He was beatnik spawn. His father was black and his mom Irish. He was a drummer and she was a painter and they had a nice little fifties bohemian romance until she got pregnant and he decided he didn't want to be tied down with all that square shit like diapers. Well, neither did she, but she didn't have much of a choice. I think she was still too much the good Catholic girl to get an abortion even if it had been legal—the shit you get brought up with stays with you a lot deeper than most people think.

I think he had a lot of that in him too. Yeah. One winter night we were drinking at my old place on 6th and B and he starts telling me he's gonna burn in hell.

222

"Yeah?" I said. "Yeah," he said. Then this Bob Marley song comes up on the tape and he starts singing along. "If a fire, mek it burn, if a blood, mek it run," he says, tipping the bottle back.

He got brought up mostly by his grandmother down on the south side of Park Slope. Not too far from here actually. Ironically. He was living evidence of his mother's sin and fuckup and she wouldn't let either of them forget it. And this was Brooklyn in the '60s so little Charlie's cafe au lait skin and tight curls were blatant evidence that his mama fucked a nigger. But he didn't fit in with the blacks either because he talked white.

I think things got a little cooler for him when he got to be a teenager. His mother married this Jamaican guy and they moved up the hill to the nicer part of the neighborhood. The kids up there were more like punks and hippies than rednecks and cugines. They used to hang out on Lenny Casiolo's stoop and get high and play guitars.

I met him on the F train in 1980. He had bleached-blonde dreads and was carrying a Fender Precision case so I started talking to him. We started the band a year later. Yeah, we did our first demo in Lenny's basement studio and the bass amp was next to the washing machine and the drums by the oil burner.

He liked to wear velvet suits. He had one black one and one electric-blue one. As fucked up as he would get, he was always polite. One night he was talking to some girl on the sidewalk in front of CBGB's—he must have drunk a pint of vodka that night—and all of a sudden he leans over and spews into the gutter. He makes some kind of tip-the-hat gesture and goes "Excuse me, madam, I appear to have experienced a brief episode of gastric distress," and goes on talking like nothing happened.

It never really affected his playing. I know they all say that but it was true for him. Well usually never. Or at least not on stage. There were a couple times he wasn't in much shape at practice. A little sloppiness was always a good thing in our music anyway. Added to the suspense. And Denise Dallesandro was always rock solid on the drums.

The weird thing about him was that he didn't do dope unless he was already drunk—once he got ripped past a certain point, anything he could grab went in his system until it all knocked him out. It was like fuel to make him burn up.

He used to find it in the weirdest places. The last time we played Philadelphia he found a rib joint across the street from where we were staying that was selling it under the counter.

That night was the first show of a tour. It was Friday before Labor Day and still steaming miasmic summer hot. We played on a rickety five-foot-high stage in the back room of some bar to 200 kids and I sweated so much it burned my eyes, I couldn't see, I broke two strings, but we ripped like we always ripped, I thought the stage was gonna cave in and we got two encores.

The party after the gig was like 20 blocks west of the club in a squat in West Philly. The lack of banisters on the stairs was a major incentive for sobriety. The walls were mostly plaster dust and lath and if you missed the third-floor toilet somebody downstairs would get a warm golden shower. It was a mix of queers, metalheads and crusty punks who looked like they hadn't taken a bath since Reagan got re-elected.

224

All sucking on 40-ounces.

I was chasing after this girl named Sarah in a black dress and spiderweb-pattern stockings. She had to drive her friend home to Upper Darby—eight months pregnant in spandex and heels—so I came for the ride. I wanted to see the MOVE house. That was where we first kissed. On Osage across from the ruins, her tongue exploring my mouth while the Africa children's bones moldered amidst the charred timbers.

Some people think being near death is romantic, like grabbing onto something before the nevermore. I don't know about that white roses and wasting-disease shit. Yeah, but part of me still wants something that's gonna make my heart beat like the drums on "Be My Baby," wash over me like a wall of violins and reverb. When I fall in love with someone I even love her old zit scars. And part of me remembers waking out of a deep hangover in 1985 to find all my stuff piled on the living room floor of my old girlfriend's apartment. She had the windows blacked out with black construction paper. She arrayed red candles on the table and was sitting there in a white nightgown with a glass of whiskey and a cigarette in one hand and a kitchen knife in the other. Marianne Faithfull was on the stereo purring with icy wrath. If you know the song you know what my sin was. The final touch was that she had been knitting.

I had to admire her sense of drama.

She always wanted to be an actress, but the closest she ever got was turning down an offer to do live sex acts on 42nd Street. That was back when she was a go-go dancer. I think she works for a publishing company now.

I always seemed to attract literate women. I don't

know why. Can't read much anymore—just don't have the attention span. Sarah showed me her stuff the next morning. It was no-future science fiction—toxic-waste concentration camps and shit like that. I'd heard it before, but at least she was trying.

We ate breakfast in a coffee shop with Denise. Charlie was still passed out—vodka bottle upside down so enough for a morning taste would drip into the cap—and Adrian our singer was a fuckin' vampire—jet-black hair, pale skin and eye makeup. We used to say he'd crumble into a pile of fine white ashes if he ever saw daylight. Our gig that night was at Mondo Trasho in Baltimore which was only 100 miles away, so we could split at 4 and still make soundcheck. Those two were always a pain in the ass once we got out West and had 400 or 500 miles between shows.

Baltimore sucked. They stuck us on a bill with one thrash-metal and two hardcore bands so the place was full of skinheads and there were about 10 people over 21. So Adrian starts posing about like he's fuckin' David Bowie and telling them they didn't appreciate true art. I was really getting to hate this I-am-a-sensitive-suffering-artiste trip he'd been on for the last year or so. Well it got him a lot of girls. Little Gothettes used to sit around for hours to catch drippings of his philosophy. Who knows what other kind of drippings they were catching too—he looked immaculate on the surface, but he only bothered to get his leather pants dry-cleaned about once a year.

I ended up screaming at him in the dressing room after the show about how he was boring and pretentious and it wasn't rock'n'roll. He screamed back that we had to grow and all I wanted to do was get drunk and play three-chord bullshit. Then Denise barged in—the spray-paint-crusted metal door slamming back against the wall—and asked if we were going to stay there all night acting like fuckin' babies while she loaded out by herself?

"You got a fuckin' filthy mouth for a girl" said a short kid in a green bomber jacket with "BALTO. SKINS" on the back.

"Don't worry. I won't be contaminating your miserable little dick with it," she spat back.

"Fuck you, bitch, I'll kick your ass" was the snappiest he could come back with. He probably didn't know what "contaminating" meant. We were in the van before he could get reinforcements. Skinheads never fight one on one. They call it solidarity.

"I shoulda kicked him in his fuckin' balls," Denise said in the van.

"Except you would've needed a microscope in the toe of your boot to find them," said Adrian.

We were staying in the promoter's girlfriend's rowhouse on the east side. Charlie was already well into a pint of vodka. There were about 20 people there and we probably would have gone over better to them than to the people at the gig. Adrian found a circle of admirers pretty fast and Denise dragged me into a back room to talk.

"Youse guys gotta work it out. You've been together for six years. You don't want to fuck it up. People know us. They know we're good. You wanna start all over again from scratch? You wanna go back to playing Tuesday nights at little shitholes for 40 bucks and then having to start all over *again* because your bass player quit? Youse guys are crazy if you quit now."

"Yeah, I know," I said. "but I wanna get people off and get myself off when we play, and it's not happening. It stops the show dead when he pulls that shit."

"Yeah, but we were on and smoking last night" she said.

"You know what Mick from the Criminal Minds told me once? He said the reason it took them so long to break up was because they still could play really well even when they couldn't be in the same room for more than like five minutes."

"That's what he told me about his old girlfriend. He said the reason it took *them* so long to break up was because they still had really good sex even when they weren't speaking to each other."

"What the fuck. I know we're a good band. I don't want to fuck it up either. But I can't write with him anymore because he wants everything to be complicated and arranged and in place. Why do you think we don't have any new songs? Every riff I bring in I get that 'three-chord bullshit' line."

Something that sounded like the Butthole Surfers was drifting through the door.

"Youse guys gotta work it out. We get through the tour, maybe we'll sell some records."

"Yeah, if fuckin' Roadkill gets it in the stores." Roadkill was the company that had so far sold about 1,500 copies of our first album. They were generally closer to getting their phone turned off than they were to good promotion.

We went on like that for about three hours. Adrian was still talking to two girls and the only other people left up were two guys nodding into their six-packs.

I crashed out on the ruptured green couch downstairs. The two girls split and I could hear Denise talking to Adrian, giving him the same youse-guys-gotta-work-it-out rap she gave me.

"He doesn't want to change, to grow," he was saying. "I'm trying to express myself, my heart, my soul and all I hear from him is 'Ah, fuck it, let's just go up there and rip.' "

I couldn't hear what she said back.

Charlie wasn't there the next morning.

The light hurt my eyes when I went out for breakfast. The shades were down when I came back and we sat around smoking cigarettes in the dim light, periodically wondering where the fuck he was. Periodically like every five minutes. We were supposed to be soundchecking at the Rebel Waltz in Richmond at 5—or failing that, onstage at 11. Nobody had seen him leave. If he went home with anyone, he was supposed to take the house number, but he could have forgotten if he was drunk enough. Adrian who didn't smoke paced, drumming his fingertips on the back of his hand. The promoter's girlfriend called around to people who'd been there last night. Daytime TV flickered, black-and-white background radiation. Nobody had seen him talking to anybody who showed enough interest.

There weren't any messages on the club's answering machine either. Nobody wanted to call the cops, but when he still wasn't back by six we did. They hadn't seen him. We cancelled Richmond. Adrian went off to stay with one of the girls he had met the night before. He got our phone number and left hers.

Monday morning the cops called. He had been picked up on the West Side Saturday night, charged with possession of two bags of dope and one vial of crack. He wasn't going to be arraigned until Tuesday morning because it was a holiday, so the Bad Seed in Greensboro wasn't going to be graced with our presence that night.

The next morning the judge, noting the defendant's lack of community ties, set bail at $1,000 cash. We had $164 between the three of us. By the time his mother and stepfather could get down from Brooklyn with it, it would be Thursday and we were supposed to be in Atlanta.

Adrian said it was my fault because I had "enabling behavior." I punched him in the face.

"I fuckin' had it with you two," said Denise. "Fuck the rest of the tour. You two are worse than my parents."

I drove the van back to New York with her. Adrian stayed with his new girlfriend through the weekend. Charlie came home on the train with his parents.

That was three years ago. Adrian joined a band called Flowers of Evil that got signed to MCA. They sounded like a cross between Guns'N'Roses and the Cure. They did a video that got on *120 Minutes* a couple times—Adrian posed in the window of an abandoned building under black clouds in a dirty red sky—but the album went down like a dead whale. I still see the CD in the $2.99 bins, its corners crudely sliced off. MCA liked him enough to give him a solo deal, but nothing's happened so far except he moved to L.A.

Denise turned out to be two months pregnant when the band broke up. She decided to keep the baby and named him Keith Moon Dallesandro. She was on welfare for awhile and then got a job in a real-estate office. She doesn't get to play very much. When I went out to Queens to see them once Keith threw a tantrum because she didn't play the tape he wanted.

"WA-MONES, MOMMY, WA-MONES," he was screaming.

Charlie was in rehab a couple times. He got on SSI too. He was in a ska band for about six months, but they broke up. Most of the time he just drinks and watches TV. He talks to me about getting back together, but I can't deal with it. I don't wanna listen to his I'm-clean bullshit.

Fire leaves an afterburn and blood leaves a clot. I may be a fuck-up, but I never missed a gig in my life.

I haven't done much worth remembering since then. I did two gigs with Piss Satan but they said I was doing rockist cliches and I said they were doing art-noise bullshit. But I'm coming back. I know I'm coming back. What the fuck else am I supposed to do?

LAST GASP?

They were evicting the squatters on East 9th Street. It was across the street from my old girlfriend Laura's old building. Somebody called me about one in the morning to come down.

I don't know what the fuck I could do about it now. They've got a fuckin' army out here. About 400 or 500 cops. Cops in black shirts, helmets, riot shields. Snipers on the roof of every building on this block and the roofs of the projects on the next. Helicopters and emergency command centers. There's about 100 of us out here. We're way outnumbered and there's some serious weaponry out there. Machine guns, 9-millimeters, tear-gas grenade launchers, who knows, probably MAC-10s, Uzis, ultra-high-frequency sound generators, nerve gas, Zyklon B dispensers, Death Ray 2000, low-yield nuclear warheads they brought back from Germany now that the Cold War is over.

All this to kick 50 people out of their homes. Two ancient tenements with lath sticking out of the walls and crumbling turn-of-the-century stonecraft, gar-goyles and crenellations, stars of David inlaid in the vestibule floor. Two ancient tenements, slowly and contentiously partially resurrected. I bet not a single person living there would have more than 50 bucks in their pocket. Fuck that, 20. Well, they committed a crime against the sanctity of private property, they committed heresy against the money-god. In the Middle Ages they would have been burned at the stake. Our society is still quite medieval when it comes to matters of religion and power.

Not a lot we can do about it now. They clear everyone out of the street at gunpoint and then a tank rolls in and crunches the barricades, old mattresses and broken refrigerators and decayed 3x12s, an aban-doned car turned over in the middle of the street. Then they hook a chain from the tank to the car's bumper and drag it out. A glorified fuckin' tow truck.

All we can do is bear witness.

All we can do is bear witness.

A bunch of us are watching it from the stoop of Laura's old building. The cops are banging on the front gate, telling Metal Pete that if he doesn't let them in they'll kick it down. Some people think it's kind of chickenshit, but all resisting would get him is a broken lock, a bust, and the satisfaction of having maintained his pose. Metal Pete is a 6' 4" 250-pound biker, but that's not much of an equalizer. The issue is academic anyway because about 30 cops just busted in through the back windows of his apartment, first-floor back, and more are coming down from the roof.

I remember when me and Laura and Osvaldo helped Pete put those windows in. "Cheetrock," Osvaldo said, the same way he'd pronounce "shit" in his Salvadoran accent. We all had a good laugh.

They kick us all off the stoop and herd us into the front room. We can still watch if we crane our necks and get the right angle. There's about 30 people standing in a line in front of the two buildings they're evicting, nonviolent resistance. They're all being carried off one by one. A hippiegirl in a Grateful Dead T-shirt and a day-glo yellow hardhat sings "We Shall Overcome." Four cops jump an emaciated guy they dragged out of one of the buildings, kicking, flailing and screaming in language that no one understands, his jeans down around his ankles. Crazy Cecil, somebody says. Someone else says he has AIDS and the cops wrap him up in a giant yellow body bag.

There's about eight of us in the room and who should I be standing next to but Ryan, the guitar player from when I was in the Suspect Devices. Weird. I just started speaking to him again, so it's still weird. "Personal and musical differences," compounded by shitty and backstabbing behavior. They went around telling people I had a drinking problem after they kicked me out. Job himself with hepatitis couldn't have stayed sober putting up with their shit. How's Courtney, he asks. You know you're a lucky man, you married a good woman. Yeah, I think so, if I didn't I'd be pretty fuckin' stupid. She had to work today. Somebody should block that tank, he says. I know him. I know he's dying to run out there and do a Tiananmen Square number in front of the tank, probably Americanizing it with a middle finger. What part is conscience and what part is ego and martyr complex, who knows. I'll be generous and say mostly conscience.

There's nothing he could do about it now. There's

about 20 cops lined up in the hall. Metal Pete wants to go back to his apartment. "Can't leave the room," says a woman cop, pointing her gun at his gut. The cops guarding us have these weird minimalist black-metal weapons, not much more than a barrel and a clip.

What kind of guns are those, Ryan asks.

You're asking me? Man, I don't know from guns. The older I get the more Jewish I sound. I know from guitars, not guns. You give me any guitar and I bet I can tell when it was made within five years. Like that's a Rickenbacker John Lennon 325, that's a '71 or '72 Gibson SG, that's a late-'60s Telecaster bass. What I am I supposed to do, go "That's a Mark David Chapman .44"? "No, it's a Son of Sam model." How the fuck should I know?

When they kick out your front door, how you gonna come? The answer here's pretty fucking obvious. None of us are ready to act the suicidal holy fool. Nobody move, nobody get hurt.

Six months later. I'm playing an abandoned glass factory, a performance space/artists' workshop on what was once the Lower East Side's most notorious heroin corner. Two sets—one with Lung, Courtney's grunge band, one with Squat City. It's a last gasp before the place gets torn down for yuppie housing. It's a fucking disaster.

Joan the promoter is primarily a journalist. She's doing this gig out of the goodness of her heart and doesn't have the dominatrix soul needed to run this kind of thing, to tell people 25 MINUTES AND NO MORE, WE'VE GOT TO BE OUT BY ONE O'CLOCK. We need that. The only place we could get a drum kit for all the bands is from Gonorrhea, a bad generic squatter-punk band. They're insisting that their friends' two equally bad generic squatter-punk bands go on before them, even though the bill is already jammed. Lung interferes, rushing on stage and setting up before anyone else can get on, and the assholes are heckling. I play well but in a fog of pure anger, hammering the bass, ripping at the guitar. Courtney's pissed off too, says the loudest one was hitting on her the minute she walked in.

An acoustic guy goes on next, and I'm in a screaming match with the bass player from Gonorrhea all through his set. YOU WANT THIS GUY TO PLAY INSTEAD OF US BECAUSE HE SOUNDS LIKE BOB DYLAN, he's yelling at me. Great. Another cretin who thinks that anything that isn't punk is part of the great homosexual conspiracy to ensure the hegemony of wimpy music and deny bad generic punk bands the success the world owes them. I was playing CBGB's and Max's before this fucking idiot ever touched a guitar. It's pointless to argue, but I don't want my band to get stuck going on 10 minutes before closing, as has happened all too many times before. Courtney pulls me away, thinking I was going to punch him. That would be most out of character for nonviolent me, but I have an intense temper. He's got the trump card anyway—the threat to take his drums and go home, which he proceeds to use.

"GET ME HIGH," I half bark, half plead at Jeanie, my lead singer's girlfriend and a solid viper. She obliges by rolling a fatty. I'm normally not so rude. I track down Joan, who needs it as much as I do, and we suck the smoke down like we're starving. Gonorrhea plays for 40 minutes, milking the audience for more. I hit Jeanie up for another one. There's a middle-class lite-punk band on next, and true to form, we don't go on till almost 1, but Joan's gotten us an extension. Between the weed and the beer I'm far more wasted than I like to be while playing. I can count on one hand (maybe two) the number of gigs I've done high on pot in the last 15 years. It fits. Seeking calm. Seeking oblivion, or at least somewhere far from reality.

The wheel has turned and the atmosphere is more settled. The Gonorrhea fans are gone but there are still people there. We do a slow-gospel version of the Specials' "Doesn't Make It All Right" and the big fat single notes I'm playing are like huge pillows surrounding my head, then I'm driving the subway-sex groove of "Trouble and Strife," one of ours born in some long-lost domestic argument. I'm slightly shocked that I'm actually producing these sounds, but when it's on, it's perfect. We're sloppy as fuck, but it goes over well. We do Merle Haggard's "The Bottle Let Me Down," kind of a hard-edged swamp-boogie version, and dedicate Patsy Cline's "She's Got You" to everyone who ever found themselves in one of the local bars with a broken heart and seven empty glasses. I'm prophesying my own fate two months in the future. It's one of those gigs that feels like playing in a church, the audience so rapt it looks dead at first sight. After we do Hooverville's "Hang the Landlord" Joan says she was almost crying, because it reminded her of what was being lost with the Glass Factory closing down. We actually moved somebody. The night is not a total disaster.

"That was one of the best gigs we ever had," my lead singer reminisces three years later.

Yeah, and a lot of piss has flowed through the sewers since then, contaminating the waters thirteen

238

miles offshore. Courtney walked out. Said I don't give a fuck about you and your fucking stupid life. Three months blind and blithering. Pain finely wrought like being stuck with a perfectly honed crystal shard, or raw and overwhelming, overpowering, inarticulate. When I quit drinking it got worse. Like it was too much trouble to pull the trigger and I'd probably fuck it up anyway.

Fuck it. If I'm gonna imitate Kurt Cobain, I'm better off writing three-chord punksongs, drop down on the verses and scream my guts out on the chorus.

She left me for dead, but I'm still alive. And the sky is blue, and the bass amp is purring like a cat who's about to get fed.

Permissions

Lyrics from the following songs were used in this book. All credits are accurate to the best of my knowledge.

"More Fun" by The Blenders (B. Sturdivent), ©1979.

"We Are the Road Crew" by Motörhead (I. Kilmister-E. Clarke-P. Taylor), ©1980 EMI Intertrax BMI.

"Book of Love" by the Monotones.

"Planet Rock" by Afrika Bambaataa and the Soulsonic Force (A. Baker, J. Robie & Soulsonic Force), ©1981 Shakin' Baker Music (BMI).

"War" by Bob Marley (A. Cole-C. Barrett), ©1976 Blue Mountain Music.

"Uh Oh" by the Avengers (P. Houston-J. Wilsey-G. Ingraham-D. Furious), ©1978 Doctor PP.

"Around and Around" by Chuck Berry, Arc Music (BMI).

"Human Being" by The New York Dolls (D. JoHansen- J. Thunders), ©1974 Lipstick Killers.

"Inner City Blues" by Marvin Gaye (M. Gaye- J. Nyx), ©1971 Jobete Music (ASCAP), administered by EMI.

"The Thrill Is Gone" by B.B. King (A. H. Benson- D. Pettite), ©1970 Grosvenor House Music.

"Means to an End" by Joy Division ©1979.

"A Change Is Gonna Come" by Sam Cooke, ©1964 Kags (BMI).

"Wear You to the Ball" byU-Roy (J. Holt), Sparta Florida Music Group Ltd.

"Queen Majesty" (a.k.a. "Minstrel and Queen" and "Chalice in the Palace") by Ranking Trevor and the Jays (C. Mayfield), Curtom Publishing (BMI).

Also available from The Imaginary Press:

Las paredes tienen la palabra y *Ataraxia maxima*
The Walls Have the Floor and *Maximum Ataraxy*

Two plays by K. Wishnia

Bilingual Spanish/English edition published by the University of Cuenca Press, Cuenca, Ecuador. Imported and distributed in the U.S.A. by The Imaginary Press.

"*Estos textos bellos se mueven entre la fina ironía antimetafísica de Woody Allen y el teatro del absurdo de Samuel Beckett.*"

"A mixture of Woody Allen's sharp anti-metaphysical irony and Samuel Beckett's theatre of the absurd."

> - from the Introduction by
> Cecilia Suárez Moreno of the
> University of Cuenca

The Walls Have the Floor - a troupe of comedians in an unidentified Latin American country put on satiric cabaret sketches lampooning their government's policies, but they have to revise their routines every night because the government changes just as often.

Maximum Ataraxy - two tribes of post-nuclear survivors struggle to learn each other's languages so that the epic tale of their final battle can be told.

"It's either a happy tragedy, or a VERY grim comedy."

Order a copy of *Exit 25 Utopia* for a friend, or just let us know that you liked this book and you'd like to see the others.

❑ Please send me __ copy(ies) of *Exit 25 Utopia* @ $7.95 each.

❑ Please send me __ copy(ies) of *Flat Rate* @ $4.95 each.

❑ Please send me __ copy(ies) of *Las paredes tienen la palabra/The Walls Have the Floor* @ $6.95 each.

Name: _____

Address: _____

City: _____ State: ___ Zip: _____

e-mail: _____

Amount enclosed: $ _____

Sales tax:
New York State residents please add applicable sales tax.
Shipping:
$2.00 for the first book and $1.00 for each additional book.

All orders from individuals must be pre-paid. Make checks payable to: The Imaginary Press.

Mail to:
The Imaginary Press, P.O. Box 509, East Setauket, NY 11733-0509 or contact us at:imaginary_press@iname.com and ask about our volume discounts.